ENTHUSIASTIC ACCLA
GIANT—*NEW YORK TIMES* BESTSELLING
GRAND MASTER

TONY HILLERMAN

"Hillerman is a master."
St. Louis Post-Dispatch

"Surely one of the finest
and most original craftsmen."
Boston Globe

"Hillerman transcends the mystery genre."
Washington Post Book World

"What he communicates better than almost any
other suspense writer is a different sense of time,
a different sense of connection to nature,
a different way of being."
Ft. Worth Star-Telegram

"An amazing writer."
Albuquerque Journal

"Hillerman's novels are like no others."
San Diego Union-Tribune

"His Leaphorn/Chee series is one of the most
original and influential in modern crime fiction."
Portland Sunday Oregonian

"We couldn't do better for a true voice of the West."
Denver Rocky Mountain News

TALKING GOD

BOOKS BY TONY HILLERMAN

FICTION

The Shape Shifter • *Skeleton Man*
The Sinister Pig • *The Wailing Wind*
Hunting Badger • *The First Eagle*
The Fallen Man • *Finding Moon*
Sacred Clowns • *Coyote Waits*
Talking God • *A Thief of Time*
Skinwalkers • *The Ghostway*
The Dark Wind • *People of Darkness*
Listening Woman • *Dance Hall of the Dead*
The Fly on the Wall • *The Mysterious West*
The Boy Who Made Dragonfly (for children)
Buster Mesquite's Cowboy Band (for children)

NONFICTION

Seldom Disappointed
Hillerman Country
The Great Taos Bank Robbery
Rio Grande
New Mexico
The Spell of New Mexico
Indian Country
Talking Mysteries (with Ernie Bulow)
Kilroy Was There
A New Omnibus of Crime

TONY HILLERMAN

HARPER

NEW YORK • LONDON • TORONTO • SYDNEY

HARPER

A hardcover edition of this book was originally published in 1989 by Harper & Row, Publishers.

HarperCollins books may be purchased for educational, business, or sales promotional use. For information, please email the Special Markets Department at SPsales@harpercollins.com.

FIRST HARPERTORCH PAPERBACK PRINTING APRIL 2002.
FIRST HARPER PREMIUM PAPERBACK PRINTING SEPTEMBER 2010.
FIRST HARPER PAPERBACKS EDITION PUBLISHED JANUARY 2020.

The Library of Congress has catalogued the hardcover edition as follows:

Hillerman, Tony
Talking God / Tony Hillerman. — 1st ed.
p. cm.
ISBN 0-06-016118-3
ISBN 0-06-016153-1 (limited)

I. Title.
PS3558.I45T35 1989
813'.54—dc20 88-45914

ISBN 978-0-06-289551-6 (pbk.)

23 24 25 26 27 LBC 7 6 5 4 3

This book is dedicated to Delbert Kedelty, Terry Teller, David Charley, Donald Tsosie, and the other kids at Tsaile School who drew the Yeibichai pictures that started me thinking about Talking God.

And to Will Tsosie, Tsosie Tsinijinnie, Tribal Councilman Melvin Bigthumb, and the others who fight to preserve Hajiinei-Dine'tah and its ruins and pictographs for future generations.

The author is grateful to Caroline L. Rose, Martin Burke, Don Ortner, Jo Allyn Archambault, and other curators, conservators, and generally good people at the Smithsonian's National Museum of Natural History for putting up with me and giving me some insight into what goes on behind the exhibits at a great museum.

TALKING GOD

All characters in this book, with the exception of Bernard St. Germain and Ernie Bulow, are figments of my imagination. Some of the job titles are more or less real, but the people who hold them are imaginary.

THROUGH THE DOORWAY which led from her receptionist-secretary's office into her own, Catherine Morris Perry instantly noticed the box on her desk. It was bulky—perhaps three feet long and almost as high. The legend printed on it said it had originally contained a microwave oven manufactured by General Electric. Strips of brown tape had been wrapped erratically around it. It was a crude box, incongruous amid the pale pastels and tasteful artifacts of Catherine Perry's stylish office.

"How was the weekend?" Markie said.

Catherine Morris Perry hung her raincoat on its peg, hung her rain hat over it, removed the transparent plastic from her shoes, and said, "Hello, Markie."

"How was Vermont?" Markie asked. "Wet up there, too?"

"Where'd that come from?" Catherine said, indicating the box.

"Federal Express," Markie said. "I signed for it."

"Am I expecting anything?"

"Not that you told me about. How was Vermont?"

"Wet," Catherine said. She did not wish to discuss Vermont, or anything else involving life outside this office, with Markie Bailey. What she did wish to discuss with Markie was taste. Or lack of taste. Putting the big box, brown and ugly, on her antique desk, as Markie had done, was typical of the problem. It squatted there, ugly, obscenely out of place. As out of place as Mrs. Bailey was in this office. But getting rid of her would be almost impossible. Certainly a huge amount of trouble under federal civil service rules. Mrs. Perry's specialty in law was not personnel, but she had learned something from the efforts to get rid of Henry Highhawk, that troublemaking conservator in the Museum of Natural History. What an unending fiasco that had been.

"You had a call," Markie said. "The cultural attaché's office at the Chilean embassy. He wanted an appointment."

"Later," Catherine Morris Perry said. "I'll return it later." She knew what that problem would be. Another Indian giver problem. General Something-or-Other wanting artifacts returned. He claimed his great-grandfather had only loaned them to some big shot in United Fruit, and he had no right to give them to the Smithsonian, and they were national treasures and must be returned. Incan, as she remembered. Gold, of course. Gold masks, encrusted with jewels, and the general would probably decide they were the general's personal treasure, if he could get his hands on them. And seeing that he didn't meant a huge amount of work for her, research into documents and into international law, which she should get working on right away.

But there sat the box taking up desk space. It was addressed to her as "Museum Spokesperson." Catherine Morris Perry didn't like being addressed as "Spokesperson." That she was so addressed probably stemmed from the statement she'd given the *Washington Post* on museum policy. It had been more or less an accident, the whole thing.

The reporter's call had been referred to her only because someone was sick in the public affairs office, and someone else was away from his desk, and whoever had handled the call had decided a lawyer should deal with it. It concerned Henry Highhawk again, obliquely at least. It concerned the trouble he was stirring up about returning aboriginal skeletal remains. And the *Post* had called and identified her incorrectly as spokesperson, and quoted her when they should have quoted the museum board of directors. The policy on skeletons was, after all, official policy of the board. And a sound policy.

The Federal Express shipping order attached to the box was correct except for the erroneous title. She was "Temporary Assistant Counsel, Public Affairs" on loan from the Department of the Interior. She sat and flipped quickly through the remainder of her mail. Nothing much. What was probably an invitation from the National Ballet Guild to an upcoming fund-raiser. Something from the American Civil Liberties Union. A memo from the museum maintenance director telling her why it was impossible for him to deal with a personnel complaint as the law required him to. Another letter concerning insurance for borrowed items going into an exhibit opening next month, and three letters which seemed to be from private outside sources, none familiar.

Catherine Morris Perry put all the envelopes aside unopened, looked at the box, and made a wry face. She opened her desk drawer and extracted her letter opener. Then she buzzed Mrs. Bailey.

"Yes'um."

"Mrs. Bailey. When packages arrive like this, don't bring them in and put them on my desk. Open them and get the contents out."

"Okay," Mrs. Bailey said. "I'll open it now. It's a heavy

thing." She paused. "Mrs. Paterson always wanted all the mail put in on her desk."

"I'll open it," Catherine said. "I meant from now on. And Mrs. Paterson is on leave. She is not in charge now."

"Okay," Mrs. Bailey said. "Did you notice the telephone messages? Two of them? On your desk, there?"

"No," Catherine said. They were probably under the box.

"Dr. Hebert called and just said he wanted to congratulate you on the way you handled the skeleton thing. On what you said in the *Post*."

With her free hand Catherine Perry was slicing the tape away with the letter opener. She thought that this box was probably a result of that story in the *Washington Post*. Any time the museum got into the news, it reminded a thousand old ladies of things in the attic that should be saved for posterity. Since she was quoted, one of them had sent this trash to her by name. What would it be? A dusty old butter churn? A set of family albums?

"The other one was somebody in the anthropology division. I put her name on the slip. Wants you to call. Said it was about the Indians wanting their skeletons back."

"Right," Catherine said. She pulled open the top flaps. Under them was a copy of the *Washington Post*, folded to expose the story that had quoted her. Part of it was circled in black.

MUSEUM OFFERS COMPROMISE
IN OLD BONE CONTROVERSY

The headline irritated Catherine. There had been no compromise. She had simply stated the museum's policy. If an Indian tribe wanted ancestral bones returned, it had only to ask for them and provide some acceptable proof that the bones in question had indeed been taken from a burial ground of the tribe. The entire argument was ridiculous and demeaning. In fact, even dealing with that Highhawk man was demeaning. Him and his Paho Society. A museum underling and an organization which, as far as anybody knew, existed only in his imagination. And only to create trouble. She glanced at the circled paragraph.

"Mrs. Catherine Perry, an attorney for the museum and its spokesperson on this issue, said the demand by the Paho Society for the reburial of the museum's entire collection of more than 18,000 Native American skeletons was 'simply not possible in light of the museum's purpose.'

"She said the museum is a research institution as well as a gallery for public display, and that the museum's collection of ancient human bones is a potentially important source of anthropological information. She said that Mr. Highhawk's suggestion that the museum make plaster casts of the skeletons and rebury the originals was not practical 'both because of research needs and because the public has the right to expect authenticity and not to be shown mere reproductions.' "

The clause "the right to expect authenticity" was underlined. Catherine Morris Perry frowned at it, sensing criticism. She picked up the newspaper. Under it, atop a sheet of brown wrapping paper, lay an envelope. Her name had been written neatly on it. She opened it and pulled out a single sheet of typing paper. While she read, her idle hand was pulling away the layer of wrapping paper which had separated the envelope from the contents of the box.

Dear Mrs. Perry:

You won't bury the bones of our ancestors because you say the public has the right to expect authenticity in the museum when it comes to look at skeletons. Therefore I am sending you

> a couple of authentic skeletons of ancestors. I went to the cemetery in the woods behind the Episcopal Church of Saint Luke. I used authentic anthropological methods to locate the burials of authentic white Anglo types—

Mrs. Morris Perry's fingers were under the wrapping paper now, feeling dirt, feeling smooth, cold surfaces.

"Mrs. Bailey!" she said. "Mrs. Bailey!" But her eyes moved to the end of the letter. It was signed "Henry Highhawk of the Bitter Water People."

"What?" Mrs. Bailey shouted. "What is it?"

> —and to make sure they would be perfectly authentic, I chose two whose identities you can personally confirm yourself. I ask that you accept these two skeletons for authentic display to your clients and release the bones of two of my ancestors so that they may be returned to their rightful place in Mother Earth. The names of these two authentic—

Mrs. Bailey was standing beside her now. "Honey," she said. "What's wrong?" Mrs. Bailey paused. "There's bones in that box," she said. "All dirty, too."

Mrs. Morris Perry put the letter on the desk and looked into the box. From underneath a clutter of what seemed to be arm and leg bones a single empty eye socket stared back at her. She noticed that Mrs. Bailey had picked up the letter. She noticed dirt. Damp ugly little clods had scattered on the polished desk top.

"My God," Mrs. Bailey said. "John Neldine Burgoyne. Jane Burgoyne. Weren't those— Aren't these your grandparents?"

2

ON THE LAST THURSDAY in August, the doctor treating Agnes Tsosie in the Public Health Service hospital at Fort Defiance told her she was dying and there was nothing he could do about it.

"I knew that," Agnes Tsosie said. And she smiled at him, and patted his hand, and asked him to call the chapter house at Lower Greasewood and leave word there for her family to come and get her.

"I won't be able to release you," the doctor said. "We have to keep you on medications to control the pain, and that has to be monitored. You won't be able to go home. Not yet."

"Not ever," Agnes Tsosie said, still smiling. "But you leave the message for me anyway. And don't you feel bad about it. Born for Water told Monster Slayer to leave Death alive to get rid of old people like me. You have to make some room for the new babies."

Agnes Tsosie came home from the hospital at Fort Defiance on the last Monday of August—overriding the objections of her doctor and the hospital establishment by force of the notorious Agnes Tsosie willpower.

In that part of the Navajo Reservation west of the Chuska mountain range and north of the Painted Desert, just about everybody knew about Agnes Tsosie. Old Woman Tsosie had twice served her Lower Greasewater Chapter on the Navajo Tribal Council. *National Geographic* had used her picture in an article about the Navajo Nation. Her iron will had a lot to do with starting tribal programs to get water wells drilled and water supplies available at every chapter house where hauling drinking water was a problem. Her stubborn wisdom had been important for years among her clansmen, the Bitter Water People. On the Bitter Water Dinee she imposed her rigid rules of peace. Once, she had kept a meeting of two Bitter Water families in session for eleven days until—out of hunger and exhaustion—they settled a grazing rights feud that had rankled for a hundred years.

"Too many people come out of these *belagaana* hospitals dead," Agnes Tsosie had told her doctor. "I want to come out alive." And no one was surprised that she did. She came out walking, helped by her daughter and her husband. She sat in the front seat of her daughter's pickup, joking as she always did, full of teasing and funny stories about hospital behavior. But on the long drive through the sagebrush flats toward Lower Greasewood the laughter died away. She leaned heavily against the pickup door and her face was gray with sickness.

Her son-in-law was waiting at her hogan. His name was Rollie Yellow and Agnes Tsosie, who liked almost everyone, liked Yellow a lot. They had worked a way around the Navajo taboo that decreed sons-in-law must avoid mothers-in-law. Agnes Tsosie decided that role applied only to mean mothers-in-law with bad sons-in-law. In other words, it applied to people who couldn't get along. Agnes Tsosie and

Yellow had gotten along wonderfully for thirty years and now it was Yellow who half carried her into her summer hogan. There she slept fitfully all afternoon and through the night.

The next morning, Rollie Yellow made the long bumpy drive around the mesa to the Lower Greasewood Chapter House and used the telephone. He called the chapter house at Many Farms and left word that Nancy Yabenny was needed.

Nancy Yabenny was a clerk-typist in the office of the Navajo Timber Industries and a crystal gazer—one of the category of Navajo shamans who specialize in answering hard questions, in finding the lost, in identifying witches, and in diagnosing illnesses so that the proper curing ceremonial can be arranged.

Nancy Yabenny arrived Thursday afternoon, driving a blue Dodge Ram pickup. She was a plump, middle-aged woman wearing a yellow pantsuit which had fit her better when she was slimmer. She carried her crystal, her four-mountains bundle, and the other paraphernalia of her profession in a briefcase. She placed a kitchen chair in the shade beside Agnes Tsosie's bed. Yellow had moved the bed out of the hogan into the brush arbor so that Agnes Tsosie could watch the thunderclouds form and blow away above the Hopi Buttes. Yabenny and Old Woman Tsosie talked for more than an hour. Then Nancy Yabenny arranged her slab of crystal on the earth, took her *jish* of sacred things out of her purse, and extracted from it a prescription bottle filled with corn pollen. She dusted the crystal with that, chanted the prescribed blessing song, held it so that the light from the sky illuminated it, and stared into it.

"Ah," she said, and held the crystal so that Agnes Tsosie could see what she was seeing. Then she questioned Agnes Tsosie about what they had seen.

It was sundown when Nancy Yabenny emerged from

the brush arbor. She talked to Tsosie's husband and daughter and to Rollie Yellow. She told them Agnes Tsosie needed a Yeibichai to be restored to harmony and beauty.

Rollie Yellow had half expected that, but still it was a blow. White men call it the Night Chant, but the ceremonial was named for its principal participant—Yeibichai, the great Talking God of Navajo metaphysics. As the maternal grandfather of all the other gods, he often serves as their spokesman. It is an expensive ceremony, nine days and nights of feeding the audience of clansmen and friends, and providing for the medicine man, his helpers, and as many as three teams of *yei* dancers. But much worse than the expense, in the mind of Rollie Yellow, was that what Yabenny had told them meant the *belagaana* doctor was probably right. Agnes Tsosie was very, very sick. No matter the cost, he would have to find a singer who knew how to do the Night Chant. Not many did. But there was time. The Yeibichai can be performed only after the first frost, after snakes have hibernated, only in the Season When Thunder Sleeps.

"I HEARD YOU DECIDED not to quit," Jay Kennedy said. "That right?"

"More or less," Lieutenant Joe Leaphorn said.

"Glad to hear it. How busy are you?"

Leaphorn hesitated, his eyes flicking over the pile of paperwork on his desk, his mind analyzing the tone of Kennedy's voice on the telephone.

"Nothing unusual," he said.

"You heard about this body out east of Gallup?"

"I heard a something-or-other," Leaphorn said—which meant a secondhand report of what had been overheard by the radio dispatcher downstairs. Just enough to know it wasn't a routine body find.

"It may not be Agency business," Kennedy said. "Except technically. But it's interesting."

Which was Kennedy's way of saying he thought it soon would be his business. Kennedy was Gallup area Federal Bureau of Investigation, and had been a friend of Leaphorn's long enough so that such things no longer had to be exactly said.

"The way I heard it, they found him beside the railroad," Leaphorn said. "That would be off the reservation. None of our business either."

"No, but it might get to be," Kennedy said.

Leaphorn waited for an explanation. None came.

"How?" he asked. "And is it a homicide?"

"Don't know the cause of death yet," Kennedy said. "And we don't have an identification. But it looks like there's some sort of connection between this bird and a Navajo." He paused. "There was a note. Well, not really a note."

"What's the interesting part? Is that it?"

"Well, that's peculiar. But what interests me is how the body got where it is."

Leaphorn's face relaxed slightly into something like a smile. He looked over the work on the desk. Through the window of his second-floor office in the Navajo Tribal Police Building he could see puffy white autumn clouds over the sandstone formation which gave Window Rock, Arizona, its name. A beautiful morning. Beyond the desk, out through the glass, the world was cool, clear, pleasant.

"Leaphorn. You still there?"

"You want me to look for tracks? Is that it?"

"You're supposed to be good at it," Kennedy said. "That's what you always tell us."

"All right," Leaphorn said. "Show me where it is."

The body was under the sheltering limbs of a clump of chamisa, protected from the slanting morning sun by an adjoining bush. From where he stood on the gravel of the railroad embankment, Leaphorn could see the soles of two shoes, their pointed toes aimed upward, two dark gray pant legs, a white shirt, a necktie, a suit coat, still buttoned, and a ground's-eye view of a pale narrow face with oddly pouched cheeks. Under the circumstances, the corpse seemed remarkably tidy.

"Nice and neat," Leaphorn said.

Undersheriff Delbert Baca thought he meant the scene of the crime. He nodded.

"Just luck," he said. "A fellow running a freight engine past here just happened to notice him. The train was rolling so he couldn't get down and stomp around over everything. Jackson here—" Baca nodded to a plump young man in a McKinley County deputy sheriff's uniform who was standing on the tracks "—he was driving by on the interstate." Baca gestured toward Interstate Highway 40, which was producing a faint rumble of truck traffic a quarter-mile to the west. "He got out here before the state police could mess everything up."

"Nobody's moved the body then?" Leaphorn asked. "What about this note you mentioned? How did you find that?"

"Baca here checked his pockets looking for identification," Kennedy said. "Reached under him to check hip pockets. He didn't find a billfold or anything, but he found this in the handkerchief pocket of his coat." Kennedy held out a small folded square of yellow paper. Leaphorn took it.

"You don't know who he is then?"

"Don't know," Kennedy said. "The billfold is missing. There wasn't anything in his pockets except some change, a ballpoint pen, a couple of keys, and a handkerchief. And then there was this note in his coat pocket."

Leaphorn unfolded the note.

"You wouldn't think to look in that coat pocket if you were stripping somebody of identification," Baca said. "Anyway, that's what I think was happening."

The note was written with what might have been a ballpoint pen with a very fine point. It said:

"Yeabechay? Yeibeshay? Agnes Tsosie (correct). Should be near Windowrock, Arizona."

Leaphorn turned the square over. "Stic Up" was printed across the top, the trade name of the maker of notepads which stick to bulletin boards.

"Know her?" Kennedy asked. "Agnes Tsosie. It sounds familiar to me."

"Tsosie's like Kennedy in Boston," Leaphorn said. He frowned. He did know one Agnes Tsosie. Just a little and from way back. An old lady who used to serve on the tribal council a long time ago. Elected from the Lower Greasewood district, if he remembered it right. A good woman, but probably dead by now. And there must be other Agnes Tsosies here and there around the reservation. Agnes was a common name and there were a thousand Tsosies. "Maybe we can find her, though. We can easy enough, if she's associated with a Yeibichai. They're not having many of those any more."

"That's the ceremony they call the Night Chant, isn't it?" Kennedy asked.

"Or Nightway," Leaphorn said.

"The one that lasts nine days," Kennedy said. "And they have the masked dancers?"

"That's it," Leaphorn said. But who was this man with the pointed shoes who seemed to know an Agnes Tsosie? Leaphorn moved past the chamisa limbs, placing his feet carefully to erase nothing not already erased in Baca's search of the victim's pockets. He squatted, buttocks on heels, grunting at the pain in his knees. He should exercise more, he thought. It was a habit he'd dropped since Emma's death. They had always walked together—almost every evening when he got home from the office. Walked and talked. But now—

The victim had no teeth. His face, narrow as it was, had the caved-in, pointed-chin look of the toothless old. But this man wasn't particularly old. Sixty perhaps. And not the sort to be toothless. His suit, blue-black with an almost microscopic gray stripe, looked old-fashioned but expensive, the attire of that social class with the time and money to keep its teeth firmly in its jaws. At this close range, Leaphorn noticed that the suit coat had a tiny patch by the middle button and the narrow lapel looked threadbare. The shirt looked threadbare, too. But expensive. So did a simple broad gold ring on the third finger of his left hand. And the face itself was an expensive face. Leaphorn had worked around white men for almost forty years, and Leaphorn studied faces. This man's complexion was dark—even with the pallor of death—but it was an aristocratic face. A narrow, arrogant nose, fine bones, high forehead.

Leaphorn shifted his position and examined the victim's shoes. The leather was expensive, and under the day's thin film of dust it glowed with a thousand polishings. Handmade shoes, Leaphorn guessed. But made a long time ago. And now the heels were worn, and one sole had been replaced by a shoemaker.

"You noticed the teeth?" Kennedy asked.

"I noticed the lack of them," Leaphorn said. "Did anyone find a set of false teeth?"

"No," Baca said. "But nobody really looked. Not yet. It seemed to me that the first question to consider was how this guy got here."

Leaphorn found himself wondering why the sheriff's office had called the FBI. Had Baca sensed something about the death of this tidy man that suggested a federal crime? He looked around him. The track ran endlessly east, endlessly west—the Santa Fe main line from the Midwest to California. North, the red sandstone ramparts of Iyanbito Mesa; south, the piñon hills which rose toward the Zuni

Mesa and the Zuni Mountains. And just across the busy lanes of Interstate 40 stood Fort Wingate. Old Fort Wingate, where the U.S. Army had been storing ammunition since the Spanish-American War.

"How did he get here? That's the question," Kennedy said. "He wasn't thrown off the Amtrak, that's obvious. He doesn't look the type to be riding a freight. So I'd guess that probably somebody carried him here. But why the hell would anybody do that?"

"Could this have anything to do with Fort Wingate?" Leaphorn asked. A half-mile or so up the main line he could see the siding that curved away toward the military base.

Baca laughed, shrugged.

"Who knows?" Kennedy said.

"I heard they were going to shut the place down," Leaphorn said. "It's obsolete."

"I heard that too," Kennedy said. "You think you can find any tracks?"

Leaphorn tried. He walked down the railroad embankment some twenty paces and started a circle through the sage, snakeweed, and chamisa. The soil here was typical of a sagebrush flat: loose, light, and with enough fine caliche particles to form a crust. An early autumn shower had moved over this area about a week ago, making tracking easy. Leaphorn circled back to the embankment without finding anything except the marks left by rodents, lizards, and snakes and confident there had been nothing to find. He walked another dozen yards down the track and started another, wider circle. Again, he found nothing that wasn't far too old or caused by an animal. Then he crisscrossed the sagebrush around the body, slowly, eyes down.

Kennedy, Baca, and Jackson were waiting for him on the embankment above the body. Behind him, far down the track, an ambulance had parked with a white sedan behind it—the car used by the pathologist from the Public Health

Service hospital in Gallup. Leaphorn made a wry face. He shook his head.

"Nothing," he said. "If someone carried him in from this side, they carried him up from way down the tracks."

"Or down from way up the tracks," Baca said, grinning.

"What were you looking for?" Kennedy asked. "Besides tracks."

"Nothing in particular," Leaphorn said. "You're not really looking for anything in particular. If you do that, you don't see things you're not looking for."

"So you think he got brought in from way down the track?" Kennedy said.

"I don't know," Leaphorn said. "Why would anyone do that? That's lots of hard work. And the risk of being seen while you're doing it. Why is this sagebrush better than any other sagebrush?"

"Maybe they hauled him in from the other side," Kennedy said.

Leaphorn stared across the tracks. There was no road over there either. "How about lifting him off a train?"

"Amtrak is going about sixty-five miles an hour here," Kennedy said. "Doesn't start slowing for Gallup for miles. I can't see that man on a freight, and they don't stop out here either. I checked with the railroad on all that."

They stood then on the embankment above the man with the pointed shoes, with nothing to say in the presence of death. The ambulance crew came down the track, carrying a stretcher, trailed by the pathologist carrying a satchel. He was a small young man with a blond mustache. Leaphorn didn't recognize him and he didn't introduce himself.

He squatted beside the body, tested the skin at the neck, tested the stiffness of the wrists, bent finger joints, looked into the toothless mouth.

He looked up at Kennedy. "How'd he get here?"

Kennedy shrugged.

The doctor unbuttoned the suit coat and the shirt, pulled up the undershirt, examined the chest and abdomen. "There's no blood anywhere. No nothin'." He unbuckled the belt, unzipped the trouser fly, felt. "You guys know what killed him?" he asked nobody in particular.

"What?" Baca said. "What killed him?"

"Hell, I don't know," the doctor said, still intent on the body. "I just got here. I was asking you."

He rose, took a step back. "Put him on the stretcher," he ordered. "Face down."

Face down on the stretcher the man with the pointed shoes looked even smaller. The back of his dark suit was floured with gray dust, his dignity diminished. The doctor ran his hands over the body, up the spine, felt the back of the head, massaged the neck.

"Ah," he said. "Here we are."

The doctor parted the hair at the back of the man's head at the point where the spine joins the skull. The hair, Leaphorn noticed, was matted and stiff. The doctor leaned back, looking up at them, grinning happily. "See?"

Leaphorn could see very little—only a small place where neck became skull and where there seemed to be the blackness of congealed blood.

"What am I seeing?" Kennedy asked, sounding irritated. "I don't see a damned thing."

The pathologist stood, brushed off his hands, and looked down at the man in the pointed shoes.

"What you see is where somebody who knows how to use a knife can kill somebody quick," he said. "Like lightning. You stick it in that little gap between the first vertebra and the base of the skull. Cut the spinal cord." He chuckled. "Zap."

"That what happened?" Kennedy asked. "How long ago?"

"Looks like it," the doctor said. "I'd say it was probably yesterday. But we'll do an autopsy. Then you'll have your answer."

"One answer," Kennedy said. "Or two. How and when. That leaves who."

And why, Leaphorn thought. Why was always the question that lay at the heart of things. It was the answer Joe Leaphorn always looked for. Why did this man—obviously not a Navajo—have the name of a Navajo woman written on a note in his pocket? And the misspelled name of a Navajo ceremonial? The Yeibichai. It was the ceremonial in which the great mystical, mythical, magical spirits who formed the culture of the Navajos and created their first four clans actually appeared, personified in masks worn by dancers. Was the murdered man headed for a Yeibichai? As a matter of fact, he couldn't have been. It was weeks too early. The Yeibichai was a winter ceremonial. It could be performed only after the snakes had hibernated, only in the Season When Thunder Sleeps. But why else would he have the note? Leaphorn pondered and found no possible answers. He would find Agnes Tsosie and ask her.

The Agnes Tsosie Leaphorn remembered proved to be—apparently—the right one. At least when Leaphorn inquired about her as the first step in what he feared would be a time-consuming hunt he learned the family was planning a Yeibichai ceremonial for her. He spent a few hours making telephone inquiries and decided he had struck it lucky. There seemed to be only three of the great Night Chant ceremonials scheduled so far. One would be held at the Navajo Nation Fair at Window Rock for a man named Roanhorse and another was planned in December over near Burnt Water for someone in the Gorman family. That left Agnes Tsosie of Lower Greasewood as the only possibility.

The drive from Leaphorn's office in Window Rock to Lower Greasewood took him westward through the ponderosa forests of the Defiance Plateau, through the piñon-juniper hills which surround Ganado, and then southeast into the sagebrush landscape that falls away into the Painted Desert. At the Lower Greasewood Boarding School those children who lived near enough to be day students were climbing aboard a bus for the trip home. Leaphorn asked the driver where to find the Agnes Tsosie place.

"Twelve miles down to the junction north of Beta Hochee," the driver said. "And then you turn back south toward White Cone about two miles and take the dirt road past the Na-Ah-Tee trading post, and about three-four miles past that, to your right, there's a road that leads off toward the backside of Tesihim Butte. That's the road that leads up to Old Lady Tsosie's outfit. About two miles, maybe."

"Road?" Leaphorn asked.

The driver was a trim young woman of perhaps thirty. She knew exactly what Leaphorn meant. She grinned.

"Well, actually, it's two tracks out through the sage. But it's easy to find. There's a big bunch of asters blooming along there—right at the top of a slope."

The junction of the track to the Tsosie place was easy to find. Asters were blooming everywhere along the dirt road past Na-Ah-Tee trading post, but the place where the track led off from the road was also marked by a post which the bus driver hadn't mentioned. An old boot was jammed atop the post, signaling that somebody would be at home. Leaphorn downshifted and turned down the track. He felt fine. Everything about this business of learning why a dead man had Agnes Tsosie's name in his pocket was working well.

"I don't have no idea who that could be," Agnes Tsosie said. She was reclining, thin, gray haired, propped up by pillows on a metal bed under a brush arbor beside her house, holding a Polaroid photograph of the man with the pointed shoes. She handed it to Jolene Yellow, who was standing beside the sofa. "Daughter, you know this man?"

Jolene Yellow examined the photograph, shook her head, handed the print back to Leaphorn. He had been in the business too long to show disappointment.

"Any idea why some stranger might be coming out here to your Yeibichai?"

"No." She shook her head. "Not this stranger."

Not this stranger. Leaphorn thought about that. Agnes Tsosie would explain in good time. Now she was looking away, out across the gentle slope that fell away from Tesihim Butte and then rose gradually toward the sharp dark outline of Nipple Butte to the west. The sage was gray and silver with autumn, the late afternoon sun laced it with slanting shadows, and everywhere there was the yellow of blooming snakeweed and the purple of the asters. Beauty before her, Leaphorn thought. Beauty all around her. But Agnes Tsosie's face showed no sign she was enjoying the beauty. It looked strained and sick.

"We have a letter," Agnes Tsosie said. "It's in the hogan." She glanced at Jolene Yellow. "My daughter will get it for you to look at."

The letter was typed on standard bond paper.

September 13

Dear Mrs. Tsosie:

I read about you in an old issue of *National Geographic*—the one with the long story about the Navajo Nation. It said you were a member of the Bitter Water Clan, which was also the clan of my grandmother, and I noticed by the picture they had of you that you two look alike. I write to you because I want to ask a favor.

I am one-fourth Navajo by blood. My grandmother told me she was all Navajo, but she married a white man and so did my mother. But I feel I am a Navajo, and I would like to see what can be done about becoming officially a member of the tribe. I would also like to come out to Arizona and talk to you about my family. I remember that my grandmother told me that she herself was the granddaughter of Ganado Mucho and that she was born to the Bitter Water People and that her father's clan had been the Streams Come Together People.

Please let me know if I can come and visit you and anything you can tell me about how I would become a Navajo.

Sincerely,
Henry Highhawk

I am enclosing a stamped, self-addressed envelope.

Leaphorn reread the letter, trying to connect these words, this odd plea, with the arrogant face of the man with the pointed shoes.

"Did you answer it?"

"I told him to come," Agnes Tsosie said. She sighed, shifted her weight, grimaced.

Leaphorn waited.

"I told him there would be a Yeibichai for me after the first frost. Probably late in November. That would be when to come. There would be other Bitter Water people there for him to talk to. I said he could talk to the *hataalii* who is doing the sing. Maybe it would be proper for him to look through the mask and be initiated like they do with boys on the last night of the sing. I said I didn't know about that. He would have to ask the *hataalii* about that. And then he could go to Window Rock and see about whether he could get on the tribal rolls. He could find out from the people there what proof he would need."

Leaphorn waited. But Agnes Tsosie had said what she had to say.

"Did he answer your letter?"

"Not yet," she said. "Or maybe he did and his letter is down at Beta Hochee. That's where we pick up our mail."

"Nobody has been by the trading post there for a while," Jolene Yellow said. "Not since last week."

"Do you think you know who this man's grandmother was?" Leaphorn asked.

"Maybe," Agnes Tsosie said. "I remember they said my mother had an aunt who went away to boarding school and never did come back."

"Anyway," Jolene Yellow said, "he's not the same man."

Leaphorn looked at her, surprised.

"He sent his picture," she said. "I'll get it."

It was about two inches square, a color photograph of the sort taken by machine to be pasted in passports. It showed a long, slender face, large blue eyes, and long blond hair woven into two tight braids. It was a face that would always look boyish.

"He certainly doesn't look like a Navajo," Leaphorn said. He was thinking that this Henry Highhawk looked even less like the man with the pointed shoes.

4

FROM BEHIND HIM in the medicine hogan, Officer Jim Chee could hear the chanting of the First Dancers as they put on their ceremonial paint. Chee was interested. He had picked a spot from which he could see through the hogan doorway and watch the personifiers preparing themselves. They were eight middle-aged men from around the Naschitti Chapter House in New Mexico, far to the east of Agnes Tsosie's place below Tesihim Butte. They had painted their right hands first, then their faces from the forehead downward, and then their bodies, making themselves ready to represent the Holy People of Navajo mythology, the *yei,* the powerful spirits. This Night Chant ceremonial was one that Chee hoped to learn someday himself. Yeibichai, his people called it, naming it for Talking God, the maternal grandfather of all the spirits. The performance was nine days long and involved five complicated sand paintings and scores of songs. Learning it would take a long, long time as would finding a *hataalii* willing to take him on as student. When the time came for that, he would have to take leave from the Navajo Tribal Police. But that was somewhere in the distant future. Now his job was watching for the Flaky Man from Washington. Henry Highhawk was the name on the federal warrant.

"Henry Highhawk," Captain Largo had said, handing him the folder. "Usually when they decide to turn Indian and call themselves something like Whitecloud, or Squatting Bear, or Highhawk, they decide they're going to be Cherokees. Or some dignified tribe that everybody knows about. But this jerk had to pick Navajo."

Chee was reading the folder. "Flight across state lines to avoid prosecution," he said. "Prosecution for what?"

"Desecration of graves," Largo said. He laughed, shook his head, genuinely amused by the irony. "Now ain't that just the ideal criminal occupation for a man who decides to declare himself a Navajo?"

Chee had noticed something that seemed to him even more ironic than a white grave robber declaring himself to be a Navajo—a tribe which happened to have a fierce religious aversion to corpses and everything associated with death.

"Is he a pot hunter?" Chee asked. "Is the FBI actually trying to catch a pot hunter?" Digging up graves to steal pre-Columbian pottery for the collector's market had been both a federal crime and big business on the Colorado plateau for generations, and the FBI's apathy about it had been both unshakable and widely known. Chee stood in front of Largo's desk trying to imagine what would have stirred the federals from such historic and monolithic inertia.

"He wasn't hunting pots," Largo said. "He's a politician. He was digging up *belagaana* skeletons back East." Largo explained what Highhawk had done with the skeletons. "So not only were they white skeletons, they were Very Important People *belagaana* skeletons."

"Oh," Chee said.

"Anyway, all you need to know about it is that you go out to the Lower Greasewood Chapter House and you find out where they're holding this Yeibichai. It will probably be at Agnes Tsosie's place. She's the one they're doing the Night Chant for. Anyway, this Highhawk nut is supposed to come to it. Probably he's already there. The FBI says he rented a Ford Bronco from Avis in Washington. A white one. They think he drove it out here. So you get yourself to Old Woman Tsosie's place. If he's there, bring him in. And if he's not there yet, then stick around and wait for him."

"Nine days?"

"Tonight's the last night of the Yeibichai," Largo said. "That's when Mrs. Tsosie said she told him to come."

"What makes us think this guy is coming all the way out here for a Yeibichai? Sounds strange to me." Chee had been looking at the sheet in the folder when he said it. When he looked up, Captain Largo was glowering at him.

"You don't get paid to make decisions on whether the feds know what they hell they're doing," the captain said. "You get paid for doing what I tell you to do. But if it makes you happier, we're told that this Highhawk told it around back in Washington that he was coming out to the Navajo Reservation to attend this specific Agnes Tsosie Yeibichai. Is that good enough for you?"

It had been good enough. And so for the past four hours Chee had been at the Agnes Tsosie place waiting for Henry Highhawk to arrive at this Yeibichai ceremonial so that he could arrest him. Chee was good at waiting. He waited at his favorite lurking point near Baby Rocks Mesa for the endless empty miles of U.S. 160 to provoke drivers into speeding. He waited at the fringe of rodeo crowds for unwary bootleggers, and in the hallways outside the various Navajo Nation Department of Justice courtrooms to be called in to testify. Deputy Sheriff Cowboy Dashee, his good friend who had tagged along on this venture, complained endlessly about the waiting their jobs required. Chee didn't mind. He had one of those minds in which curiosity is constantly renewed. Wherever he waited, Chee's eyes wandered. They always found something that interested him. Here, waiting for the white Ford Bronco to appear (or fail to appear), Chee was first fascinated with the ceremonial itself. And then he'd noticed the Man with Bad Hands.

Bad Hands was curious indeed.

He had arrived early, as had Chee, a little before sundown in that recess between the afternoon singing in the medicine hogan and the dancing of the *yeis,* which would begin only when the night was totally dark. He was driving a green four-door Jeep Cherokee which bore a Farmington car rental company's sticker. Chee had identified him at first as a *belagaana,* that grab bag of social-ethnic types which included whites plus all those who were neither fellow members of the Dineh (Navajos), nor Nakai (Mexicans), nor Zunis, nor Hopis, nor Apaches, nor Utes, nor members of any of the other Indian tribes who lived near enough to the Navajos to have earned a name in the Navajo language—which had no noun for "Indian." Thus Bad Hands was *belagaana* by default. Bad Hands wasn't the only white attracted by this ceremonial, but he was the only one who defied Chee's personal classification system.

The handful of other whites standing around the bonfires or keeping warm in their vehicles fit neatly enough. Two were "friends." They included a lanky, bald-headed man from whom Chee sometimes bought hay at a Gallup feed store, and Ernie Bulow, a towering, gray-bearded desert rat who'd been raised on the Big Reservation and had written a book about Navajo taboos. Bulow spoke coherent Navajo and had developed close personal relationships with Navajo families. He had brought with him today in his dusty station wagon a fat Navajo man and three middle-aged white women, all of whom stood beside the vehicle looking cold, nervous, and uncomfortable. Chee put the women in his "tourist" category. The remainder of the *belagaana* delegation were mostly "Lone Rangers"—part of the liberal/intellectual covey. They had flocked into the Navajo Mountain territory and declared themselves spokesmen for, and guardians of, the Navajo families facing eviction from their lands in what had become the Hopi part of the old Joint Use Reservation. Lone Rangers were a nuisance, but also a source of anecdotes and amusement. There were three of these, two males not much older than Chee and a pretty young blonde woman with her hair rolled atop her head. All wore the ragged jeans, jean jacket, and horse-blanket uniform of their clique.

Bad Hands' necktie, his neatly fitted business suit, his white shirt, his gloves of thin black leather, his snap-brim felt hat, his fur-collared overcoat, all disqualified him as a Lone Ranger. Like them he was a city person, but without the disguise. Total disinterest in the ceremonial ruled him out as tourist, and he seemed to know no one here—most of them Bitter Water People of the patient's maternal clan. Like Jim Chee, Bad Hands was simply waiting. But for Bad Hands, waiting was a joyless matter of enduring. He showed no sign of pleasure in it.

Chee had first noticed him when he emerged from the Jeep Cherokee. He'd parked it amid a cluster of shabbier vehicles a polite distance from the dance grounds. He had stretched, rotated his shoulders in his overcoat, bent his knees, bowed his back, went through those other movements of people who have been confined too long in a car. He gave no more than a glance to the men who were unloading sawmill waste from the tribe's lumbermill to help fuel the fires which would warm the spectators and illuminate the dancing tonight. He was more interested in the parked vehicles. These he inspected carefully, one after another. He had noticed Chee noticing him, and he had noticed Chee's police uniform, but he showed no special interest. After stretching his muscles he climbed back into his vehicle and sat. It was then that Chee noticed his hands.

He had opened the door by grasping the handle with two fingers of his left hand, then pressing in the release button with a finger of his right hand. It was obviously a practiced motion. Still it was clumsy. And as he did it, Chee noticed that the thumb and little finger of the right glove jutted out stiffly. The man was either missing that thumb and finger, or they were immobilized. Why then didn't he open the door with the other hand? Chee couldn't get a look at it.

But now Chee's curiosity was clicked up a notch. He prowled the dance ground the Tsosie family had cleared, he chatted with people, he watched the fire builders build the stacks of logs and waste wood which would line the dancing area with flames. He talked to the husband of the woman whose mother was the patient. Yellow was his name. Yellow was worrying about everything going right.

Chee helped Yellow check the wiring from the little generator he'd rented to provide the electric lighting he'd rigged up behind the medicine hogan. Chee kept an eye on five boys wearing Many Farms football jackets who might become trouble if their group became large enough to reach teenage critical mass. Chee prowled among the parked vehicles on the lookout for drunks or drinking. He stopped where Cowboy Dashee was parked in his Apache County Sheriff's Department patrol car to see if Cowboy was still asleep. ("Wake me when your criminal gets here, or wake me when the dancing gets going," Dashee said. "Otherwise, I need my rest.") But always he wandered back to where he could see the Jeep Cherokee and its driver.

The man was sometimes sitting in it, sometimes leaning against it, sometimes standing beside it.

He's nervous, Chee decided, but he's not the sort who

allows himself to show his nerves in the usual ways. When the light of an arriving car lit his face, Chee noticed that he might be part Indian. Or perhaps Asiatic. Certainly not Navajo, or Apache, or a Pueblo man. In the same light he saw his hands again, gloved, both of them this time resting lightly on the steering wheel. The thumbs and little fingers of both hands jutted out stiffly as if their joints were frozen.

Chee was standing beside the medicine hogan thinking of these odd hands and what might have happened to them when Henry Highhawk arrived. Chee noticed the vehicle coming over the rim of the mesa and jolting toward the parking area. In the reflected light from the fires it seemed to be small and white. As it parked he saw it was the white Ford Bronco he had been waiting for.

". . . Wind Boy, the holy one, paints his form," the voices behind him chanted in rhythmic Navajo.

"With the dark cloud, he paints his form.

With the misty rain, he paints his form. . . ."

The vehicle disappeared from sight in an irregular row of mostly pickup trucks. Chee strolled toward it, remaining out of the firelight when he could. It was a Bronco, new under its heavy coating of dust. Its only occupant seemed to be the driver. He opened the door, lighting the overhead bulb. He swung his legs out, stretched, emerged stiffly, and closed the door behind him. In no hurry, apparently.

Neither was Jim Chee. He leaned against the side of an old sedan and waited.

The cold breeze moved through the sage around him, whispering just loud enough to obscure the ceremonial chanting. The fires that lined the sides of the dance ground between the hogan and the little brush-covered medicine lodge were burning high now. The light reflected from the face of Henry Highhawk. Or, to be more accurate, Chee thought, the man I presume to be Henry Highhawk. The man, at least, who drove the prescribed white Bronco. He wore a shirt of dark blue velvet with silver buttons—the shirt a traditional Navajo would have proudly worn about 1920. He wore an old-fashioned black felt hat with a high crown and a band of silver conchas—a "reservation hat" as old-fashioned as the shirt. A belt of heavy silver conchas hung around his waist, and below it he wore jeans and boots—the left boot, Chee now noticed, reinforced with a metal brace and thickened sole. He stood for a long time beside the car in his shirt sleeves, oblivious of the cold, engrossed in what he was seeing. In contrast to Bad Hands, this visitor was obviously fascinated by this ceremonial event. Finally, he reached inside, pulled out a leather jacket, and put it on. The jacket had leather fringes. Of course it would have fringes, Chee thought. Hollywood's Indian.

Chee strolled past him to Cowboy's patrol car and rapped on the window.

Cowboy sat up, looked at him. Chee opened the door and slid in.

"They ready to dance?" Cowboy asked, the question muffled by a yawn.

"Any minute now," Chee said. "And our bandido has arrived."

Cowboy felt around for his gun belt, found it, straightened to put it on. "Okay," he said. "Away we go."

Deputy Sheriff Cowboy Dashee climbed out of his patrol car and followed Navajo Tribal Policeman Jim Chee toward the crowd gathering around the fires. Dashee was a citizen of Mishhongnovi on the Hopi Second Mesa, born into the distinguished Side Corn Clan, and a valuable man in the ancient Hopi Antelope Society. But he was also a friend of Jim Chee from way back in their high school days.

"There he is," Chee said. "The cat with the reservation hat, leather jacket with the Buffalo Bill fringes."

"And the braids," Dashee said. "He trying to set a new style for you guys? Replace buns with braids?"

The driver of the Bronco was standing very close to a squat, elderly man in a red plaid coat, leaning over him as he first talked, then listened attentively. Chee and Dashee edged through the crowd toward him.

"Not now," Plaid Coat was saying. "Old Lady Tsosie she's sick. She's the patient. Nobody can talk to her until this sing is over."

Why would this *belagaana* grave robber want to see Agnes Tsosie? Chee had no idea. That irritated him. The big shots never told working cops a damned thing. Captain Largo certainly didn't. Nobody did. Someday he would walk into something and get his head shot off because nobody had told him something. There was absolutely no excuse for it.

Bad Hands walked past him, approached Highhawk, waited for the polite moment, touched the man's shoulder. Highhawk looked startled. Bad Hands seemed to be introducing himself. Highhawk offered a hand, noticed Bad Hands' glove, listened to what might have been an explanation, shook the glove gingerly. "Let's get him," Dashee said. "Come on."

"What's the hurry?" Chee said. "This guy's not going anyplace."

"We arrest him, we put him in the patrol car, and we don't have to worry about him," Dashee said.

"We arrest him, and we have to baby-sit him," Chee said. "We have to haul him down to Holbrook and book him into jail. We miss the Yeibichai dance."

Dashee yawned a huge yawn, scrubbed his face with both palms, yawned again. "To tell the truth," he said, "I forget how you talked me into coming out here anyway. It's us Hopi that have the big tourist-attraction ceremonials. Not you guys. What am I doing here, anyway?"

"I think I told you something about all the Miss Navajo and the Miss Indian Princess contestants always coming to these Yeibichais," Chee said. "They haul them in from Albuquerque and Phoenix and Flagstaff on buses."

"Yeah," Dashee said. "You did say something about girls. Where the hell are they?"

"Be here any minute," Chee said.

Dashee yawned again. "And speaking of women, how you doing with your girlfriend?"

"Girlfriend?"

"That good-looking lawyer." Dashee created curves in the air with his hands. "Janet Pete."

"She's not my girlfriend," Chee said.

Dashee put on his skeptical expression.

"I'm her confidant," Chee said. "The shoulder upon which she weeps. She's got a boyfriend. In Washington. Her old law professor down at the University of Arizona decided to quit teaching and be a millionaire. Now she's back there working for him."

Dashee's disappointment showed. "I liked her," he said. "For a Navajo, that is. And for a lawyer, too. Imagine liking a lawyer. But I thought you two had something going."

"No," Chee said. "She tells me her troubles. I tell her mine. Then we give one another bad advice. It's one of those things."

"Your troubles? You mean that blue-eyed little schoolteacher. I thought she'd kissed you off and moved back to Milwaukee or some place. Is she still your trouble?"

"Mary Landon," Chee said.

"That sure has dragged along," Dashee said. "Is she back out here again?"

"She did move back to Wisconsin," Chee said, thinking he really didn't much want to talk about this. "But we write. Next week, I'm going back there to see her."

"Well," Dashee said. The breeze had shifted now and

was moving out of the north, even colder than it had been. Dashee turned up his coat collar. "None of my business, I guess. It's your funeral."

The screen of blankets had been dropped over the doorway of the patient's hogan now and all the curing activities were going on in privacy. The bonfires that lined the cleared dance ground burned high. Spectators huddled around them, keeping warm, gossiping, renewing friendships. There was laughter as a piñon log collapsed and the resulting explosion of sparks routed a cluster of teenagers. Mr. Yellow had built a kitchen shelter behind the hogan, using sawed telephone poles as roof posts, two-by-fours and particle board for its walls. Through its doorway, Chee could see dozens of Mrs. Tsosie's Bitter Water clansmen drinking coffee and helping themselves from stacks of fry bread and a steaming iron pot of mutton stew. Highhawk had drifted that way too, with Bad Hands trailing behind. Chee and Dashee followed Highhawk into the kitchen shelter, keeping him in sight. They sampled the stew and found it only fair.

Then the curtain drew back and the *hataalii* backed out through it. He walked down the dance ground to the *yei* hogan. A moment later he made the return trip, walking slowly, chanting. Old Woman Tsosie emerged from the medicine hogan. She was bundled in a blanket, her hair bound in the traditional fashion. She stood on another blanket spread on the packed earth and held out her hands toward the east. The kitchen shelter emptied as diners became spectators. The socializing at the bonfires quieted. Then Chee heard the characteristic call of Talking God.

"Huu tu tu. Huu tu tu. Huu tu tu. Huu tu tu."

Talking God led a row of masked *yei,* moving slowly with the intricate, mincing, dragging step of the spirit dancers. The sound of the crowd died away. Chee could hear the tinkle of the bells on the dancers' legs, hear the *yei* singing in sounds no human could understand. The row of stiff eagle feathers atop Talking God's white mask riffled in the gusty breeze. Dust whipped around the naked legs of the dancers, moving their kilts. Chee glanced at Henry Highhawk, curious about his reaction. He noticed the man with the crippled hands had moved up beside Highhawk.

Highhawk's lips were moving, his expression reverent. He seemed to be singing. Chee edged closer. Highhawk was seeing nothing but Talking God dancing slowly toward them. "He stirs. He stirs," Highhawk was singing. "He stirs. He stirs. Now in old age wandering, he stirs." The words were translated from the ceremony called the Shaking of the Masks. That ritual had been held four days earlier in this ceremonial, awakening the spirits which lived in the masks from their cosmic dreams. This white man must be an anthropologist, or a scholar of some sort, to have found a translation.

Talking God and his retinue were close now and Highhawk was no longer singing. He held something in his right hand. Something metallic. A tape recorder. *Hataalii* rarely gave permission for taping. Chee wondered what he should do. This would be a terrible time to create a disturbance. He decided to let it ride. He hadn't been sent here to enforce ceremonial rules, and he was in no mood to be a policeman.

The hooting call of the Yeibichai projected Chee's imagination back into the myth that this ceremony reenacted. It was the tale of a crippled boy and his compact with the gods. This was how it might have been in those mythic times, Chee thought. The firelight, the hypnotic sound of the bells and pot drum, the shadows of the dancers moving rhythmically against the pink sandstone of the mesa walls behind the hogan.

Now there was a new smell in the air, mixing with the perfume of the burning piñon and dust. It was the smell of dampness, of impending snow. And as he noticed it, a flurry of tiny snowflakes appeared between him and the fire, and as quickly disappeared. He glanced at Henry Highhawk to see how the grave robber was taking this.

Highhawk was gone. So was Bad Hands.

Chee looked for Cowboy Dashee. But where was Cowboy when you needed him? Never in sight. There he was. Talking to a young woman bundled in a down jacket. Grinning like an ape. Chee jostled his way through the crowd. He grabbed Dashee's elbow.

"Come on," he said. "I lost him."

Deputy Sheriff Dashee was instantly all business.

"I'll check Highhawk's car," he said. And ran.

Chee ran for Bad Hands' car. The two men were standing beside it, talking.

No more waiting, Chee thought. He could see Dashee approaching.

"Mr. Highhawk," Chee said. "Mr. Henry Highhawk?"

The two men turned. "Yes," Highhawk said. Bad Hands stared, his lower lip clenched nervously between his teeth.

Chee displayed his identification.

"I'm Officer Chee, Navajo Tribal Police. We have a warrant for your arrest and I'm taking you into custody."

"What for?" Highhawk said.

"Flight across state lines to avoid prosecution," Chee said. He sensed Dashee at his elbow.

"You have the right to remain silent," Chee began. "You have the right to—"

"It's for digging up those skeletons, isn't it?" Highhawk said. "It's okay to dig up Indian bones and put 'em on display. But you dig up white bones and it's a felony."

"—can and will be used against you in a court of law," Chee concluded.

"I heard the law was looking for me," Highhawk said. "But I wasn't sure exactly why. Is it for sending those skeletons through the mail? I didn't do that. I sent them by Federal Express."

"I don't know anything about it," Chee said. "All I know is you're Henry Highhawk and I got a warrant here to arrest you on. As far as I know you shot eighteen people in Albuquerque, robbed the bank, hijacked airplanes, lied to your probation officer, committed treason. They don't tell us a damned thing."

"What do you do to him?" Bad Hands asked. "Where do you take him?"

"Who are you?" Dashee asked.

"We take him down to Holbrook," Chee said, "and then we turn him over to the sheriff's office and they hold him for the federals on the fugitive warrant, and then he goes back to somewhere or other. Wherever he did whatever he did. Then he goes on trial."

"Who are you?" Dashee repeated.

"My name is Gomez," Bad Hands said. "Rudolfo Gomez."

Cowboy nodded.

"I'm Jim Chee," Chee said. He held out his hand.

Bad Hands looked at it. Then at Chee.

"Pardon the glove, please," he said. "I had an accident."

As he shook it, Chee felt through the thin black leather an index finger and, perhaps, part of the second finger. All else inside the glove felt stiff and false.

That was the right hand. If his memory was correct, the right hand was Bad Hands' better hand.

LEROY FLECK ENJOYED having his shoes shined. They were Florsheims—by his standards expensive shoes—and they deserved care. But the principal reason he had them shined each morning at the little stand down the street from his apartment was professional. Fleck, who was often after other people, felt a need to know if anyone was after him. Sitting perched these few minutes on the Captain's shoeshine throne gave him a perfect opportunity to rememorize the street. Each morning except Sunday Fleck examined every vehicle parked along the shady block his apartment house occupied. He compared what he saw with what he remembered from previous days, and weeks, and months of similar studies.

Still, he enjoyed the shine. The Captain had gradually grown on him as a person. Fleck no longer thought of him as a nigger, and not even as one of Them. The Captain had gradually become—become what? Somebody who knew him? Whatever it was, Fleck found himself looking forward to his shoeshine.

This morning, though, Fleck had other things on his mind. Things to do. A decision to make. He examined the street through habit. The cars were familiar. So was the bakery truck making its delivery to the coffee shop. The old man limping down the sidewalk had limped there before. The skinny woman was another regular walking her familiar dog. Only the white Corvette convertible parked beside the Texaco station down the street and the dark green Ford sedan immediately across from the entrance to the apartments were strangers. The Corvette was not the sort of car that interested Fleck. The Ford he would check and remember. It was one of those nondescript models that cops liked to use.

Fleck glanced down at the top of the head of the shoeshine man. The hair was a thick mass of tight gray curls. Darky hair, Fleck thought. "How you doing there, Captain?"

"About got 'em."

"You notice that green Ford yonder? Across the street there? You know who belongs to that?"

The man glanced up, found the Ford, examined it. Once his face had been a shiny, coffee black. Age had grayed it, broken it into a wilderness of lines. "I don't know it," the Captain said. "Never noticed it before."

"I'll get a check on the license number down at headquarters," Fleck said. "You tell me if you see it around here again."

"Sure," the Captain said. He whipped his shine cloth across the tip of Fleck's right shoe. Snapped it. Stood up and stepped back. "Done," he said.

Fleck handed him a ten-dollar bill. The Captain folded it into his shirt pocket.

"See if you can get a look at who gets into it," Fleck said.

"Your man, maybe?" the Captain said, his expression somewhere between skeptical and sardonic. "You think it's that dope dealer you been after?"

"Maybe," Fleck said.

He walked the five blocks down to the telephone booth he was using today, thinking about that expression on the Captain's face, and about Mama, and about what he was going to tell The Client. The Captain's expression made it clear that he didn't really believe Fleck was an undercover cop. The old man had seemed convinced enough last summer when Fleck had first taken this job and moved into the apartment. He'd shown the Captain his District of Columbia police detective credentials the third morning he had his shoes shined. The man had seemed properly impressed then. But weeks ago—how many weeks Fleck couldn't quite decide—Fleck's subconscious began registering some peculiarities. Now he was pretty sure the old man didn't believe Fleck was a cop. But he was also fairly sure the Captain didn't give a damn. The old man was playing lookout partly because he enjoyed the game and partly because of the money. The Captain was a neutral. He didn't give a damn whether Fleck was part of the law, or outside it, or the Man from Mars.

At that point, Fleck had even considered talking to the Captain about Mama. He was a nigger, but he was old and he knew a lot about people. Maybe he'd have some ideas. But talking about Mama was complicated. And painful. He didn't know what to do about her. What could he do? She hadn't been happy out there at Bluewater Home outside Cleveland, and she wasn't happy at this place he'd put her when he came to D.C.—Eldercare Manor. Maybe she wouldn't be happy anywhere. But that wasn't the point right now. The point was Eldercare wanted to be shut of her. And right away.

"We just simply can't put up with it," the Fat Man had told him. "Simply cannot tolerate it. We have to think of our other clients. Look after their welfare. We can't have that woman harassing them."

"Doing what?" Fleck had asked. But he knew what Mama was doing. Mama was getting even.

"Well," the Fat Man had said, trying to think how to put it. "Well, yesterday she put out her hand and tripped Mrs. Oliver. She fell right on the floor. Might have broken her bones." The Fat Man's hands twisted together at the thought, anxiously. "Old bones break easily, you know. Especially old ladies'."

"Mrs. Oliver has done something to Mama," Fleck said. "I can tell you that right now for dead certain." But he knew he was wasting his breath when he said it.

"No," Fat Man said. "Mrs. Oliver is a most gentle person."

"She did something," Fleck had insisted.

"Well," Fat Man said. "Well, I hadn't meant to say anything about this because old people do funny things and this isn't serious and it's easy to deal with. But your mother steals the silverware at the table. Puts the knives and forks and such things up her sleeve, and in her robe, and slips them into her room." Fat Man smiled a depreciatory smile to tell Fleck this wasn't serious. "Somebody collects them and brings them back when she's asleep, so it doesn't matter. But Mrs. Oliver doesn't know that. She tells us about it. Maybe that was it."

"Mama don't steal," Fleck had said, thinking that would be it all right. Mama must have heard the old woman telling on her. She would never tolerate anybody snitching on her, or on anybody in the family. Snitching was not to be tolerated. That was something you needed to get even for.

"Mrs. Oliver fell down just yesterday," Fleck had said. "You called me before then."

"Well," Fat Man said. "That was extra. I told you on the phone about her pulling out Mr. Riccobeni's hair?"

"She never did no such thing," Fleck had said, wearily, wondering what Mr. Riccobeni had done to warrant such retribution, wondering if pulling out the old man's hair would be enough to satisfy Mama's instinct for evening the score.

But there was no use remembering all that now. Now he had to think of what he could do with Mama, because the Fat Man had been stubborn about it. Get Mama out of there by the end of next week or he would lock her out on the porch. The Fat Man had meant it, and he had gotten that much time out of the son of a bitch only by doing a little very quiet, very mean talking. The kind of talk where you don't say a lot, and you don't say it loud, but the other fellow knows he's about to get his balls cut off.

With the phone booth in view ahead, Fleck slowed his brisk walk to a stroll, inspecting everything. He glanced at his watch. A little early, which was the way he liked it. The booth was outside a neighborhood movie theater. There was a single car in the lot, an old Chevy which Fleck had noticed before and presumed was owned by the morning cleanup man. Nothing unusual on the street, either. Fleck went into the booth, felt under the stand, found nothing more sinister than dried chewing gum wads. He checked the telephone itself. Then he sat and waited. He was thinking he would just have to be realistic about Mama. There was simply no way he could keep her with him. He'd have to just give up on that idea. He'd tried it and tried it, and each time Mama had gotten even with somebody or other, things had gone to hell, and he'd had to move her. The last time, the police had come before he'd gotten her out, and if he hadn't skipped they probably would have committed her.

The phone rang. Fleck picked it up.

"This is me," he said, and gave The Client his code name. He felt silly doing it—like kids playing with their Little Orphan Annie code rings.

"Stone," the voice said. It was an accented voice which

to Fleck's ear didn't match an American name like Stone. A Spanish accent. "What do you have for me today?"

"Nothing much," Fleck said. "You gotta remember, there's one of me and seven of them." He paused, chuckled. "I should say six now."

"We're interested in more than just six," the voice said. "We're interested in who they're dealing with. You understand that?"

Fleck didn't like the tone of voice. It was arrogant. The tone of a man used to giving orders to underlings. Mama would call The Client one of Them.

"Well," Fleck said. "I'm doing the best I can, just being one man and all. I haven't seen nothing interesting though. Not that I know of."

"You're getting a lot of money, you know. That's not just to pay for excuses."

"When we get right down to it," Fleck said, "you're owing me some money. There was just two thousand in that package Monday. You owed me another ten."

"The ten is if the job was done right," The Client said. "We don't know that yet."

"What the hell you mean? It's been almost a month and not a word about anything in the papers." Fleck was usually very good at keeping his emotion out of his voice. It was one of the skills he prided himself in, one of the tricks he'd learned in the recreation yards of detention centers and jails and, finally, at Joliet. But now you could hear the anger. "I need that money. And I'm going to get it."

"You will get it when we decide nothing went wrong with that job," The Client said. "Now shut up about it. I want to talk to you about Santero. We still don't know where he went when he left the District. That worries us."

And so the man who called himself Stone talked about Santero and Fleck half listened, his mouth stiff and set with his anger. Stone outlined a plan. Fleck told him the number of the pay phone where he would be next Tuesday, blurting it out because he had some things to say to this arrogant son of a bitch. Some rules to lay down, and some understanding that Fleck was nobody's nigger.

"So that'll be the number and now I want you to listen—" Fleck began, but he heard the line disconnect. He stared at the phone. "You son of a bitch," he said. "You dirty son of a bitch." His voice squeaked with the anger. The rage. This was what Mama had told them about. Him and Delmar. About the ruling class. The way they put you down if you let them. Treated you like niggers. Like dogs. And the only way you kept your head up, the only way to keep from being a bum and a wino, was by getting even. Always keeping things even. Always keeping your pride.

He walked back toward his apartment thinking about how he would go about it. Lot of work to be done. They knew who he was, he'd bet a million dollars on that. The shyster pretended otherwise. Elkins pretended that what he called "protective insulation" worked both ways. But lawyers lied. Lawyers were part of Them. Leroy Fleck would be expendable, something to be thrown to the police when he wasn't useful. Safer for everybody to have Fleck dead, or back in lockup. But The Client was where the money came from, so The Client would know everything he wanted to know.

There would be plenty of time to even that up, Fleck thought, because there was nothing he could do until he had Mama taken care of. He had to have another place for her, and that always meant a big advance payment. While he was hunting a place for Mama, he'd find out just who The Client was and where he could find him. Now he was almost certain The Client was an embassy. Spanish-speaking. Some country that had revolution problems, judging from the work they had him doing.

THE TROUBLE WAS nobody was interested. November had become December and the man with the pointed shoes remained nameless, an unresolved problem. Somewhere someone worried and waited for him. Or, if they had guessed his fate, they mourned him. The man had taken on a personality in Joe Leaphorn's mind. Once he would have discussed him with Emma, and Emma would have had something sensible to say.

"Of course no one is interested," Emma would have said in that small, soft voice. "The Agency doesn't have to take jurisdiction so it's not an FBI problem. And McKinley County has had about five bodies since then to worry about and these bodies are local with relatives who vote. And it didn't happen on the reservation, and it wouldn't be your problem even if it had because it's clearly a homicide, and reservation homicides are the FBI's problem. You're just interested because it's an interesting puzzle." To which he would have said: Yes. You're right. Now tell me why he was put under those chamisa bushes when it was so tough to get him there, carrying him all the way down the railroad tracks, and explain the Yeibichai note. And Emma would have said something like, They wanted the body seen from the train and reported and found, or they stopped the train and put him off.

But Leaphorn couldn't imagine what Emma would have said about the Yeibichai and Agnes Tsosie. He felt the old, painful, overwhelming need to talk to her. To see her sitting in that old brown chair, working on one of those endless making-something-for-somebody's-baby projects which always kept her hands busy while she thought about whatever problem he'd presented her. A year now, a little more than a year, since she had died. This part of it seemed to get no better.

He turned off the television, put on his coat and walked out on the porch. It was still snowing a little—just an occasional dry flake. Enough to declare the end of autumn. Inside again, he got his winter jacket from the closet, dropped it on the sofa, turned on the TV again, and sat down. Okay, Emma, he thought, how about the missing dentures? They don't just pop out when one is struck. They're secured. He'd told the pathologist he was curious about those missing false teeth and the man had done some checking during the autopsy. There was not just one question, the doctor had said, but two. The gums showed the victim secured his teeth with a standard fixative. Therefore either the fellow had been killed while his teeth were out, or they had been removed after his death. In light of the way the man was dressed the first seemed improbable. So why remove the teeth? To avoid identification of the victim? Possibly. Would Emma have any other ideas? The second question was exactly the sort which intrigued Leaphorn.

"I didn't find any sign of any of those gum diseases, or those jawbone problems, which cause dentists to remove teeth. Everything was perfectly healthy. There was some sign of trauma. The upper right molars, upper left incisor, had been broken in a way that caused some trauma to the bone and left resulting bone lesions." That's what the pathologist had said. He had looked up from his report at Leaphorn and said: "Do you know why his teeth are missing?"

So tell me, Emma, Leaphorn thought. If you're so smart, you tell me why such a high-class gentleman got his teeth extracted. And why.

As he thought it, he heard himself saying it aloud. He pushed himself out of the chair, embarrassed. "Crazy," he said, also aloud. "Talking to myself."

He switched off the TV again and retrieved the coat. It was colder but no longer snowing. He brushed the feathery deposit from the windshield with his sleeve, and drove.

Eastbound through Gallup, he saw Kennedy's sedan parked at the Zuni Truck Stop Cafe. Kennedy was drinking tea.

"Sit," Kennedy said, indicating the empty bench across the booth table from him. He extracted the tea bag from his cup and held it gingerly by its string. "Peppermint," he said. "You ever drink this stuff?"

Leaphorn sat. "Now and then," he said.

"What brings you off the reservation on such an inclement Saturday evening?"

What, indeed? Old friend, I am running from Emma's ghost, Leaphorn thought. I am running from my own loneliness. I am running away from craziness.

"I'm still curious about your man with the pointed shoes," Leaphorn said. "Did you ever get him identified?"

Kennedy gazed at him over the cup. "Nothing on the fingerprints," he said. "I think I told you that. Nothing on anything else, either."

"If you found his false teeth, could you identify him from that?"

"Maybe," Kennedy said. "If we knew where he was from, then we could find out who made that sort of denture. Probably we could."

The waitress appeared with a menu. "Just coffee," Leaphorn said. He had no appetite this evening.

"My wife tells me coffee is giving me the night sweats. The caffeine is making me jumpy," Kennedy said. "She's got me off on tea."

Leaphorn nodded. Emma used to do such things to him.

"That guy's sheriff's office business anyway," Kennedy said. "I had a hunch he'd be my baby if he was identified. Just by the looks of him. He looked foreign. Looked important." He grinned. "Kinda nice, not having him identified."

"How hard did you try?"

Kennedy glanced at him over the teacup, mildly surprised at Leaphorn's tone.

"The usual," he said. "Prints. Clothes were tailor-made. So were the shoes. We sent them all back to Washington. Sent photographs, too. They didn't match anyone on the missing list." He shook his head. "Nothing matched anywhere. *Nada.* Absolutely nothing."

"Nothing?"

"Lab decided the clothes were foreign made. European or South American probably. Not Hong Kong."

"That's a big help," Leaphorn said. He sipped the coffee. It was fresh. Compared to the instant stuff he'd been drinking at home it was delicious.

"It confirmed my hunch, I think," Kennedy said. "If we ever get that sucker identified, it will be a federal case. He'll be some biggie in drugs, or moving money illegally. Something international."

"Sounds like it," Leaphorn said. He was thinking of a

middle-aged woman sitting somewhere wondering what had happened to Pointed Shoes. He was wondering what circumstances brought a man in old, worn, lovingly polished custom-built shoes to die amid the chamisa, sage, and snakeweed east of Gallup. He was wondering about the fatal little puncture at the base of his skull. "Anything new about the cause of death? The weapon?"

"Nothing changed. It's still a thin knife blade inserted between the first vertebra and the base of the skull. Still a single thrust. No needless cuts or punctures. Still a real pro did it."

"And what brings a real pro to Gallup? Does the Agency have any thoughts on that?"

Kennedy laughed. "You caught me twenty-eight years too late, Joe. When I was on the green side of thirty and still bucking for J. Edgar's job, then this one would have worried me to death. Somewhere back there about murder case three hundred and nine it dawned on me I wasn't going to save the world."

"You ran out of curiosity," Leaphorn said.

"I got old," Kennedy said. "Or maybe wise. But I'm curious about what brings you off the reservation in this kind of weather."

"Just feeling restless," Leaphorn said. "I think I'm going to drive out there where the body was."

"It'll be dark by the time you could get out there."

"If the pathologist is right, it was dark when that guy got knifed. The night before we found him. You want to come along?"

Kennedy didn't want to come along. Leaphorn cruised slowly down Interstate 40, his patrol car causing a brief bubble of uneasy sixty-five-mile-an-hour caution in the flood of eastbound traffic. The cold front now was again producing intermittent snow, flurries of small, feathery flakes which seemed as cold and dry as dust, followed by gaps in which the western horizon glowed dully with the dying day. He angled off the highway at the Fort Wingate interchange and stopped where the access road met the old fort's entrance route. He sat a moment, reviving the question he raised when he'd seen the body. Any link between this obsolete ammunition depot—long on the Pentagon's list for abandonment—and a corpse left nearby wearing clothing cut by a foreign tailor? Smuggling out explosives? From what little Leaphorn knew about the mile after mile of bunkers here, they held the shells for heavy artillery. There was nothing one would sneak out in a briefcase—or find a use for if one did. He restarted the car and drove under the interstate to old U.S. Highway 66, and down it toward the Shell Oil Company's refinery at Iyanbito. The Santa Fe railroad had built the twin tracks of its California-bound main line here, paralleling the old highway with the towering pink ramparts of Nashodishgish Mesa walling in this corridor to the north. Leaphorn parked again, pulling the car off in the snakeweed beside the pavement. From this point it was less than four hundred yards to the growth of chamisa where the body of Pointed Shoes had been laid. Leaphorn checked the right-of-way fence. Easy enough to climb through. Easy enough to pass that small body over. But that hadn't been done. Not unless whoever did it could cross four hundred yards of soft, dusty earth without leaving tracks.

Leaphorn climbed through the fence and walked toward the tracks. A train was coming from the east, creating its freight train thunder. Its locomotive headlight made a dazzling point in the darkness. Leaphorn kept his eyes down, the brim of his uniform hat shading his face, walking steadily across the brushy landscape. The locomotive flashed past, pushed by three other diesels and trailing noise, towing flatcars carrying piggyback truck trailers, and then a parade of tank cars, then hopper cars, then cars carrying new automobiles stacked high, then old slab-side freight cars, and finally a caboose. Leaphorn was close enough now to see light in the caboose window. What could the brakeman in it see? Could some engineer have seen two men (three men? four men? The thought was irrational) carrying Pointed Shoes along the right of way to his resting place?

He stood watching the disappearing caboose lights and the glare of an approaching eastbound headlight on the next track. The snow was a little heavier now, the wind colder on his neck. He pulled up his jacket collar, pulled down the hat brim. What he didn't know about this business had touched something inside Leaphorn—a bitterness he usually kept so submerged that it was forgotten. Under this dreary cold sky it surfaced. If Pointed Shoes had been something different than he was, someone too important to vanish unmissed and unreported, someone whose tailored suit was not frayed, whose shoe heels were not worn, then the system would have answered all these questions long ago. Train schedules would have been checked, train crews located and interviewed. Leaphorn shivered, pulled the jacket tighter around him, looked down the track trying to get a reading on what an engineer could see along the track in the glare of his headlight. From the high vantage point of the cabin, he could see quite a lot, Leaphorn guessed.

The freight rumbled past, leaving silence. Leaphorn wandered down the track, and away from it back toward the road. Then he heard another train coming from the east. Much faster than the freights. It would be the Amtrak, he thought, and turned to watch it come. It whistled twice, probably for the crossing of a county road up ahead. And then it was roaring past. Seventy miles an hour, he guessed. Not yet slowing for its stop at Gallup. He smiled, remembering the suggestion he had put into Emma's voice—that maybe they stopped the Amtrak and put him off. He was close enough to see the heads of people at the windows, people in the glass-roofed observation car. People with a fear of flying, or rich enough to afford not to fly. Maybe they stopped the Amtrak and put him off, he thought. Well, maybe they did. It seemed no more foolish than his vision of a platoon of men carrying Pointed Shoes down the tracks.

Bernard St. Germain happened to be the only railroader who Leaphorn knew personally—a brakeman-conductor with the Atchison, Topeka and Santa Fe Railroad Company. Leaphorn called him from the Fina station off the Iyanbito interchange and got the recording on St. Germain's answering machine. But while he was leaving a message, St. Germain picked up the receiver.

"I have a very simple question," Leaphorn said. "Can a passenger stop an Amtrak train? Do they still have that cord that can be pulled to set the air brakes, like you see in the old movies?"

"Now there's a box in each car, like a fire alarm box," St. Germain said. "They call it the 'big hole lever.' A passenger can reach in there and pull it."

"And it stops the train?"

"Sure. It sets the air brakes."

"How long would it be stopped?"

"That would depend on circumstances. Ten minutes maybe. Or maybe an hour. What's going on?"

"We had a body beside the tracks east of Gallup last month. I'm trying to figure out how it got there."

"I heard about it," St. Germain said. "You think somebody stopped the Amtrak and took the body off?"

"Just a thought. Just a possibility."

"What day was it? I can find out if somebody pulled the big hole lever."

Leaphorn gave him the date of the death of Pointed Shoes.

"Yeah. All that stuff has to be reported," St. Germain said. "Any time a train makes an unscheduled stop for any reason you have to turn in a delay report. And that has to be radioed in immediately. I'll find out for you Monday."

7

ONE IS NOT supposed to deal with one's personal mail while on duty in the Navajo Tribal Police Office at Shiprock. Nor is one supposed to receive personal telephone calls. On Monday, Officer Jim Chee did both. He had a fairly good reason.

The post office would not deliver mail to Chee's little aluminum house trailer parked under the cottonwoods beside the San Juan River. Instead, Chee picked it up at the post office each day during his lunch break. On Monday his portion was an L. L. Bean catalog for which he had sent off a coupon, and a letter from Mary Landon. He hurried back to the office with them, put the catalog aside, and tore open the letter.

"Dearest Jim," it began. From that excellent beginning, it went downhill fast.

When your letter arrived yesterday, I was thrilled at the thought of your visit, and seeing you again. But now I have had time to think about it and I think it is a mistake. We still have the same problem and all this will do is bring all the old pain back again. . . .

Chee stopped reading and stared at the wall across from his desk. The wall needed painting. It had needed painting for years. Chee had stuck a calendar to it, and an eight-by-ten photograph of Mary Landon and himself, taken by Cowboy Dashee with the two of them standing on the steps of the little "teacherage" where she had lived when she taught at the Crownpoint Elementary School. Like many of Cowboy's photographs it was slightly out of focus but Chee had treasured it because it had managed to capture Mary's key ingredient: happiness. They had been out all night, watching the final night of an Enemy Way ceremonial over near the Whippoorwill Chapter House. Looking back on it, Chee had come to realize that it was that night he decided he would marry Mary Landon. Or try to marry her.

He read the rest of the letter. It was short—a simple recitation of their problem. She wouldn't want her children raised on the reservation, bringing them up as strangers to her own culture. He wouldn't be happy away from the reservation. And if he made the sacrifice for her, she would be miserable because she had made him miserable. It was an impossible dilemma, she said. Why should they revive the pain? Why not let the wound heal?

Why not, indeed? Except it wasn't healing. Except he couldn't seem to get past it. He put the letter aside. Think of something else. What he had to do today. He had pretty well cleaned up everything pending, getting ready for this vacation. There was a man he was supposed to find out behind Toh-Atin Mesa, a witness in an assault case. The trial had been postponed and he'd intended to let that hang until he came back from Wisconsin and seeing Mary. But he would do it today. He would do it right now. Immediately.

The telephone rang. It was Janet Pete, calling from Washington.

"Ya et eeh," Janet Pete said. "You doing all right?"

"Fine," Chee said. "What's up?"

"Our paths are crossing again," she said. "I've got myself a client and it turns out you arrested him."

Chee was puzzled. "Aren't you in Washington?"

"I'm in Washington. But you arrested this guy on the rez. Out at a Yeibichai, he tells me."

Henry Highhawk. "Yeah," Chee said. "Guy with his hair in braids. Like a blond Kiowa."

"That's him," Janet said. "But he noticed he wasn't in style on the reservation. He changed it to a bun." There was a pause. "You doing all right? You sound sort of down."

"Even Navajos get the blues," Chee said. "No. I'm okay. Just tired. Tomorrow my vacation starts. You're supposed to be tired just before vacation. That's the way the system's supposed to work."

"I guess so," Janet said. She sounded tired, too. "When you arrested him, do you remember if there was another man with him? Slender. Latin-looking."

"With crippled hands? He said his name was Gomez. I think it was Gomez. Maybe Lopez."

"It was Gomez. What did you think of him?"

The question surprised Chee. He thought. "Interesting man. I wondered how he managed to lose so many fingers."

There was a long silence.

"How did he lose those fingers?"

"I don't know," Janet said. "I'm just trying to get some sort of handle on this man. On my client, really. I like to understand what I'm getting into."

"How did you manage to get involved with this Highhawk bird anyway?" Chee asked. "Are you specializing in really weird cases?"

"That's easy. Highhawk is part Navajo and very proud of it. He wants to be whole Navajo. Anyway, he talks like he does. So he wants a Navajo attorney."

"Totally his idea then," Chee said, sounding skeptical. "You didn't volunteer?"

Janet laughed. "Well, there's been a lot about the case in the papers here. Highhawk's a conservator at the Smithsonian and he'd been raising hell about them keeping a million or so Native American skeletons in their warehouse, and last year they tried to fire him. So he went and filed a suit and won his job back. It was a First Amendment case. First Amendment cases get a lot of space in the *Washington Post*. Then he pulls this caper you arrested him for. He dug up a couple of graves up in New England, and of course he picked a historically prominent couple, and that got him a lot more publicity. So I knew about him, and I had read about the Navajo connection . . ." Her voice trailed off.

"I think you have a strange one for a client," Chee said. "Any chance to get him off?"

"Not if he gets his way. He wants to make it a political debate. He wants to put the *belagaana* grave robbers on trial for robbing Indian graves while he's on trial for digging up a couple of whites. It might work in Washington, if I could pick the right jury. But the trial will be up in New Haven or someplace up in New England. Up in that part of the country everybody's happy memories are of hearing great-granddaddy tell about killing off the redskins."

Another pause. Chee found himself looking at the picture. Mary Landon and Jim Chee on the doorstep, clowning. Mary's hair was incredibly soft. Out on the malpais that day they went on the picnic, it had blown around her face. He had used his first finger to brush it away from her forehead. Mary's voice saying: "You have a choice. You know if you go to the FBI Academy, then you'll do well, and you know they'll offer you a job. They need some Navajo agents. It's not as if you didn't have any choice." And he had said, you have a choice, too, or something like that. Something inane.

"You're probably supposed to be working," Janet Pete was saying, "and I don't know what I called about exactly anyway. I think I just hoped you could tell me something helpful about Gomez. Or about Highhawk."

Or wanted to hear a friendly voice, Chee thought. It was his own feeling, exactly. "Maybe I'm overlooking something," Chee said. "Maybe if I understood the problem better—"

"I don't understand the problem myself," Janet said. She exhaled noisily. "Look. What would you think if you're talking to your client and it went like this. This guy's going on trial for desecrating a grave. You are being very cool, trying to talk some sense into him about how to handle it if he actually did what they accuse him of, and all of a sudden he says: 'Of course I did it. I'm proud I did it. But would you be my lawyer for another crime?' And I say, 'What crime?' And he says, 'It hasn't been committed yet.' And I don't know what to say to that so I say something flippant. If you're going to dig up another grave, I don't want to hear about it, I say. And he says, 'No, this one would be something better than that.' And I look at him, surprised, you know. I'm thinking it's a joke, but his face is solemn. He's not joking."

"Did he tell you what crime?"

"I said, What crime? How serious? And he said *we* can't talk about it. And, if *we* told you, you would be an accessory before the fact. He was smiling when he said that. Notice, he said *we.*"

"We," Chee repeated. "Any idea who? Is he part of some sort of Indian Power organization? Is somebody working with him on this 'free the bones' project?"

"Well, he's always talking about his 'Paho Society' but I think he's the only member. This time I think he meant Gomez."

"Why Gomez?"

"I don't know. Gomez brings him to my office. I call Highhawk at Highhawk's place, and Gomez answers the telephone. Gomez always seems to be around. Did you know Gomez bonded him out after you picked him up in Arizona?"

"I didn't," Chee said. "Maybe they're just friends."

"I wanted to ask you about that," Janet said. "Did they come to the Yeibichai together? Did you get the feeling they were friends? Old friends?"

"They were strangers," Chee said. "I'm sure of that." He remembered the scene, described it to Janet—Gomez arriving first, waiting in the rental car, disinterested, making contact with Highhawk. He described the clear, obvious fact that Highhawk didn't know Gomez. "I'd say that Gomez came to the Yeibichai just to find Highhawk. But how could he have known Highhawk was coming, if they were really strangers?"

"That's easy. The same way the FBI knew where to arrest him," Janet said. "He told everybody, the woman he rents his apartment from, his neighbors, his drinking buddies, the people he works with at the Smithsonian, told everybody, that he was coming out to Arizona to attend a Yeibichai for his *shima'sa'ni'."*

"He used that word? Maternal grandmother?"

"Well, he told them he had found this old woman in his Bitter Water Clan. He claims his maternal grandmother was a Bitter Water Dineh. And he claims the old woman had invited him to her Yeibichai."

Chee found he was getting interested in all this. "Well, whatever, when I saw them, Gomez was trying to get acquainted with a stranger. Either that, or they're both good actors. And who would they be trying to fool?" Chee didn't wait for an answer to that rhetorical question. He was thinking about what Janet had said about the crime not yet committed. Something serious. Something *"we"* couldn't talk about.

"I'd say you have a very flaky client," Chee added. "Any reason to think this isn't just some neurotic Lone Ranger trying to impress a pretty lawyer?"

"There's a little bit more," Janet Pete said. "His telephone is tapped."

"Oh," Chee said. "He tell you that?"

"I heard the click. The interference on the line. I called him just before I called you. In fact, that's what actually motivated me to make this call."

"Oh," Chee said. "I thought maybe you were missing me."

"That too," Janet said. "That, and somebody's been following me."

"Ah," Chee said. He was remembering Janet Pete. How she had handled him when she thought he was mishandling one of her clients the first time they had met; how she had dealt with the situation when he'd damaged a car she was buying. Janet Pete was not a person who would be easy to spook.

"If not exactly following me, then keeping an eye on my place. And on me. I see this guy outside my apartment. I see him in the newsstand below where we work. I see him too often. And I never saw him until I got tied up with this Highhawk business."

Chee had been holding Mary Landon's letter in his left hand, folding and unfolding it between his fingers. Now he dropped it into his out-basket on top of the little folder which held his round-trip Continental Airlines ticket to Milwaukee. He thought he might go to Washington, drop in at the J. Edgar Hoover Building in Washington. See what it looked like. Talk to a couple of people he knew back there. See what it would feel like to work for the Agency.

"Tell you what," he said. "I'm coming to Washington anyway. Next day or two. I have some business at the FBI office. I'll let you know exactly when and you set it up for me to talk to Highhawk. And Gomez, too, if you can. That is, if you want to see what I think of it."

"I do." A long pause. "Thanks, Jim."

"It'll be good to see you," he said. "And I want to meet your boyfriend, the rich and famous attorney."

At least it would be better than two weeks lying around the trailer. And he had detected something in Janet Pete's voice that he'd never heard before. She sounded frightened.

8

SUNDAY LIEUTENANT JOE LEAPHORN had felt a lot better about the man with pointed shoes. His sense of the natural order of things had been restored. While in many ways Joe Leaphorn had moved into the world of the whites, his Navajo requirement for order and harmony remained. Every effect must have its cause, every action its necessary result. Unity existed, universal and eternal. And now it seemed that nothing violating this natural order had happened in the sagebrush plain east of Gallup. Apparently Pointed Shoes had flashed his bankroll in the wrong place, perhaps at a poker game in the observation car. The man with the knife had killed him, stopped the train, put the body under a convenient cover of chamisa brush, and gotten back on with the victim's wallet.

There were some holes in that theory, some unanswered questions. For example, what the devil had happened to the false teeth? What was the connection with the Agnes Tsosie Yeibichai? But basically much of the disharmony had seeped out of this homicide. Leaphorn could think of other things. He thought about cleaning his house, and getting ready for his vacation. As with most Navajo Tribal Policemen, vacation time for Leaphorn came after the summer tourist season ended and before winter brought its blizzards with their heavy work load of rescue operations. If Leaphorn wanted to take his vacation, now was the time. He had already postponed it once, simply because in the absence of Emma he could think of nothing he would enjoy doing. But he should take it. If he didn't, his friends would notice. He would see more of those subtle little indications of their kindness and their pity that he had come to dread. So he would think of someplace to go. Something to do. And he would think of it today. Just as soon as he got the dishes done, and the dirty clothes down to the laundromat.

But when the phone rang just as he was getting ready to go to lunch Monday he still hadn't thought of anything. Lunch was going to be with Kennedy. Kennedy was in Window Rock on some sort of Agency records-checking business and was waiting for him at the coffee shop of the Navajo Nation Motor Inn. He had decided he would ask Kennedy for suggestions about what to do with eighteen days off. Leaphorn picked up the receiver and said "Leaphorn," in a tone which he hoped expressed hurry.

The voice was Bernard St. Germain's. Leaphorn had time for this call.

"Pretty good guess you made," St. Germain said. "Not perfect, but close."

"Good," Leaphorn said. Now, he thought, Pointed Shoes becomes a homicide committed in interstate commerce. A federal case. Now the Agency would be involved. More than eleven thousand FBI agents, well dressed, well trained, and highly paid, would be unleashed to attach an identity to the man with pointed shoes. The world's most expensive crime lab would be involved. And if Pointed Shoes was important and a solution seemed imminent, law enforcement's best-funded and most successful public relations machinery would spring into action. Kennedy, his old friend, with whom he was about to have lunch, would have to get to work.

"What do you mean, close but not perfect?" Leaphorn asked.

"Close because the Amtrak did stop that evening, and right about where your body was found. But nobody pulled the big hole lever," St. Germain said. "The ATS system malfunctioned and stopped it."

"ATS?"

"They used to call it the dead man's switch," St. Germain said. "If the engineer doesn't push the button periodically, it automatically applies the air brakes. It's just in case the engineer has a heart attack or a stroke or something. Or maybe goes to sleep. Then he doesn't push the button and the ATS stops the train automatically."

"That means it was just an accident? A passenger couldn't cause that? No question about it?"

"No question at all. Such things have to be reported in writing. It's all there on the delay report. The Amtrak was seven minutes behind schedule. Then, a few miles east of the Fort Wingate spur, the ATS shorted out or something and put on the brakes."

Leaphorn stared at the map on the wall behind his desk, rethinking his theory.

"How long was it stopped?"

"I knew you'd ask that," St. Germain said. "It was stopped 38 minutes. From 8:34 until 9:12 P.M. That would be about average, I think. The engineer has to get the air pressure up and the brakes have to be reset. So forth."

"Could passengers get off?"

"Not supposed to."

"But could they?"

"Sure. Why not?"

"And get back on again?"

"Yep."

"Would anybody see if someone did? Anybody on the train crew?"

"You mean at night? After dark? It would depend. But probably not. Not if the guy didn't want to be seen. It would be simple enough. You'd just have to wait until everybody was busy. Nobody looking."

"Bernard, what happens to the luggage if a passenger gets off before his destination and leaves it?"

"They take it off at the end of the line—the turnaround point when they're cleaning out the cars. It goes into the claims office. The Lost and Found. Or, if it comes out of a reserved compartment on the sleeper, or a roomette, then they'd do a tracer on it and send it back to the point of origin. So the passenger could pick it up there."

"This Amtrak that comes through here, would the turnaround point be Los Angeles?"

"Not exactly. There's an eastbound and a westbound each day. West is Number 3. East is Number 4."

"Who would I call there to find out about left-behind luggage?"

St. Germain told him.

Kennedy could wait a minute to have lunch with him. He called the Amtrak claims office in Los Angeles, and told the man who answered who he was, what he needed, and why he needed it. He gave the man the train and the date. Then he waited. It didn't take long.

"Yeah. There was a suitcase and some personal stuff left in a roomette on that train. We held it here to see if somebody would claim it. But now it's gone back to Washington," the man said.

"Washington?"

"That's where the passenger boarded. He transferred to Number 3 in Chicago."

Leaphorn took the cap off his ballpoint, pulled his note pad toward him.

"What was his name?"

"Who knows? I guess you could get it from the claims office in Washington. Or from the reservations office. Wherever they keep that sort of records. That's not my end of the business."

"How about locating the train crew? That possible?"

"That's Washington, too. That's where that crew is based. I'd think it would be easy enough to get their names out of Washington."

Kennedy had already ordered when Leaphorn reached his table. He was eating a club sandwich.

"You running on Navajo time?" he asked.

"Always," Leaphorn said. He sat, glanced at the menu, ordered green chili stew. He felt great.

"I've learned a few things about that body," he said. He told Kennedy about the Amtrak being stopped that night at the place where the body was left, and about what St. Germain had told him, and about the passenger's baggage being left in the roomette.

Kennedy chewed, looking thoughtful. He grinned, but the grin was faint. "If you don't quit this, you know, you're going to make a federal case out of it," he said. "What do you want me to do?"

"Do your famous FBI thing," Leaphorn said.

Kennedy swallowed, took a sip of water, nodded. "Okay. I'll get somebody in Washington to go down and take a look at the luggage. We'll see if they can get an identification. We'll see where that leads us."

"What more could anyone ask?"

"I can think of a few more things you're going to ask," Kennedy said. "Based on our past experiences with you. It'll turn out this luggage belongs to an alcoholic who has a habit of falling through cracks. So we will sensibly decide he's not the body, but you won't be happy with that." Kennedy held up a hand, all fingers extended. He bent down one. "One. You'll want some sort of latent fingerprint check on the luggage." He bent down another. "Two. You'll want identification of the eighty-two people who have handled it since the owner." He bent down a third. "Three. You'll want a rundown on everybody who was on that particular Amtrak trip." Kennedy bent down the surviving finger. "Four. You'll want interviews with the train crews. Five—" Kennedy had exhausted his supply of fingers. He extended his thumb. "In summation, you'll want the same sort of stuff we'd do if the Emperor of Earth had been kidnapped by the Martians. Cost eighty-six billions in overtime and then it turns out that your body is a car dealer who got in an argument with somebody in the bar of the train and it's not the business of the Agency."

Leaphorn nodded.

"It's none of your business, either," Kennedy added. "You know that, don't you?"

Leaphorn nodded again. "Not my business yet." He took a spoonful of the stew, ate it. "But I wonder why he was going to the Yeibichai," he said. "Don't you?"

"Sure," Kennedy said. "That seems strange."

"And if he was going, why was he almost a month early?"

"I wonder about a lot of things," Kennedy said. "I wonder why George Bush picked what's-his-name for vice president. I wonder why the Anasazis walked away from all those cliff dwellings. I wonder why the hell I ever got into law enforcement. Or had lunch with you when I knew you'd be wanting a favor."

"And I wonder about that guy's false teeth," Leaphorn said. "Not so much where the false ones went as what happened to his original teeth."

Kennedy laughed. "I'm not that deeply into the wondering game," he said.

"There was nothing wrong with his gums, or his jawbone," Leaphorn said. "That's what the autopsy showed. And that's why people have their teeth pulled."

Kennedy sighed, shook his head. "You get the check," he said. "I'll get somebody to check on the luggage in Washington."

He did. Leaphorn got the call Tuesday.

"Here's what they found," Kennedy said. "The reservation was made in the name of Hilario Madrid-Peña. Apparently it was a bogus name. At least both the address and the telephone number were phony and the name isn't in any of the directories."

"That puts us back to square one," Leaphorn said, trying to keep the disappointment out of his voice. "Unless they found something in the luggage."

"Just a second," Kennedy said. "One large suitcase and one briefcase," he read. "Suitcase contained the expected articles of underwear, shirts, socks, one pair trousers, ceramic pottery, toilet articles. Briefcase contained magazines and newspapers in Spanish, books, small notebook, stationery, envelopes, stamps, fountain pen, package Tums, incidentals. Nothing in notebook appeared helpful in establishing identity." Kennedy paused. "That's it. That's all she wrote."

Leaphorn thought about it. "Well," he said, "I don't know what to think."

"I'm waiting for you to say 'Thank you Mr. Kennedy,' " Kennedy said.

"Do you know the agent who checked?" Leaphorn asked.

"You mean personally? Or what was his name? No to both. It could have been anybody."

"You think it would have been somebody who knew what he was doing?"

"I wouldn't think so," Kennedy said. "Some rookie you'd want to get out of the office. A deal like this one wouldn't be high priority." Kennedy laughed. "Neither am I."

"What's the chance of getting the Agency to run down the train crew, find out who picked up the luggage, cleaned up the roomette, that sort of thing?"

"I don't know. Probably about the same as you pitching the opening game of the World Series next year."

"I'm told that train crew works out of Washington."

"So what?" Kennedy said. "Before they put a man on something like that, they have to have a reason."

"I guess so," Leaphorn said. He was thinking that he knew a man in Washington who might do it for him. Out of friendship. If Leaphorn was willing to impose on the friendship. He said, "Well, thank you Mr. Kennedy," and hung up, still thinking about it. P. J. Rodney would do it out of friendship, but it would be a lot of work for him—or at least it might be. And maybe Rodney was retired by now. Leaphorn tried to remember what year it had been when Rodney left the Duluth Police Department and signed on at Washington. He must have enough years in to qualify for retirement, but when Leaphorn had written Rodney to tell him about Emma, he had still been on the District of Columbia force.

Leaphorn glanced at his watch. Time for the news. He walked into the living room, turned on the television, flicked it to channel seven, turned off the sound to avoid the hysterical screaming of the Frontier Ford commercial, then turned it up to hear the newscast. Nothing much interesting seemed to be happening and he found his thoughts returning to Rodney. A good man. They had become friends when they were both country-cousin outsiders attending the FBI Academy. One of those all-too-rare cases when you know almost at first glance that you're going to like someone, and the liking is mutual. And when Rodney had stopped off at Window Rock to visit them on his way to California, he'd had the same effect on Emma. "You make good friends," Emma had told him.

Rodney was a good friend. Leaphorn watched Howard Morgan warning about a winter storm moving across southern Utah toward northeastern Arizona and New Mexico. "Watch out for blowing snow," Morgan said.

Leaphorn thought it would be good to see Rodney again. He knew what he would do with his vacation time.

JANET PETE MET HIM at the Continental gate at National Airport, looking trim, efficient, tense, and happy to see him. She hugged him and shepherded him through the mob to the taxi stands.

"Wow," Chee said. "Is it always this crowded?"

"Anthill East," Janet said. She's tired, he thought. But pretty. And very sophisticated. The suit she wore was pale gray and might have been made out of silk. Whatever it was made of it reminded Chee that Janet Pete had a very nice shape. It also reminded him that his town jeans, leather jacket, and bolo tie did not put him in the mainstream of fashion in Washington, D.C., as they did in Farmington or Flagstaff. Here every male above the age of puberty wore a dark three-piece suit, a white shirt, and a dark tie. To Chee, the suits seemed to be identical. His eyes shifted back to Janet, studying her.

"Nobody ever looks at anyone," Chee said, who had been caught by Janet staring at her. "You notice that?"

"Avoid eye contact," Janet said. "That's the first rule of

survival in an urban society. I hear it's even worse in Tokyo and Hong Kong and places like that. And for the same reason. Too damn many people crowded together." She gave the driver the address of Chee's hotel. "It was nice of you to come," she said, and her tone told Chee she meant it.

It was a gray, chilly, drizzling day, a "female rain" in Chee's Navajo vocabulary. Janet asked about the reservation, about tribal politics, about their very few mutual acquaintances. Chee answered, wondering now why he had come, wondering if he should have gone to Wisconsin despite Mary's letter. He'd told the travel agency at Farmington to get him a hotel in the "moderate to economical" range. The one where the cab stopped looked economical at best. He checked in. The price was seventy-six dollars per day—approximately triple a good room in the Four Corners country. This room was tiny, with a small double bed, a single chair, a TV set mounted on a wall bracket with one of the control knobs missing, a single narrow window looking out at the windows of a building across the street. Chee motioned Janet to the chair and sat on the bed.

"Here I am," Chee said. "What can I do?"

Janet made a wry face. "The trouble is I don't know what's going on. Or even if *anything* is going on."

"You said someone was following you. Tell me about that."

"That doesn't take long," Janet said. "The first time I went to see Henry Highhawk, I couldn't find his place at first. I walked right past it, and then back again. There was a car parked up the block a ways with a man sitting in it. He was staring at me, so I noticed him. Medium to small apparently. Maybe forty-five or so. Red hair, a lot of freckles, sort of a red face." She paused and glanced at Chee with an attempt at a smile. "Do you ever wonder why they call *us* redskins?" she asked.

"Go on," Chee said. "I'm interested."

"Highhawk lives out on Capitol Hill, in a neighborhood they call Eastern Market. It's easy to get there on the Metro. That's the subway. So I took the Metro and walked to his house. About seven or eight blocks, maybe. I happened to walk past this guy twice sitting in his parked car, so I noticed him. Then when—"

"Hold it," Chee said. "You mean he'd moved the car after you passed him the first time? He moved it up ahead of you?"

"Apparently. And then, when I left Highhawk's place, he was still there. Still sitting in that car. Again, I noticed him twice more while I was walking back to the subway. He was walking the second time. Like he wanted to know where I was going and he left his car parked and followed me on foot. But he didn't get on the subway. Or if he did, I didn't see him."

She paused, looked at him for reaction.

"Hmm," Chee said, trying to sound thoughtful. He was thinking there were plenty of nonsinister reasons a man might follow Janet Pete.

"Since then, three or four times, I've seen him," she added.

Chee apparently didn't looked sufficiently impressed by this. Janet flushed.

"This isn't Shiprock," she said. "You don't just keep seeing a stranger in Washington. Not unless you work in the same place. Or eat in the same place. Millions of people. But I saw this man outside the building where we have our law offices. Once in the parking lot and once outside the lobby. And not counting the Eastern Market Metro business, I saw him out at the Museum of Natural History. Too much to be a coincidence."

"The very first time was at Highhawk's place," Chee said. "Is that right? And again out in his neighborhood. Maybe he's interested in Highhawk. And you're Highhawk's lawyer. Maybe he's interested in you because of that."

"Yes," Janet said. "I thought of that. That's probably it."

"I'd offer you some refreshments if I had any," Chee said. "In Farmington, in a seventy-five-dollar hotel, if they had anything that expensive, you'd have a little refrigerator with all those snacks and drinks in it. Or you'd have room service."

"In Washington that comes in the three-hundred-dollar-per-day hotels," Janet said. "But I don't want anything. I want to know what you think of Highhawk. What do you think of all of this?"

"He struck me as slightly bent," Chee said. "Big, good-looking *belagaana,* but he wants to be a Navajo. Or that's the impression I got. And I guess he dug up those bones he's accused of digging up to be a militant Indian."

Janet Pete looked at him, thoughtfully. "Do you know anything that connects him with the Tano Pueblo?"

"Tano? No. Really, I know damned little. I just got stuck with the job of taking the federal warrant and going out to the Yeibichai and arresting the guy. They don't tell you a damn thing. If they don't give you the 'armed and dangerous' speech, then you presume he's not armed or dangerous. Just pick him up, take him in, let the federals handle the rest of it. It was a fugitive warrant. You know, flight to avoid. But I heard he was wanted somewhere East for desecrating a graveyard, vandalism. So forth."

Janet sat with her lower lip caught between her teeth, looking troubled.

"Jim," she said, "I think I'm being used."

"Oh?"

"Maybe it's just I'm the token Navajo and Highhawk wanted a Navajo lawyer. That would make sense. Washington is lousy with lawyers but not with Navajo lawyers."

"Guess not."

"But I've got a feeling," she added. She shook her head, got up, tried to pace. The room was, by Chee's quick estimate, about nine feet wide and sixteen feet long, with floor space deleted for a bathroom and a closet. Pacing was not just impractical, it was impossible. Janet sat down again. "This Highhawk, he's a publicity hound. Oh, that's not really fair. Just say he knows how to make his point with the press and he knows the press is important to him and the press loves him. So when he waived extradition and came back here, he said he wanted a Navajo lawyer and that made the *Post.*" She paused, glanced at Chee. "You know me," she said.

Chee had known her on the reservation as a lawyer on the staff of the Dinebeiina Nahiilna be Agaditahe, which translated loosely into English as "People Who Talk Fast and Help the People Out" but was more often called the DNA or Tribal Legal Aid, and which had earned a hard-nosed reputation for defending the underdog. In fact, Chee had gotten to know her when she nailed him for trying to keep one of her clients locked up in the San Juan County jail longer than Janet thought was legal or necessary.

"Knowing you, I bet you volunteered," Chee said.

"Well, I called him," she said. "And we talked. But I didn't make any commitments. I thought the firm wouldn't like it."

"Let's see," Chee said. "It's Dalman, MacArthur, Fenix, and White, isn't it? Or something like that. They sound like they'd be a little too dignified to be representing somebody who vandalizes graveyards."

"Dalman, MacArthur, White, and Hertzog," Janet said. "And yes, it's a dignified outfit. And it doesn't handle criminal defense cases. I thought they'd want to avoid Highhawk. Especially when the case is going to make the *Post* every day and the client is a notorious grandstander. And I didn't think John would like it either. But it didn't work that way."

"No," Chee said. John was John McDermott. Professor John McDermott. Ex-professor. Ex–University of Arizona law faculty. Janet Pete's mentor, faculty advisor, boss, lover, father figure. The man she'd quit her job with the Navajo Tribe to follow to Washington. Ambitious, successful John. "It doesn't sound like John's sort of thing."

"It turned out I was wrong about that," Janet said. "John brought it up. He asked me if I'd like to represent Highhawk."

Chee made a surprised face.

"I said I didn't think the firm would like it. He said it would be fine with the firm. It would demonstrate its social consciousness."

Chee nodded.

"Bullshit," Janet said. "Social consciousness!"

"Why then?"

Janet started to say something but stopped. She got up again and walked to the window and looked out. Rain streaked the glass. In the office across the street the lights were on. A man was standing at his window looking across at them. Chee noticed he had his coat off. Vest and tie but no coat. It made Chee feel more cheerful.

"You have an idea why, don't you?" Chee said.

"I don't know," Janet said to the window.

"You could guess," Chee said.

"I can guess," she agreed. "We have a client. The Sunbelt Corporation. It's a big factor in real estate development, apartment complexes, that sort of thing. They bought a ranch outside Albuquerque. From what little I know about it, I think they have some sort of big development planned there." She turned away from the window, sat down again, stared at her hands. "Sunbelt is interested in where an interstate bypass is located. It makes a lot of difference in their land values. From what I hear the route Sunbelt favors runs across Tano Pueblo land. The Tano tribal council is split on whether to sell the right of way. The traditionals say no; the progressives see economic development, money." She glanced up at Chee. "The old familiar story."

"It does sound familiar," Chee said. When she got around to it, Janet Pete would explain to him how all this involved Henry Highhawk, and her being followed. It was still raining outside. He looked at the man in the tie and vest in the window across the street who seemed to be looking at him. Funny town, Washington.

"They're having their tribal election sometime this winter," Janet said. "Youngish guy named Eldon Tamana is a contender against one of the old guard. Tamana favors granting the right of way." There was another long pause.

"Good chance of winning?" Chee asked.

"I'd guess not," Janet said. She turned and looked at him.

"I'm getting to be like a white man," Chee said. "I'm getting in a hurry for you to tell me what this is all about."

"I'm not sure I know myself. What I know is that the Smithsonian seems to have in its collection a Tano fetish. It's a figure representing one of their Twin War Gods. Somehow Tamana found out about it, and I think he knew John at Arizona, and he came to John to talk about how to get it returned."

Janet hesitated, looked down at her hands.

"I'd think that would be fairly simple," Chee said. "You'd have the Tano tribal council adopt a resolution asking for it back—or maybe have it come from the elders of the kiva society that owned the fetish. Then you'd ask the Smithsonian to return it, and they'd take it under advisement, and do a study to find out where they'd got their hands on it, and after about three years you'd either get it back or you wouldn't."

"I don't think that would work. Not for Tamana," Janet said, still studying her hands.

"Oh?"

Janet sighed. "Did I tell you he's running for a position on the tribal council? I guess he wants to just walk in and present the War God, sort of prove he's a young man who can get things done while the old-timers just talk about it. I doubt if the council knows the museum has the fetish."

"Ah," Chee said. "Are you representing Sunbelt interests in this? I guess Sunbelt has an interest in getting Tamana elected."

"I'm not," Janet said. "John is. John is the law firm's Southwestern expert. He gets the stuff which involves public land policy, Indians, uranium, water rights, all the cases like that."

"Did he tell you all this?"

"Mostly he was asking me. I'm the firm's Indian. Indians are supposed to know about Indians. All us redskins are alike. Mother Earth and Father Sun and all that Walt Disney crap." She smiled a wan smile. "That's really not fair to John. He's not as bad as most. Mostly he understands the cultural differences."

"But you think he's using you?"

"I think the law firm would like to use me," Janet corrected. "John works for them. So do I."

The gray rain outside, the form of the shirt-sleeved man standing in the window across from them, the narrow, shabby room, all of it was depressing Chee. He got off the bed and tried to pull the drape fully across the window. It helped some.

"I'm going to wash up," Chee said. "Then let's get out of here and get some coffee somewhere." He wanted to think about what Janet had told him. He could understand her suspicion. The firm wanted her to represent Highhawk because Highhawk worked in a sensitive position for the museum which held Tano sacred objects. Why? Did they want

Highhawk to steal the War Twin? Was Janet, as his lawyer, supposed to talk him into doing that?

"Fine," Janet said. "We have an appointment with Highhawk. I don't think I told you about that. Out at his place in Eastern Market."

There were two bare bulbs above the wash-basin mirror, one of which worked. Chee rinsed his face, looked at himself in the mirror, wondered again what the hell he was doing here. But in some subconscious way he knew now. He was looking forward to another conversation with the man who wanted to be a Navajo.

LEAPHORN HAD LEFT his umbrella. He'd thought of it as he boarded the plane at Albuquerque—the umbrella lying dusty in the trunk of his car and the plane flying eastward toward Washington and what seemed to Leaphorn to be inevitable rain. The umbrella had never experienced rain. He'd bought it last year in New York, the second of two umbrellas he'd purchased on the same trip—the first one having been forgotten God knows where. He'd tossed the second one into the trunk of his car with his luggage on his return to the Albuquerque airport. There it had rested for a year.

Now, with the rain drumming down on his neck, he paid the cabby. He pulled his hat lower over his ears, and hurried across the sidewalk to the Amtrak office. He had an appointment with Roland Dockery, who was the person in the Amtrak bureaucracy stuck with handling such nondescript problems as Leaphorn represented.

Dockery was waiting for him, a plump, slightly bald, and slightly disheveled man of perhaps forty. He examined

Leaphorn's Navajo Tribal Police identification through bifocal glasses with obvious curiosity and invited Joe to sit with a wave of his hand. He pointed to the luggage on his desk—a shabby leather suitcase and a smaller, newer briefcase.

"The FBI's already been through them," Dockery said. "Like I told you on the phone. I guess they would have told you if they found anything."

"Nothing useful," Leaphorn said. "What we're looking for is anything that might connect the bags to a homicide we have out in New Mexico. I hope you won't mind me going over some questions the FBI probably already covered."

"No problem," Dockery said. He laughed. "No trouble about keys. The FBI already opened them." He flipped open both cases with a flourish. Dockery was obviously enjoying this. It represented something unusual in a job that must be usually routine.

Leaphorn sorted through the big case first. It held a spare suit, dark gray and of some expensive fabric, but looking much used. A sweater. Two dark blue neckties. White, long-sleeved shirts, some clean and neatly folded, some used and folded into a laundry sack. Eight altogether. Three used. Five clean. Leaphorn checked his notes. The neck and arm sizes matched the shirt on the corpse. Shorts and undershirts, also white. Same total, same breakdown. Same with socks, except the color now was black. He thought about the numbers and the timetable. He'd check but it seemed about right. If this was indeed the luggage of Pointed Shoes, then he had in fact been about three shirts west of Washington by the time he reached Gallup. Wearing shirt four when he was stabbed, with five clean ones to take him to where he was going. Or—if he was simply going to see Agnes Tsosie—home again to Washington.

The smaller bag contained a jumble of things. Leaphorn glanced up from it but Dockery didn't give him a chance to ask the question.

"One of the cleanup crew packed it," Dockery said. "Just dumped all the stuff that was around the roomette into the bag. I've got his name somewhere. The FBI had him in and talked to him when they checked on it."

"So this would be everything left lying around?" Leaphorn asked. And Dockery nodded his agreement. But it wasn't everything, of course, Leaphorn knew. Odds and ends that seemed to have no value would have been discarded. Old newspapers, notes, empty envelopes, just the sort of stuff that might be most helpful would have been thrown away.

But what hadn't been thrown away was also helpful. First, Leaphorn noticed an almost empty tube of Fixodent and a small can of denture cleaner. He had expected to find them. If he hadn't he would have doubted that this was the luggage of a man who wore false teeth. Three books, all printed in Spanish, added another bit of support. The clothing Pointed Shoes had been wearing had looked old-fashioned and foreign. So did the clothing in the suitcase. He found a thin little notebook, covered in black plastic, glanced at it, and set it aside. Under a sweater in the bag he found two pots, each wrapped in newspaper. He examined them. They were the sort Pueblo Indians made to sell to tourists—small, one with a black-on-white lizard design, the other geometric. Probably they had been purchased as gifts at the Amtrak station in Albuquerque, where such things were sold beside the track. But the pots interested Leaphorn less than the newspaper pages in which the purchaser had cushioned them.

Spanish again. Leaphorn unfolded a wad of pages, looking for the name and the date. The name was *El Crepúsculo de Libertad.* Something-or-other of Liberty. Leaphorn's working vocabulary in Spanish was mostly the Gallup-

Flagstaff wetback variety. Now he ransacked his memory of the twelve credit hours he'd taken at Arizona State. He came up with "sunrise," or perhaps "twilight." Dawn seemed more likely. The Dawn of Liberty. The date on the page was late October, about two weeks before Pointed Shoes had been knifed. Leaphorn glanced at the headlines, getting only a word or two, but enough to guess the subject was politics. Neither of the crumpled pages included a place of publication.

Leaphorn folded them into his pocket and sorted through the odds and ends in the bottom of the bag. He extracted a sheet of white notepaper, folded vertically as if to fit into a pocket. On it, someone had written what seemed to be a checklist.

Pockets
Prescription bottles
eyeglasses (check case, too)
dentures (if any)
labels in coats
address books, etc.
letters, envelopes
book plats (plates?) stuff written in books
addresses on mags, etc.

Leaphorn stared at the list, thinking. He showed it to Dockery. "What do you think of this?"

Dockery looked at it. "Looks like some sort of shopping list," Dockery said. "No, it's not that. Reminders, maybe. Things to do."

Leaphorn put the list on the desk. He picked up the notebook he'd set aside, opened it. Several pages had been torn out. The writing in it was in Spanish, done with blue ink in a small, careful hand. He got out his wallet, extracted the note he'd found in the dead man's shirt pocket. The handwriting matched the small, neat penmanship in the notebook. And it looked nothing at all like the handwriting on the list.

"Do you happen to know if that fellow had a roommate?" he asked.

"Just the single occupant," Dockery said.

"Any sign somebody broke in?"

"Not that I know of," Dockery said. "And I think I would have heard. I'm sure I would have. That's the sort of thing that would get around." He fished a pack of Winstons from his desk drawer, offered one to Leaphorn.

"I finally managed to quit," Leaphorn said.

Dockery lit up, exhaled a blue cloud. "What are you fellows looking for, anyway?"

"What did the FBI tell you?"

Dockery laughed. "Not a damned thing. It was some young fella. He didn't tell me squat."

"We found the body of a man beside the tracks east of Gallup. Stabbed. All identification gone. False teeth missing." Leaphorn tapped the Fixodent with a finger. "Turns out the Amtrak had an emergency there at the right time. Turns out the baggage unclaimed from this roomette has also been stripped of all identification. The clothing we have here in this bag is the same size and type the corpse was wearing. So we think it's likely that the man who reserved this roomette under the phony name was the victim."

"Hey, now," Dockery said. "That's interesting."

"Also," Leaphorn added slowly, looking at Dockery, "we think that someone—probably the person who knifed our victim—got into this roomette, searched through his stuff, and took out everything that would help identify the corpse."

"Have you talked to the attendant?" Dockery asked.

"I'd like to," Leaphorn said. "And whoever it was who cleaned up the room, and packed up the victim's stuff."

"He saw somebody in that roomette," Dockery said.

Leaphorn stopped leafing through the notebook and stared at Dockery. "He told you that?"

"Conductor on that run's a guy named Perez, an old-timer. He used to be our chapter chairman in the Brotherhood of Railroad Trainmen. He told me he and the guy traveling in that roomette would chat in Spanish now and then. You know, just polite stuff. He said the guy was a nice man, and kind of sickly. Had some sort of heart condition and the altitude out there had been bothering him. So when they had that nonscheduled stop there in New Mexico, after they got the train rolling again, Perez checked at the roomette to see if this guy needed any help getting off at Gallup." Dockery paused, ashed his cigarette into something invisible in his desk drawer, inhaled more smoke. Through the window behind him Leaphorn noticed it was raining hard now.

"There was a man in there. Perez said that he tapped on the door and when nobody answered it, he was uneasy about this sick passenger so he unlocked it. And he said there was a man in there. He asked Perez what he wanted, and Perez told him he was checking to see if the passenger needed any help. The man said 'no help needed' and shut the door." Dockery blew a smoke ring. "Seemed funny to Perez because he said he couldn't see his passenger back in the roomette and he'd never seen the passenger and this guy together. So he was watching for the passenger when they made the Gallup stop. Didn't see him get off so he tapped at the door again and nobody answered. So he unlocked the door and went in and all this stuff was in there but no passenger." Dockery stopped, waiting for reaction.

"Odd," Leaphorn said.

"Damn right," Dockery agreed. "It's the sort of thing you remember."

"You tell the FBI agent about this?"

"Didn't really get a chance. He just wanted to look at the bags and be on his way."

"Could I talk to Perez?"

"He's on the same run," Dockery said. He fished a timetable out of his drawer and handed it to Leaphorn. "Call some station a stop ahead where they stop long enough to get him to the telephone. He'll call you back. He'd be damned interested in what happened to his passenger."

Leaphorn was thumbing his way through the notebook a second time, making notes in his own notebook. Most of the pages were blank. Some contained only initials and what seemed to be telephone numbers. Leaphorn copied them off. One page contained only two letter-number combinations. Most of the notations seemed to concern meetings. The one Leaphorn was looking at read, "Harrington. *Cuarto* 832. 3 p."

"Harrington," Leaphorn said. "Would that be a hotel?"

"It's downtown," Dockery said. "Over on E Avenue and not far from the Mall. Sort of lower middle class. They let it run down. Usually when that happens somebody buys it and turns it into offices."

Leaphorn wrote the address and room number in his notebook. At the top of the next page "AURANOFIN" was written in capital letters, followed by "W1128023." He jotted that down, too. Below, on the same page, a notation touched a faint chord in Joe Leaphorn's excellent memory. It was a name, slightly unusual, that he'd seen somewhere before.

The man with the pointed shoes had written: "Natl. Hist. Museum. Henry Highhawk."

JANET PETE DECIDED they would take the Metro from the Smithsonian Station up to Eastern Market. It cost only eighty cents a ticket, and was just as fast as a taxi. Then, too, it would give Jim Chee a chance to see the Washington subway. As Chee was wise enough to guess, Janet wanted to play city mouse to his country mouse. That was okay with Chee. He could see that Janet Pete's self-esteem could use a little burnishing.

"Not like New York," Janet said. "It's clean and bright and fast and you feel perfectly safe. Not at all like New York." Chee, who had only heard rumors of the New York subway, nodded. He'd always wanted to ride the New York subway. But maybe this trip would be interesting, too.

It was. The soaring waffled ceiling, the machines which dispensed paper slips as tickets along with the proper change, the gates which accepted those paper slips, opened, and then returned the slips, the swarm of people conditioned to avoid human contact—eye, knee, or elbow. Chee clung to the bracket by the sliding door and inspected them.

It surprised him, at first, that he wasn't being inspected in return. He must look distinctly different: his best felt reservation hat with its silver band, his best leather jacket, his best boots, his rawboned, weather-beaten, homely Navajo face. But the only glances he drew were quick and secretive. He was politely ignored. That seemed odd to Chee.

And there were other oddities. He'd presumed the subway would be used by the working class. The blue-collar people were here, true enough, but there was more than that. He could see three men and one woman in navy uniforms, with enough stripes on their sleeves to indicate membership in the privileged class. Since rank had come young for them, they would be graduates of the Naval Academy. They would be people with political connections and old family money. At least half the white men, and about that mix of blacks, wore the inevitable dark three-piece suit and dark tie of the Eastern Establishment, or perhaps here it was the Federal Bureaucracy. The women wore mostly skirts and high heels. Chee's study of anthropology at the University of New Mexico had led him into sociology courses. He remembered a lecture on those factors which condition humans and thereby form culture. He felt detached from this subway crowd, an invisible entity looking down on a species that had evolved to survive overcrowding, to endure aggression, to survive despite what old Professor Ebaar called "intraspecies hostility."

On the long ride up the escalator to what his own Navajo Holy People would have called the Earth Surface World, Chee mentioned these impressions to Janet Pete.

"Will you ever feel at home here?" he asked. She didn't answer until they reached the top and walked out into the dim twilight, into what had become something between drizzle and mist.

"I don't know," she said. "I thought so once. But it's hard to handle. A different culture."

"And you don't mean different from Navajo?"

She laughed. "No. I don't mean that. I guess I mean different from the empty West."

Henry Highhawk's place was about seven blocks from the Metro station—a narrow, two-story brick house halfway down a block of such narrow houses. Tied to the pillar just beside the mailbox was something which looked like a paho. Chee inspected it while Janet rang the bell. It was indeed a Navajo prayer stick, with the proper feathers attached. If Highhawk had made it, he knew what he was doing. And then Highhawk was at the door, inviting them in. He was taller than Chee remembered him from the firelight at Agnes Tsosie's place. Taller and leaner and more substantial, more secure in his home territory than he had been surrounded by a strange culture below the Tsosies' butte. The limp, which had touched Chee with a sense of pity at the Tsosie Yeibichai, seemed natural here. The jeans Highhawk wore had been cut to accommodate the hinged metal frame that reinforced his short leg. The brace, the high lift under the small left boot, the limp, all of them seemed in harmony with this lanky man in this crowded little house. He had converted his Kiowa-Comanche braids into a tight Navajo bun. But nothing would convert his long, bony, melancholy face into something that would pass for one of the Dineh. He would always look like a sorrowful white boy.

Highhawk was in his kitchen pouring coffee before he recognized Chee. He looked at Chee intently as he handed him his cup.

"Hey," he said, laughing. "You're the Navajo cop who arrested me."

Chee nodded. Highhawk wanted to shake hands again—a "no hard feelings" gesture. "Policeman, I mean," Highhawk amended, his face flushed with embarrassment. "It was very efficient. And I appreciated you getting that guy to drive that rent-a-car back to Gallup for me. That saved me a whole bunch of money. Probably at least a hundred bucks."

"Saved me some work, too," Chee said. "I would have had to do something about it the next morning." Chee was embarrassed, too. He wasn't accustomed to this switch in relationships. And Highhawk's behavior puzzled him a little. It was too deferential, too—Chee struggled for the word. He was reminded of a day at his uncle's sheep camp. Three old dogs, all shaggy veterans. And the young dog his uncle had won somewhere gambling. His uncle lifting the young dog out of the back of the pickup. The old dogs, tense and interested, conscious that their territory was being invaded. The young dog walking obliquely toward them, head down, tail down, legs bent, sending all the canine signals of inferiority and subjection, deferring to their authority.

"I'm Bitter Water Dinee," Highhawk said. He looked shy as he said it, tangling long, slender fingers. "At least my grandmother was, and so I guess I can claim it."

Chee nodded. "I am one of the Slow Talking Dineh," he said. He didn't mention that his father's clan was also Bitter Water, which made it Chee's own "born for" clan. That made him and Highhawk related on their less important paternal side. But then, after two generations under normal reservation circumstances, that secondary paternal link would have submerged by marriages into other clans. Chee considered it, and felt absolutely no kinship link with this strange, lanky man. Whatever his dreams and pretensions, Highhawk was still a *belagaana.*

They sat in the front room then, Chee and Janet occupying a sofa and Highhawk perched on a wooden chair. Someone, Chee guessed it had been Highhawk, had enlarged the room by removing the partition which once had separated it from a small dining alcove. But most of this space was occupied by two long tables, and the tables were occupied by tools, by what apparently had been a section of tree root, by a roll of leather, a box of feathers, slabs of wood, paint jars, brushes, carving knives—the paraphernalia of Highhawk's profession.

"You had something to tell me," Highhawk said to Janet. He glanced at Chee.

"Your preliminary hearing has been set," Janet said. "We finally got them to put it on the calendar. It's going to be two weeks from tomorrow and we have to get some things decided before then."

Highhawk grinned at her. It lit his long, thin face and made him look even more boyish. "You could have told me that on the telephone," he said. "I'll bet there was more than that." He glanced at Chee again.

Chee got up and looked for a place to go. "I'll give you some privacy," he said.

"You could take a look at my kachina collection," Highhawk said. "Back in the office." He pointed down the hallway. "First door on the right."

"It's not all that confidential," Janet said. "But I can imagine what the bar association would say about me talking about a plea bargain with a client right in front of the arresting officer."

The office was small and as cluttered as the living area. The desk was a massive old rolltop, half buried under shoeboxes filled with scraps of cloth, bone fragments, wood, odds and ends of metal. A battered cardboard box held an unpainted wooden figure carved out of what seemed to be cottonwood root. It stared up at Chee through slanted eye sockets, looking somehow pale and venomous. Some sort of fetish or figurine, obviously. Something Highhawk must be replicating for a museum display. Or could it be the Tano War God? Another box was beside it. Chee pulled back the flaps and looked inside. He looked into the face of Talking God.

The mask of the Yeibichai was made as the traditions of the Navajos ruled it must be made—of deerskin surmounted by a bristling crown of eight eagle feathers. The face was painted white. Its mouth protruded an inch or more, a narrow tube of rolled leather. Its eyes were black dots surmounted by painted brows. The lower rim of the mask was a ruff of fox fur. Chee stared at it, surprised. Such masks are guarded, handed down in the family only to a son willing to learn the poetry and ritual of the Night Chant, and to carry the role his father kept as a Yeibichai dancer.

Keepers of such masks gave the spirits that lived within them feedings of corn pollen. Chee examined this mask. He found no sign of the smearing pollen would have left on the leather. It was probably a replica Highhawk had made. Even so, when he closed the cardboard flaps on the box, he did so reverently.

Three shelves beside the only window were lined with the wooden figures of the kachina spirits. Mostly Hopi, it seemed to Chee, but he noticed Zuni Mudheads and the great beaked Shalako, the messenger bird from the Zuni heavens, and the striped figures of Rio Grande Pueblo clown fraternities. Most of them looked old and authentic. That also meant expensive.

Behind him in the front room, Chee heard Janet's voice rise in argument, and Highhawk's laugh. He presumed Janet was telling her client during this ironic gesture at confidentiality what she had already told Chee on the walk from the subway. The prosecutor with jurisdiction over crime in Connecticut had more important things on his mind than disturbed graves, especially when they involved a minority political gesture. He would welcome some sort of plea-bargain compromise. Highhawk and attorney would be welcome to come in and discuss it. More than welcome.

"I don't think this nut of mine will go for it," Janet had

told Chee. "Henry wants to do a Joan of Arc with all the TV cameras in sharp focus. He's got the speech already written. 'If this is justice for me, to go to jail for digging up your ancestors, where then is the justice for the whites who dug up the bones of my ancestors?' He won't agree, not today anyway, but I'll make the pitch. You come along and it will give you a chance to talk to him and see what you think."

And, sure enough, from the combative tone Chee could hear in Highhawk's voice, Janet's client wasn't going for it. But what the devil was Chee supposed to learn here? What was he supposed to think? That Highhawk was taller than he remembered? And had changed his hairstyle? That wasn't what Janet expected. She expected him to smell out some sort of plot involving her law firm, and a fellow following her, and a big corporation developing land in New Mexico. He looked around the cluttered office. Fat chance.

But it was interesting. Flaky as he seemed, Highhawk was an artist. Chee noticed a half-finished Mudhead figure on the table and picked it up. The traditional masks, as Chee had seen them at Zuni Shalako ceremonials, were round, clay-colored, and deformed with bumps. They represented the idiots born after a daughter of the Sun committed incest with her brother. Despite the limiting conventions of little round eyes and little round mouth, Highhawk had carved into the small face of this figurine a kind of foolish glee. Chee put it down carefully and reinspected the kachinas on the shelf. Had Highhawk made them, too? Chee checked. Some of them, probably. Some looked too old and weathered for recent manufacture. But perhaps Highhawk's profession made him skilled in aging, too.

It was then he noticed the sketches. They were stacked on the top level of the rolltop desk, done on separate sheets of heavy artist's paper. The top one showed a boy, a turkey with its feathers flecked with jewels, a log, smoke rising from it as it was burned to hollow it into a boat. The setting was a riverbank, a cliff rising behind it. Chee recognized the scene. It was from the legend of Holy Boy, the legend reenacted in the Yeibichai ceremony. It showed the spirit child, still human, preparing for his journey down the San Juan River with his pet turkey. The artist seemed to have captured the very moment when the illness which was to paralyze him had struck the child. Somehow the few lines which suggested his naked body also suggested that he was falling, in the throes of anguish. And above him, faintly in the very air itself, there was the blue half-round face of the spirit called Water Sprinkler.

The sound of Highhawk's laugh came from the adjoining room, and Janet Pete's earnest voice. Chee sorted through the other sketches. Holy Boy floating in his hollow log, prone and paralyzed, with the turkey running on the bank beside him—neck and wings outstretched in a kind of frozen panic; Holy Boy, partially cured but now blind, carrying the crippled Holy Girl on his shoulders; the two children, hand in hand, surrounded by the towering figures of Talking God, Growling God, Black God, Monster Slayer, and the other *yei*—all looking down on the children with the relentless, pitiless neutrality of the Navajo gods toward mortal men. There was something in this scene—something in all these sketches now that he was aware of it—that was troubling. A sort of surreal, off-center dislocation from reality. Chee stared at the sketches, trying to understand. He shook his head, baffled.

Aside from this element, he was much impressed both by Highhawk's talent and by the man's knowledge of Navajo metaphysics. The poetry of the Yeibichai ceremonial usually used didn't include the role of the girl child. Highhawk had obviously done his homework.

The doorbell rang, startling Chee. He put down the sketch and went to the office door. Highhawk was talking to someone at the front door, ushering him into the living room.

It was a man, slender, dark, dressed in the standard uniform of Washington males.

"As you can see, Rudolfo, my lawyer is always on the job," Highhawk was saying. The man turned and bowed to Janet Pete, smiling.

It was Rudolfo Gomez, Mr. Bad Hands.

"I've come at a bad time," Bad Hands said. "I didn't notice Miss Pete's car outside. I didn't realize you were having a conference."

Jim Chee stepped out of the office. Bad Hands recognized him instantly, and with a sort of controlled shock that seemed to Chee to include not just surprise but a kind of dismay.

"And this is Jim Chee," Highhawk said. "You gentlemen have met before. Remember? On the reservation. Mr. Chee is the officer who arrested me. Jim Chee, this is Rudolfo Gomez, an old friend."

"Ah, yes," Bad Hands said. "Of course. This is an unexpected pleasure."

"And Mr. Gomez is the man who put up my bail," Highhawk said to Chee. "An old friend."

Bad Hands was wearing his gloves. He made no offer to shake hands. Neither did Chee. It was not, after all, a Navajo custom.

"Sit down," Highhawk said. "We were talking about my preliminary hearing."

"I've come at a bad time," Bad Hands said. "I'll call you tomorrow."

"No. No," Janet Pete said. "We're finished. We were just leaving." She gave Chee the look.

"Right," Chee said. "We have to go."

A cold wind out of the northwest had blown away the drizzle. They walked down the steps from Highhawk's porch and passed a blue Datsun parked at the sidewalk. It wasn't the car Bad Hands had been driving at the Agnes Tsosie place, but that had been three thousand miles away. That one was probably rented. "What'd you think?" Janet Pete asked.

"I don't know," Chee said. "He's an interesting man."

"Gomez or Highhawk?"

"Both of them," Chee said. "I wonder what happened to Gomez's hands. I wonder why Highhawk calls him an old friend. But I meant Highhawk. He's interesting."

"Yeah," Janet said. "And suicidal. He's flat determined to go to jail." They walked a little. "Stupid son-of-a-bitch," she added. "I could get him off with some community service time and a suspended sentence."

"You know anything about this Gomez guy?" Chee asked.

"Just what I told you and what Highhawk said. Old friends. Gomez posted his bail."

"They're not old friends," Chee said. "I told you that. I saw them meet at that Yeibichai where I arrested him. Highhawk had never seen the guy before."

"You sure of that? How do you know?"

"I know," Chee said.

Janet put her hand on his arm, slowed. "There he is," she said in a tiny voice. "That car. That's the man who's been following me."

The car was parked across the street from them. An aging Chevy two-door, its medium color hard to distinguish in the shadows.

"You sure?" Chee said.

"See the radio antenna? Bent like that? And the dent in the back fender? It's the same car." Janet was whispering. "I really looked at it. I memorized it."

What to do? His inclination was to ignore this situation, to simply walk past the car and see what happened. Nothing would happen, except Janet would think he was a nerd. He felt uneasy. On the reservation, he would have simply trotted across the street and confronted the driver. But confront him with what? Here Chee felt inept and incompetent. This entire business seemed like something one saw on television. It was urban. It seemed dangerous but it was probably just silly. What the devil would the Washington Police Department recommend in such a circumstance?

They were still walking very slowly. "What should we do?" Janet asked.

"Stay here," Chee said. "I'll go see about it."

He walked diagonally across the street, watching the dim light reflecting from the driver's-side window. What would he do if the window started down? If he saw a gun barrel? But the window didn't move.

Beside the car now, Chee could see a man behind the steering wheel, looking at him.

Chee tapped on the glass. Wondering why he was doing this. Wondering what he would say.

Nothing happened. Chee waited. The man behind the wheel appeared to be motionless.

Chee tapped on the window again, rapping the glass with the knuckles of his right hand.

The window came down, jerkily, squeaking.

"Yeah?" the man said. He was looking up at Chee. A small face, freckled. The man had short hair. It seemed to be red. "Whaddaya want?"

Chee wanted very badly to get a better look at the man. He seemed to be small. Unusually small. Chee could see no sign that he was armed, but that would be hard to tell in the darkness of the front seat.

"The lady I'm with, she thinks you've been following her," Chee said. "Any reason for her to think that?"

"Following her?" The man leaned forward toward the

window, looking past Chee at Janet Pete waiting across the street. "What for?"

"I'm asking if you've been following her," Chee said.

"Hell, no," the man said. "What is this anyway? Who the hell are you?"

"I'm a cop," Chee said, thinking as he said it that it was the first smart thing he'd said in this conversation. And it was more or less true. A good thing to have said as long as this guy didn't ask for identification.

The man looked up at him. "You sure as hell don't look like a cop to me," he said. "You look like an Indian. Let's see some identification."

"Let's see your identification," Chee said.

"Ah, screw this," the man said, disappearing from the window. The glass squeaked as he rolled it up. The engine started. The headlights came on. The car rolled slowly away from the curb and down the street. It made a careful right turn and disappeared. Absolutely no hurry.

Chee watched it go. Through the back window he noticed that only the top of the driver's head protruded above the back of the seat. A very small driver.

12

SINCE BOYHOOD Fleck had been one of those persons who like to worry about one thing at a time. This morning he wanted to worry only about Mama. What the devil was he going to do about her? He was up against the Fat Man's deadline. Get her out of that nursing home. *"Get her out now!"* the Fat Man had shouted it at him. "Not one more day!" The only place he'd found to put her wanted first month and last month in advance. With all those so-called incidental expenses they always stuck you with for the private room, that added up to more than six thousand dollars. Fleck had most of it. Plus he had ten thousand coming, and overdue. But that didn't help him right now. He'd scared the Fat Man enough to hold him a day or two. But he couldn't count on much more than that. The son of a bitch was the kind who just might call the cops in on him. That wasn't something Fleck wanted to deal with. Not with Mama involved. He had to get the ten thousand.

There was another problem. He had to give some thought to that cowboy who'd walked over to his car last night and tapped at the window. What the hell did that mean? The guy looked like an Indian, and he was with that Indian woman who'd been visiting Highhawk. But what did it mean to Fleck? Fleck smelled cop. He sensed danger. There was more going down here than he knew about. That worried him. He needed to know more, and he intended to.

Fleck pulled into the Dunkin' Donuts parking area. He was a little early but he noticed that the Ford sedan with the telephone company symbol was already parked. His man was on a stool, the only customer in the place, eating something with a fork. Fleck took the stool next to him.

"You got it?" Fleck asked.

"Sure. You got fifty?"

Fleck handed the man two twenties and a ten and received a folded sheet of paper. He felt foolish as he did it. If he was smart, he could probably have found a way to get this information free without paying this creep in the telephone company. Maybe it was even in the library. He unfolded the paper. It was a section torn from a Washington Convention and Visitors Bureau map of the District of Columbia.

"I circled the area where they use the 266 prefix," the man said. "And the little *x* marks are where the public phone booths are."

Only a few *x*'s, Fleck noticed. Less than twenty. He commented on it.

"It's mostly a residential district," the man explained, "and part of the embassy row. Not much business for pay phones out there. You want a doughnut?"

"No time," Fleck said, getting up.

"Haven't heard much from you lately," the man said. "You going out of business?"

"I'm in a little different line of work right now," Fleck said, walking toward the door. He stopped. "Would you happen to know of any good nursing homes? Where they take good care of old people?"

"Don't know nothing about 'em," the man said.

Fleck hurried, even though he had until two P.M. He started on Sixteenth Street, because that's where the countries without enough money to build on Massachusetts Avenue mostly located their embassies. None of the numbers matched there, although he found two booths with 266 numbers The Client had used earlier. He moved to Seventeenth Street and then Eighteenth. It was there he found the number he was scheduled to call at two P.M. Fleck backed out of the booth and looked up and down the street. No other pay booths in sight. He'd have to rent the car equipped with a mobile telephone. He'd reserved one at Hertz last night, just in case it worked out this way.

Fleck spent the next two hours driving out to Silver Springs and checking on a rest home he'd heard about out there. It was a little cheaper but the linoleum on the floors was cracked and streaked with grime and the windows hadn't been washed and the woman who ran the place had a mean-looking mouth. He picked up the rent-a-car a little after one, a black Lincoln town car which was too big and too showy for Fleck's taste but which would look natural enough in Washington. He made sure the telephone worked, put his Polaroid camera on the front seat beside him, and drove back to Eighteenth Street. He parked across the street and a little down the block from the phone booth, called it, left his receiver open, and walked down the sidewalk far enough to hear the ringing in the booth. Then he sat behind the wheel, slumped down to be less visible. He waited. While he waited, he thought.

First he went over his plan for this telephone call. Then he thought about the cowboy walking across the street and rapping at his window. If he was an Indian—and he looked like one—it might tie back to the killing. He'd left the train at the little town in New Mexico. Gallup, it was. Indians everywhere you looked. Probably they even had Indian cops and maybe one of them was looking into it. If that was true it meant they had tracked him back to Washington and somehow or other tied something together with that silly-looking bastard who wore his hair in a bun. That meant they must know a hell of a lot more about what Fleck was involved with than Fleck knew himself.

That thought made him uneasy. He shifted in the seat and looked out the window at the weather, getting his mind off what would happen to him if the police ever had him in custody, with his fingerprints matched and making the circuit. If it ever got that far, he could kiss his ass good-bye. He could never, ever let that happen. What would Mama do if it did?

If he could only find someplace where her always getting even didn't get Mama into trouble. She was too old for that now. She couldn't get away with it like when she was healthy. Like that time when they were living down there near Tampa when Mama was young and the landlord got the sheriff onto them to make them move out. He remembered Mama down on her stomach behind the stove loosening up something or other on the gas pipe with Delmar standing there handing her the tools. "You can't let the bastards get up on you," she was saying. "You hear that, Delmar? If you don't even it up, they grind you down even more. They spit on you ever' living time if you don't teach them you won't let them do it."

And they had almost spit on them that time, if Mama hadn't been so smart. Some of the neighbors had seen Delmar down there that night just before the explosion and the big fire. And they told on him, and the police came there to the Salvation Army shelter where Mama was keeping them and they took Delmar off with them. And then he and Mama had gone down to the sheriff's office and he told them it was him, not Delmar, the neighbors had seen. And it had worked out just like Mama had said it would. They had to go easy on him because he was only thirteen and it was a first offense on top of that, and they'd have to handle him in juvenile court. But with Delmar being older, and with shoplifting and car theft and assault already on his books, they would try him as an adult. Fleck had only got sixty days in the D Home and a year's probation out of that one. Mama had always been good at handling things. But now she was just too old and her mind was gone.

Fleck's reverie was ended by a woman hurrying around the corner toward him. She wore a raincoat, something shiny and waterproof over her head, and was carrying a plastic sack. She walked past Fleck's Lincoln without a glance. While he watched her in the rearview mirror, another figure appeared at the corner ahead of him. A man in a dark blue raincoat and a dark gray hat. He carried an umbrella and as he hesitated at the curb, looking for traffic, he opened it.

It had started to rain, streaking the car windows, pattering against the windshield. Fleck glanced at his watch. Seventeen minutes until two. If this was his man, the man was early. He crossed the street, slanting the umbrella against the rain, and hurried down the sidewalk toward the telephone booth. He walked past it.

Fleck slumped down in the seat, too low to see or be seen. He waited. Then he pushed himself up. He used the electric control to adjust the side mirror, found the man just as he turned the corner behind the car. Probably someone with nothing to do with this business, Fleck thought. He relaxed a little. He glanced at his watch again. Waited.

What Mama had always taught Delmar and him had saved him there in the Joliet State Penitentiary, that was certain enough. It had been hard to do it. Things are always hard when you're a little man, and you're young. He thought they'd kill him if he tried it. But it had saved him. He couldn't have lived through those years if he'd let them spit on him. He'd have died. Or worse than that, been like the little pet animals they turned their baby dolls into. Three of them had been after him. Cassidy, Neal, and Dalkin, those were their names. Cassidy had been the biggest, and the one Fleck had been the most afraid of, and the one he'd decided he had to kill first. But looking back on it, knowing what he knew now, Dalkin was really the dangerous one. Because Dalkin was smart. Cassidy had made the move on him first, and when he got away from that, the three of him had got him into a corner in the laundry. He'd never forget that. Never tried to in fact, because that had been the black, grim, hard-rock bottom of his life and he needed to think of it whenever things were tough, like today. They'd held him down and raped him, Cassidy first. And when they were all finished with him, he had just laid there a moment, not even feeling the pain. He remembered vividly exactly what he had thought. He'd thought: Do I want to stay alive now? And he absolutely didn't want to. But he remembered what Mama had taught him. And he thought, I'll get even first. I'll get that done before I die. And he'd got up and told them all three they were dead men. Three or four other cons had been in the laundry by then. He hadn't noticed them. He wouldn't have noticed anyone then, but they got the word out in the yard. Cassidy had beaten him after that, and Dalkin had beaten him, too. But getting even had kept him alive.

It was raining harder now. Fleck turned on the ignition and started the windshield wipers. As he did, the man with the umbrella turned the corner again. He'd circled the block and was walking again down the opposite sidewalk toward the telephone booth. Fleck turned off the wipers and glanced at his watch. Five minutes until two. The Client was punctual. He watched him enter the booth, close the umbrella and the door. Cassidy had been punctual, too. Fleck had gotten the note to him. Printed on toilet paper. "I'll have something just for you five minutes into the work break. Behind the laundry."

He gambled that Cassidy would think only of sex. He gambled that a macho two-hundred-and-forty-pounder who could bench press almost four hundred pounds wouldn't be nervous about a hundred-and-twenty-pounder, the kid the yard called Little Red Shrimp. Sure enough, Cassidy wasn't nervous. He came around the corner, grinning. He had walked out of the sunlight into the shadow, squinting, reaching out for Fleck when he saw Fleck smiling at him, walking into the shank.

Fleck dialed all but the final digit of the 266 number, glanced at his watch. Almost a minute early. Fleck could still remember the sensation. Holding the narrow blade flat, just as he'd practiced it, feeling it slide between the ribs, flicking the handle back and forth and back again as it penetrated to make certain it cut the artery and the heart. He hadn't really expected it to work. He expected Cassidy to kill him, or the thing to end with him on trial for premeditated murder and getting nothing better than life and probably the gas chamber. But there was no choice. And Eddy had told him it would be like Cassidy was being struck by lightning if he did it right.

"Do it right, he shouldn't make a sound," Eddy had said. "It's the shock that does it."

Now it was time. Fleck punched the final digit, heard the beginning of the ring, then The Client's voice.

Fleck brought him up to date, told him about checking on Highhawk, about the woman lawyer showing up there with the cowboy, about Santero driving up and going in and the woman and the cowboy coming out a minute later. He told him about the cowboy walking right up and tapping on his window. "I circled the block and followed them back to the Eastern Market Metro station, and then I dropped it. There's just one of me. Now I want to know who that cowboy is. He's tall. Slender. Dark. Looks like an Indian to me. Narrow face. Leather jacket, boots, cowboy hat, all that. Who the hell is he? Something about him smells like cop to me."

"What did he say?"

"He said the woman thought I was following her. I told him he was crazy. Told him to screw off."

"Amateurs!" The Client's voice was full of scorn. It took a moment for Fleck to realize he meant Fleck.

Fleck pressed it. "You know anything at all about the cowboy? Know who he is?"

"God knows," The Client said. "This is the product of you letting Santero slip away from you. We don't know where he went or who he talked to and we don't know what he did. I warned you about that."

"And I told you about it," Fleck said. "Told you there's just one of me and seven of them, not counting the womenfolk. I can't watch them all all the time."

"Seven?" The Client said. "Was that a slip? You told us you had subtracted one. The old man. You're expecting us to pay you for that."

"Six is the correct number," Fleck said. "Old Man Santillanes is definitely off the list. Did you send the ten thousand?"

"We wait for the full month. Now I wonder if we should also ask to see a little more proof."

"I sent you the goddamn billfold. And the false teeth." Fleck sighed. "You're just stalling," he said. "I can see that now. I want that money by tomorrow night."

There was a period of silence from the other end. Fleck noticed the rain had stopped. With his free hand he rolled down the window beside him. Then he picked up the camera and checked the settings.

"The deal is no publicity, no identification for one full month. Then you get the money. After a month. Now I want you to think about Santero. I think he needs to go. The same deal. But remember it can't happen in the District. We can't risk that. It should be a long way outside the Beltway. A long way from here. And no chance of identification. No chance at all of identification."

"I have got to have the ten thousand now," Fleck said. Never lose your temper, Mama had said. Never show them a thing. About all we got going for us, Mama had always told Delmar and him, is they never expect us to do anything at all but crawl there on the ground on our bellies and wait to get stepped on again.

"No," The Client said.

"Tell you what. If you'll have three thousand of it delivered to me tomorrow, then I can wait for the rest of it."

"You can wait anyway," The Client said. And hung up.

Fleck put down the telephone and picked up the camera. It rattled against the door, making him aware that he was shaking with rage. He took a deep breath. Held it. Through the rangefinder he saw The Client emerge from the telephone booth, umbrella folded. He stood with hand outstretched, looking around, confirming that the rain had stopped. Fleck had taken four shots before he walked down the sidewalk away from him.

Fleck let The Client get well around the corner before he left the car to follow. He kept a block behind him down Eighteenth Street, and then east to Sixteenth. There The Client turned again. He walked down the row of second-string embassies and disappeared down a driveway.

Fleck walked past it with only a single sidelong glance. It was just enough to tell him who he was working for.

SINCE JOE LEAPHORN and Dockery had arrived a little early, and the Amtrak train had arrived a little late, Leaphorn had been given the opportunity to answer a lot of Dockery's questions. He'd presumed that Dockery had volunteered to come down to Union Station on his day off because Dockery was interested in murder. And clearly Dockery was interested in that. And he was interested in what Perez might have seen in the roomette of his doomed passenger. But Dockery seemed even more interested in Indians.

"Sort of a fascination with me ever since I was a kid," Dockery began. "I guess it was all those cowboy and Indian movies. Indians always interested me. But I never did know any. Never had the opportunity." And Leaphorn, not knowing exactly what to say to this, said: "I never knew any railroad people, either."

"They have this commercial on TV. Shows an Indian looking at all this trash scattered around the landscape. There's a tear running down his cheek. You seen that one?"

Leaphorn nodded. He had seen it.

"Are Indians really into that worshiping Mother Earth business?"

Leaphorn considered that. "It depends on the Indian. The Catholic bishop at Gallup, he's an Indian."

"But in general," Dockery said. "You know what I mean."

"There are all kinds of Indians," Leaphorn said. "What religion are you?"

"Well, now," Dockery said. He thought about it. "I don't go to church much. I guess you'd have to say I'm a Christian. Maybe a Methodist."

"Then your religion is closer to some Indians' than mine is," Leaphorn said.

Dockery looked skeptical.

"Take the Zunis or the Hopis or the Taos Indians for example," said Leaphorn, who was thinking as he spoke that this sort of conversation always made him feel like a complete hypocrite. His own metaphysics had evolved from the Navajo Way into a belief in a sort of universal harmony of cause and effect caused by God when He started it all. Inside of that, the human intelligence was somehow intricately involved with God. By some definitions, he didn't have much religion. Obviously, neither did Dockery, for that matter. And the subject needed changing. Leaphorn dug out his notebook, opened it, and turned to the page on which he'd reproduced the list from the folded paper. He asked Dockery if he'd noticed that the handwriting on that paper was different from the fine, careful script in the passenger's notebook.

"I didn't take a really close look at it," Dockery said.

About what Leaphorn had expected. But it was better than talking religion. He turned another page and came to the place he had copied "AURANOFIN W1128023" from the passenger's notebook. That had puzzled him. The man apparently spoke Spanish, but it didn't seem to be a Spanish word. *Aura* meant something more or less invisible surrounding something. Like a vapor. *No fin* in Spanish, if it held such a phrase, would mean something like "without end." No sense in that. The number looked like a license or code designation. Perhaps that would lead him to something useful.

He showed it to Dockery. "Can you make any sense out of that?"

Dockery looked at it. He shook his head. "Looks like the number off an insurance policy, or something like that. What's the word mean?"

"I don't know," Leaphorn said.

"Sounds like a medicine my wife used to take. Former wife, that is. Expensive as hell. I think it cost about ninety cents a capsule."

The sound of the train arriving came through the wall. Leaphorn was thinking that in a very few minutes he would be talking to a conductor named Perez, and that there was very little reason to believe Perez could tell him anything helpful. This was the final dead end. After this he would go back to Farmington and forget the man who had kept his worn old shoes so neatly polished.

Or try to forget him. Leaphorn knew himself well enough to recognize his weakness in that respect. He had always had difficulty leaving questions unanswered. And it had become no better with the age that, in his case, hadn't seemed to have brought any wisdom. All he had gotten out of Dockery was more evidence of how careful the killer of Pointed Shoes had been. That catalog of things on the folded paper must have been intended as a checklist, things to be checked off to avoid leaving behind any identification. The dentures were gone. So were the glasses, and their case, which might have contained a name and address, and prescription bottles which would certainly have a name on them. Prescription bottles were specifically mentioned on the checklist. And judging from the autopsy report the man must have taken medications. But no prescription bottles were in the luggage. He didn't need more evidence of the killer's cleverness. What he needed was some clue to the victim's identity. He would talk to Perez but it would be more out of courtesy—since he had wasted everyone's time to arrange this meeting—than out of hope.

Perez didn't think he'd be much help.

"I just got one look at him," the attendant said, after Dockery had introduced them and led them back to a cold, almost unfurnished room, where the passenger's luggage sat on a long, wooden table. "I'd noticed this passenger wasn't feeling all that great so I went by his compartment to see if he needed any help. I heard somebody moving in there but when I tapped on the door, nobody answered. I thought that was funny."

Perez pushed his uniform cap back to the top of his head and looked at them to see if that needed explanation. It didn't seem to.

"So, I unlocked it. There's this man in there, standing over a suitcase. I told him I'd come by to see if my passenger needed a hand and he said something negative. Something like he'd take care of it, or something like that. I remember he looked sort of hostile."

Perez stopped, looking at them. "Now when I think about that I think I was talking to the guy who had already knifed my passenger to death. And what he was probably thinking about right that moment was whether he should do it to me, too."

"What'd you do then?" Dockery asked.

"Nothing. I said, Okay. Or let me know if he needs a hand, or something like that. And then I got out." Perez looked slightly resentful. "What was I supposed to do? I didn't know anything was wrong. Far as I know this guy really is just a friend."

"What did he look like?" Leaphorn asked. He had remembered now why the name Henry Highhawk scribbled in the notebook struck a chord. It was the name of the man who had written Agnes Tsosie about coming to the Yeibichai. The man who had sent his photograph. He felt that odd sort of relief he had come to expect when unconnected things that troubled him suddenly clicked together. Perez would describe a blond man with braided hair and a thin, solemn face—the picture Agnes Tsosie had shown him. Then he'd have another lead away from this dead end.

"I just got a glance at him," Perez said. "I'd say sort of small. I think he had on a suit coat, or maybe a sports coat. And he had short hair. Red hair. Curly and close to his head. And a freckled face, like a lot of redheads have. Sort of a round face, I think. But he wasn't fat. I'd say sort of stocky. Burly. Like he had a lot of muscles. But small. Maybe hundred and thirty pounds, or less."

The good feeling left Leaphorn.

"Any other details? Scars? Limp? Anything like that? Anything that would help identify him?"

"I just got a glance at him," Perez said. He made a wry face. "Just one look."

"When did you check the room again?"

"When I didn't see the passenger get off at Gallup. I sort of was watching for him, you know, because Gallup was his destination. And I didn't see him. So I thought, well, he got off at another door. But it seemed funny, so when we was ready to pull out west, I took a look." He shrugged. "The roomette was empty. Nobody home. Just the luggage. So I looked for him. Checked the observation car, and the bar. I walked up and back through all the cars. And then I went back and looked in the room again. Seemed strange to me.

But I thought maybe he had got sick and just got off and left everything behind."

"Everything was unpacked."

"Unpacked," Perez agreed. "Stuff scattered around." He pointed to the bags. "I took it and put it in the bags and closed them."

"Everything?"

Perez looked surprised, then offended.

"Sure, everything. What'd ya think?"

"Newspapers, magazines, empty candy wrappers, paper cups, everything?" Leaphorn asked.

"Well, no," Perez said. "Not the trash."

"How about some magazine that might have been worth saving?" Leaphorn phrased the question carefully. Perez was obviously touchy about the question of him taking anything out of the passenger's room. "Some magazine, maybe, that might have something interesting in it and shouldn't be thrown away. If it was something he had subscribed to, then it would have an address label on it."

"Oh," Perez said, understanding. "No. There wasn't anything like that. I remember dumping some newspapers in the waste container. I left the trash for the cleaners."

"Did you leave an empty prescription bottle, or box, or vial, or anything?"

Perez shook his head. "I would have remembered that," he said. He shook his head again. "Like I'm going to remember that red-headed guy. Standing there looking at me and he had just killed my passenger a few minutes before that."

In the taxi heading back for his hotel, Leaphorn sorted it out. He listed it, put it in categories, tried to make what little he knew as neat as he could make it. The final summation. Because this was where it finished. No more leads. None. Pointed Shoes would lie in his anonymous grave, forever lost to those who cared about him. If such humans existed, they would go to their own graves wondering how he had vanished. And why he had vanished. As for Lieutenant Joe Leaphorn of the Navajo Tribal Police, who had no legitimate interest in any of this anyway, he would make a return flight reservation from the hotel. He would return the call of Rodney, who had missed him returning Leaphorn's call, and take Rodney out to dinner tonight if that was possible. Then he would pack. He would get to the airport tomorrow, fly to Albuquerque, and make the long drive back home to Window Rock. There would be no Emma there waiting for him. No Emma to whom he would report this failure. And be forgiven for it.

The cab stopped at a red light. The rain had stopped now. Leaphorn dug out his notebook, flipped through it, stared again at "AURANOFIN" and the number which followed it. He glanced at the license of the cab driver posted on the back of the front seat. Susy Mackinnon.

"Miss Mackinnon," he said. "Do you know where there's a pharmacy?"

"Pharmacy? I think there's one in that shopping center up in the next block. You feeling okay?"

"I'm feeling hopeful," Leaphorn said. "All of a sudden."

She glanced back at him, on her face the expression of a woman who is long past being surprised at eccentric passengers. "I've found that's better than despair," she said.

The pharmacy in the next block was a Merit Drug. The pharmacist was elderly, gray-haired, and good-natured. "That looks like a prescription number all right," he said. "But it's not one of ours."

"Is there any way to tell from this whose prescription it is? Name, address, so forth?"

"Sure. If you tell me where it was filled. If it was ours, see—any Merit Drug anywhere—then we'd have it on the computer. Find it that way."

Leaphorn put the notebook back in his jacket pocket. He made a wry face. "So," he said. "I can start checking all the Washington, D.C., drugstores."

"Or maybe the suburbs. Do you know if it was filled in the city?"

"No way of guessing," Leaphorn said. "It was just an idea. Looks like a bad one."

"If I were you, I'd start with Walgreen's. There was a *W* at the start of the numbers, and that looks like their code."

"You know where the nearest Walgreen's might be?"

"No. But we'll look that sucker up," the pharmacist said. He reached for the telephone book. It proved to be just eleven blocks away.

The pharmacist at Walgreen's was a young man. He decided Leaphorn's request was odd and that he should wait for his supervisor, now busy with another customer. Leaphorn waited, conscious that his cab was also waiting, with its meter running. The supervisor was a plump, middle-aged black woman, who inspected Leaphorn's Navajo Tribal Police credentials and then the number written in his notebook.

She punched at the keyboard of the computer, looking at Leaphorn over her glasses.

"Just trying to get an identification? That right? Not a refill or anything?"

"Right," Leaphorn said. "The pharmacist at another drugstore told me he thought this was your number."

"It looks like it," the woman said. She examined whatever had appeared on the screen. Shook her head. Punched again at the keyboard.

Leaphorn waited. The woman waited. She pursed her lips. Punched a single key.

"Elogio Santillanes," she said. "Is that how you pronounce it? Elogio Santillanes." She recited a street address and a telephone number, then glanced at the computer screen again. "And that's apartment three," she added. She wrote it all on a sheet of note paper and handed it to Leaphorn. "You're welcome," she said.

Back in the cab Leaphorn read the address to Miss Susy Mackinnon.

"No more going to the hotel?" she asked.

"First this address," Leaphorn said. "Then the hotel."

"Your humor has sure improved," Miss Mackinnon said. "They selling something in Walgreen's that you couldn't get in that other drugstore?"

"The solution to my problem," Leaphorn said. "And it was absolutely free."

"I need to remember that place," Miss Mackinnon said.

The rain had begun again—as much drizzle as rain—and she had the wipers turned to that now-and-then sequence. The blades flashed across the glass and clicked out of sight, leaving brief clarity behind. "You know," she said, "you're going to have a hell of a tab. Waiting time and now this trip. I hope you're good for about thirty-five or forty dollars when you finally get where you're going. I wouldn't want to totally tap you out. My intention is to leave you enough for a substantial tip."

"Um," Leaphorn said, not really hearing the question. He was thinking of what he would find at apartment number three. A woman. He took that for granted. And what he would say to her? How much would he tell her? Everything, he thought, except the grisly details. Leaphorn's good mood had been erased by the thought of what lay ahead. But in the long run it would be better for her to know everything. He remembered the endless weeks which led to Emma's death. The uncertainty. The highs of hope destroyed by reality and followed by despair. He would be the destroyer of this woman's hope. But then the wound could finally close. She could heal.

Miss Mackinnon seemed to have sensed he no longer wanted conversation. She drove in silence. Leaphorn rolled a window down an inch in defiance of the rain, letting in the late-autumn smell of the city. What would he do next, after the awful interview ahead? He would notify the FBI. Better to call Kennedy in Gallup, he thought, and let him initiate the action. Then he would call the McKinley County Sheriff's office and give them the identification. Not much the sheriff could do with such information but professional courtesy required it. And then he would go and call Rodney. It would be good to have some company this evening.

"Here you are," Miss Mackinnon said. She slowed the cab to avoid an old Chevy sedan which was backing into a parking space, and then stopped the cab in front of a two-story brick building with porches, built in a U shape around a landscaped central patio. "You want me to wait? It's expensive."

"Please wait," Leaphorn said. When he had broken the news here, he didn't want to wait around.

He walked down the pathway, following the man who had disembarked from the Chevy. Apartment one seemed to be vacant. The driver of the Chevy unlocked the door of apartment two and disappeared inside after a backward glance at Leaphorn. At apartment three, Leaphorn looked at the doorbell button. What would he say? I am looking for the widow of Elogio Santillanes. I am looking for a relative of Elogio Santillanes. Is this the residence of Elogio Santillanes?

From inside the apartment Leaphorn heard voices, faintly. Male and then female. Then he heard the sound of music. He rang the bell.

Now he heard only music. Abruptly that stopped. Leaphorn removed his hat. He stared at the door, shifting his weight. From the eaves of the porch behind him there came the sound of water dripping. On the street in front of the apartment a car went by. Leaphorn shifted his feet again. He pushed the doorbell button again, heard the ringing break the silence inside. He waited.

Behind him, he heard the door of apartment two opening. The man who had parked the Chevy stood in the doorway peering out at him. He was a small man and on this dim, rainy afternoon his form was backlit by the lamps in his apartment, making him no more than a shape.

Leaphorn pushed the button again and listened to the ring. He reached into his coat and got out the folder which held his police credentials. He sensed that behind him the man was still watching. Then he heard the sound of a lock being released. The door opened about a foot. A woman looked out at him, a middle-aged woman, slender, a thin face with glasses, black hair pulled severely back.

"Yes," she said.

"My name is Leaphorn," he said. He held out the folder, letting it drop open to reveal his badge. "I am looking for the residence of Elogio Santillanes."

The woman closed her eyes. Her head bent slightly forward. Her shoulders slumped. Behind her, from some part of the room beyond Leaphorn's vision, came the sound of a sharp intake of breath.

"Are there relatives of Mr. Santillanes living here?" Leaphorn asked.

"Yo soy," the woman said, her eyes still closed. And then, in English: "Yes." She was pale. She reached out, felt for the door, clutched it.

Leaphorn thought, the news I am bringing her is not news. It is something she anticipated. Something her instincts told her was inevitable. He knew the feeling. He had lived with it for months, knowing that Emma was dying. It was a fate already faced. But that didn't matter. There was still no humane way to tell her even though her heart had already given her the warning.

"Mrs. Santillanes?" he said. "Is there someone here with you? Some friend or relative?"

The woman opened her eyes. "What do you want?"

"I want to tell you about your husband." He shook his head. "It's bad news."

A man wearing a loose blue sweater appeared beside the woman. He was as old as Leaphorn, gray and stocky. He stood rigidly erect and peered at Leaphorn through the thick lenses of dark-rimmed glasses. A soldier, Leaphorn thought. "Sir," he said, in a loud, stern voice. "What can I do for you?"

The woman put her hand on the man's arm. She spoke in Spanish. Leaphorn didn't catch her words. The man said *"Callate!"* sharply, and then, more gently, something that Leaphorn didn't understand. The woman looked at Leaphorn as if remembering his face would be terribly important to her. Then she nodded, bit her lip, bowed, and disappeared from the room.

"You asked about a man named Santillanes," the man said. "He does not live here."

"I came looking for his relatives," Leaphorn said. "I'm afraid I bring bad news.

"We do not know him," the man said. "No one of that name lives here."

"This was the address he gave," Leaphorn said.

The man's expression became totally blank—a poker player staring at his cards. "He gave an address to you?" he asked. "And when was that?"

Leaphorn didn't hurry to answer that. The man was lying, of course. But why would he be lying?

"He gave this address to the pharmacist where he buys his medicine," Leaphorn said.

"Ah," the man said. He produced a slight smile. "Then

he has been sick. I trust this man, this Santillanes, is feeling better now."

"No," Leaphorn said. They stood there in the doorway, both of them waiting. Leaphorn had sensed some motion behind him. He shifted his weight enough to see the entrance of apartment two. The door was almost closed now. But not quite. Through it he could see the shadow of the small man, listening.

"He is not better? Then he is worse?"

"I should not be wasting your time with this," Leaphorn said. "Did Elogio Santillanes live here once and move away? Do you know where I might find any of his relatives? Or a friend?"

The gray man shook his head.

"I will go then," Leaphorn said. "Thank you very much. Please tell the lady I am sorry I disturbed her."

"Ah." The man hesitated. "You have made me curious. What happened to this fellow, this Santillanes?"

"He's dead," Leaphorn said.

"Dead." There was no surprise. "How?"

"He was stabbed," Leaphorn said.

"When did this happen?" Still there was no surprise. But Leaphorn could see the muscle along his jaw tighten. "And where did it happen?"

"Out in New Mexico. About a month ago." Leaphorn put his hand on the man's arm. "Listen," he said. "Do you know why this man Santillanes would have gone to New Mexico? What interest did he have in going to see a woman named Agnes Tsosie?"

The man pulled his arm away. He swallowed, his eyes misty with grief. He looked away from Leaphorn, toward his feet. "I don't know Elogio Santillanes," he said. And he carefully shut the door.

Leaphorn stood for a moment staring at the wood, sorting this out. The puzzle that had brought him here was solved. Clearly solved. No doubt about it. Or only the shadow of a doubt. The man with the worn, pointed shoes was Elogio Santillanes, the husband (perhaps brother) of this dark-haired woman. The brother (perhaps friend) of this gray-haired man. No more question of the identity of Pointed Shoes. Now there was another puzzle, new and fresh.

He walked down the porch, noticing that the door to apartment two was now closed but the light still illuminated the drapery. A dark afternoon, the kind of weather Leaphorn rarely saw on the Arizona–New Mexico border, and which quickly affected his mood. His taxi was waiting at the curb. Miss Mackinnon sat with a book propped on the steering wheel, reading.

Leaphorn turned and walked back to apartment two. He pushed the doorbell button. This one buzzed. He waited, thinking that people in Washington are slow to come to their doors. The door opened and the small man stood in it, looking at him.

"I need some information," Leaphorn said. "I'm looking for Elogio Santillanes."

The small man shook his head. "I don't know him."

"Do you know those people in that apartment over there?" Leaphorn nodded toward it. "I understand Santillanes lives in this building."

The man shook his head. Behind him in the apartment Leaphorn could see a folding card table with a telephone on it, a folding lawn chair, a cardboard box which seemed to contain books. A cheap small-screen television set perched on another box. The sound was turned off but the tube carried a newscast, in black and white. Otherwise the room seemed empty. A newspaper was on the floor beside the lawn chair. Perhaps the man had been reading there when the doorbell rang. Leaphorn suddenly found himself as interested in this small man as he was in the slim chance of getting information that had brought him here.

"You don't know the names of the people?" Leaphorn asked. He asked it partly to extend this conversation and see where it might lead. But there was a note of disbelief in his voice. Old as he was, Leaphorn still found it incredible that people could live side by side, see each other every day, and not be acquainted.

"Who are you?" the small man asked. "Are you an Indian?"

"I'm a Navajo," Leaphorn said. He reached for his identification. But he thought better of that.

"From where?"

"Window Rock."

"That's in—" The man hesitated, thinking. "Is it in New Mexico?"

"It's in Arizona," Leaphorn said.

"What are you doing here?"

"Looking for Elogio Santillanes."

"Why? What do you want with him?"

Leaphorn's eyes had been locked with the small man's. They were a sort of greenish blue and Leaphorn sensed in them, in the man's tone and his posture, a kind of hostile resentment.

"I just need information," Leaphorn said.

"I can't help you," the man said. He closed the door. Leaphorn heard the security chain rattle into place.

Miss Mackinnon started the motor as soon as he climbed into the backseat of the taxi. "I hope you got a lot of money," she said. "Back to the hotel now? And get your traveler's checks out of the safe-deposit box."

"Right," Leaphorn said.

He was thinking of the small man's strange, intent eyes, of his freckles, of his short, curly red hair. There must be thousands of short men in Washington who fit the Perez description of the man searching the roomette of Elogio Santillanes. But Leaphorn had never believed in coincidence. He had found the widow of Santillanes. He was sure of that. The widow or perhaps a sister. Certainly, he had found someone who had loved him.

And almost as certainly, he had found the man who had killed him. Going back to Window Rock could wait a little. He wanted to understand this better.

OVER LUNCH, the day after their visit to Highhawk's house, Chee and Janet Pete had discussed the man waiting in the sedan. "I think he was watching Highhawk, not you," Chee had said. "I think that's why he was parked out there." And Janet had finally said maybe so, but he could tell she wasn't persuaded by his logic. She was nervous. Uneasy about it. So he didn't tell her something else he had concluded—that the little man was one of the sort policemen call "freaks." At least the desert-country cops with whom Chee worked called them that—those men who have been somehow damaged beyond fear into a species that is unpredictable, and therefore dangerous. Finding a strange man tapping at his window in the darkness hadn't shaken the small man in the slightest. That was obvious. It had only aroused curiosity, and then provoked a sort of aggressive macho anger. Chee had seen that in such men before.

He had given Janet his analysis of Highhawk. ("He's nuts. Perfectly normal in some ways, but his sketches, they show you he's tilted about nine degrees. Slightly crazy.")

And he told her of the carving of the fetish he'd seen in Highhawk's office-studio.

"He was carving it out of cottonwood root—which is what the Pueblo people like to use, at least the ones I know. The Zunis and the Hopis," Chee had said. "No reason to believe Tano would be any different. Maybe he was making a copy of the Twin War God."

And Janet, of course, was way ahead of him. "I've thought about that," she said. "That maybe John would hire him to make a copy of the thing. Maybe I guessed right about that." She looked sad as she said it, not looking at Chee, studying her hands. "Then I guess we would give it to our man in the Tano Pueblo. And he'd use it to get himself elected."

"Tell him it's the real thing?"

"Depending on how honest our Eldon Tamana is," Janet said glumly. "If he's honest, then you lie to him. If he's not, then you tell the truth and let him do the lying."

"I wonder if anyone at the Pueblo could tell the copy from the real thing," Chee said. "How long has the thing been missing?"

"Since nineteen three or four, I think John said. Anyway, a long time."

"You'd probably be safe with a substitute then," Chee said. He was thinking about Highhawk. It didn't seem within the artist's nature to use his talent in a conspiracy to cheat an Indian Pueblo. But perhaps Highhawk would be another one considered honest enough to require that he be lied to. Maybe he didn't know why he was making the replica. In fact, maybe that carving wasn't a replica at all. Maybe that cottonwood fetish in his office was something else. Or maybe it was the genuine fetish itself. Or maybe this whole theory was nonsense.

"Jim," Janet said. "What do you think? Do you think they're sort of being—that I'm getting sort of led into something?" She was looking down at her hands, gripped tightly in her lap. "What do you think?"

Jim Chee thought the way she had changed that question was interesting. He thought it was interesting that she didn't ever actually pronounce the name of John McDermott. He wanted to say "Led by whom?" and force her at least to put some sort of name to it—if only the name of the law firm.

"I think something's going on," Chee said. "And I think we should go somewhere quiet, and eat dinner and talk it over." He glanced at her. "Maybe even hold hands. I could use a little handholding."

She had been looking down at her hands. Now she gave him a quick sidelong glance, and then turned away. "I can't tonight," she said. "I promised John I would meet him. Him and the man from Tano."

"Well, then," Chee said. "I'll ask you another question. Has Highhawk said anything more to you about this crime that hasn't been committed yet? You remember that? You mentioned it when you called me at Shiprock. I think it was sort of vague. Some reference to needing a lawyer in the future for something that hadn't yet happened. Do you remember?"

"Of course I remember," Janet said, looking at her hands again. "And tonight it's really law firm business. John arranged to have Tamana come. He said he wants to get me involved in how to handle the problem. He wants me to talk to Tamana. So I could hardly get out of it."

"Of course not," Chee said. He was disappointed. He had counted on this evening stretching on. But it was more than disappointment. There was resentment, too.

Janet sensed it. "I guess I could," she said. "I don't know how long this man's going to be in Washington. But I can try to call John and cancel it. Or leave a message for him at the restaurant."

"No, no," Chee said. "Business is business." But he didn't want to think about Janet and John McDermott having dinner and about what would happen after dinner. If I was honest with her, he thought, I would tell her that of course McDermott was using her. That he had probably used her when she was his student in law school, and ever since, and would always use her. He had never seen McDermott, but he knew professors who used their graduate students. Used them for slave labor to do their research, used them emotionally.

"Back to my question," Chee said. "Did you ever ask Highhawk what he meant by that reference to the uncommitted crime? Did he ever explain what he meant by that?"

Janet seemed happy to shift the subject. "I said something like I hoped he wasn't intending to dig up any more old bones. And he just laughed. So I said—frankly, this whole thing bothered me, so I said I didn't think it was laughable if he was planning to commit a felony. Something stuffy-sounding like that. And he laughed again and said he didn't intend to be guilty of making his attorney a co-conspirator. He said the less I knew the better."

"He seems to know something about the law."

"He knows a lot about a lot of things," Janet agreed. "Nothing wrong with the man's mind."

"Except for being crazy."

"Except for that," Janet agreed.

"Can you arrange for me to see him again?" Chee said. "And I'd like to get a look at that genuine Tano fetish figure. You think that's possible?"

"I'm sure there's no problem seeing Highhawk. About the fetish, I don't know. It's probably stored somewhere in a basement. And the Smithsonian must be pretty selective about who has access to what."

"Maybe because I'm a cop," Chee said, wondering as he said it what in the world he could say to make anyone believe the Navajo Tribal Police had a legitimate interest in a Pueblo Indian artifact.

"More likely because you're a shaman," Janet Pete said. "You still are, aren't you?"

"Trying to be," Chee said. "But being a medicine man doesn't fit very well with being a policeman. Don't get much business." Even that was an overstatement. The curing ceremonial Chee had learned was the Blessing Way. In the four years since he had declared himself a *hataalii* ready to perform that most popular ceremonial he'd had only three customers. One had been a maternal cousin, whom Chee had suspected of hiring him only as an act of family kindness. One had been the blessing of a newly constructed hogan owned by the niece of a friend, and one had been for a fellow policeman, the famous Lieutenant Joe Leaphorn. "Did I tell you about singing a Blessing Way for Joe Leaphorn?"

Janet looked shocked. "The famous Leaphorn? Grouchy Joe? I thought he was—" She searched for the word to define Lieutenant Joe Leaphorn. "Agnostic. Or skeptical. Or—what is it? Anyway, I didn't think he believed in curing ceremonials and things like that."

"He wasn't so bad," Chee said. "We had worked together on a case. People were digging up Anasazi graves and then there were a couple of homicides. But I think he asked me to do it because he wanted to be nice."

"Nice," Janet said. "That doesn't sound like the Joe Leaphorn I always used to hear about. Seems like I was always hearing Navajo cops bitching about Leaphorn never being quite satisfied with anything."

But it had, in fact, been nice. More than nice. Beautiful. Everything had gone beautifully. Not many of Leaphorn's relatives had been there. But then the old man was a widower and he didn't think Leaphorn had much family. Leaphorn was a Red Forehead Dinee and that clan was pretty much extinct. But the curing itself had gone perfectly. He had forgotten nothing. The sand paintings had been exactly correct. And when the final singing had been finished Old Man Leaphorn had, in some way difficult for Chee to define, seemed to be healed of the sickness that had been riding him. The bleakness had been gone. He had seemed back in harmony. Content.

"I think he just always wants things to be better than they naturally are," Chee said. "I got used to him after a while. And I've got a feeling that all that talk about him being a smart son-of-a-bitch is pretty much true."

"I used to see him in court there at Window Rock now and then, and in the police building, but I never knew him. I heard he was a real pragmatist. Not a traditional Navajo."

And how about you, Janet Pete? Chee thought. How traditional are you? Do you believe in what Changing Woman taught our ancestors about the power we are given to heal ourselves? How about you leaving Dinetah and the Sacred Mountains because a white man wants you to keep him happy in Washington? But that was none of his goddamn business. That was clear enough. His role was to be a friend. No more. Well, why not? For that matter, he could use a friend himself.

"What did you mean about getting to see the fetish as a shaman?" he asked.

"Highhawk would be very impressed if he knew you were a Navajo *hataalii,*" she said. "Tell him you're a singer and let him know you would like to see his work. He's setting up a mask exhibition, you know. Tell him you'd like to see the Navajo part of the show."

"And then ask to see the fetish," Chee said.

Janet looked at him, studying his expression. "Why not?" she asked, and the question sounded a little bitter. "You think I'm thinking too much like a lawyer?"

"I didn't say that."

"Well, I am a lawyer."

He nodded. "You think I could see Highhawk tonight?"

"He's working tonight," she said. "On that exhibit. I'll call him at the museum and see if I can set something up. Will you be at your hotel?"

"Where else?" Chee said, noticing as Janet glanced at him that his tone, too, sounded a little bitter.

"I'll try to hurry it up," she said. "Maybe you can do it tomorrow."

It proved to be quicker than that.

Janet had shown him the Vietnam Memorial wall, the Jefferson Memorial, and the National Air and Space Museum, and then dropped him off at his hotel. Chee ate a cheese omelet in the hotel coffee shop, took a shower in his bathroom tub (which, small as it was, was huge compared to the bathing compartment in Chee's trailer home), and turned on the television. The sound control was stuck somewhere between loud and extremely loud and Chee spent a futile five minutes trying to adjust the volume. Failing that, he found an old movie in which the mood music was lower-decibel and sprawled across the pillow to watch it.

The telephone rang. It was Henry Highhawk.

"Miss Pete said you wanted to see the exhibit," Highhawk said. "Are you doing anything right now?"

Chee was available.

"I'll meet you at the Twelfth Street entrance to the Museum of Natural History building," Highhawk said. "It's just about five or six blocks from your hotel. I hate to rush you but I have another appointment later on."

"I'll be there in twenty minutes," Chee said. He turned off the TV and reached for his coat.

Perhaps Janet's idea of being followed had made him edgy. He looked for the car and he saw it almost as soon as he left the hotel entrance. The old Chevy sedan with the bent antenna was parked across the street and down the block. He stood motionless studying it, trying to see if the small man was in it. Reflection from the windshield made it impossible to tell. Chee walked slowly down the sidewalk, thinking that the small man hadn't made any effort at concealment. What might that mean? Did he want Chee to know he was being watched? If so, why? Chee could think of no reason for that. Perhaps it was simply carelessness. Or arrogance. Or perhaps he wasn't watching Chee at all.

His route to the Museum of Natural History would take him the other way, but Chee detoured to walk past the sedan. It was empty. He leaned against the roof, looking in. On the front seat there was a folded copy of today's *Washington Post* and a paper cup. A street map of the District of Columbia was on the dash. The backseat was empty except that an empty plastic bag with a Safeway logo was crumpled on the floor. The car was locked.

Chee looked up the street and down it. Two teenaged black girls were walking toward him, laughing at something one had said. Otherwise, no one was in sight. The rain had stopped now but the streets and sidewalks still glistened with dampness. The air was damp too, and chill. Chee pulled his jacket collar around his throat and walked. He listened. He heard nothing but occasional traffic sounds. He was on Tenth Street now, the gray mass of the Department of Justice building beside him, the Post Office building looming across the street. Justice seemed dark but a few of the windows in the postal offices were lit. What did post office bureaucrats do that kept them working late? He imagined someone at a drafting table designing a stamp. He stopped at the intersection of Constitution Avenue waiting for the Don't Walk signal to change. Two men and a woman, all wearing the Washington uniform, were walking briskly down the sidewalk toward him. Each held a furled umbrella. Each carried a briefcase. The little man was nowhere in sight. Then, under the shrubbery landscaping the corner of the Justice building to Chee's left, he saw a body.

Chee sucked in his breath. He stared. It was a human form, drawn into the fetal position and partially covered by what seemed to be a cardboard box. Near the head was a sack. Chee made a tentative step toward it. The trio walked past the body. The man nearest glanced at it and said something unintelligible to Chee. The woman looked at the body and looked quickly away. They walked past Chee. ". . . at least GS 13," the woman was saying. "More likely 14, and then before you know it . . ." Probably a wino, Chee thought. Chee had seen a thousand or so unconscious drunks since his swearing-in as an officer of the Navajo Tribal Police, seen them sprawled in Gallup alleys, frozen in the sagebrush beside the road to Shiprock, mangled like jackrabbits on the asphalt of U.S. Highway 666. But he could see the floodlit spire of the Washington Monument just a few blocks behind him. He hadn't expected it here. He walked over the dead autumn grass, knelt beside the body. The cardboard was damp from the earlier rain. The body was a man. The familiar and expected smell of whiskey was missing.

Chee reached his hand to the side of the man's throat, feeling for a pulse.

The man screamed and scrambled into a crouching position, trying to defend himself. The cardboard box bounced to the sidewalk.

Chee jumped back, totally startled.

The man was bearded, bundled in a navy peacoat many sizes too large for him. He struck at Chee, feebly, screaming incoherently. Two men in the Washington uniform hurrying down Constitution Avenue glanced at the scene and hurried even faster.

Chee held out empty hands. "I thought you needed help," he said.

The man fell forward to hands and knees. "Get away, get away, get away," he howled.

Chee got away.

Highhawk was waiting for him at the employees' entrance on Twelfth Street. He handed Chee a little rectangle of white paper with the legend VISITOR printed and Chee's name written on it.

"What do you want to see first?" he asked. Then paused. "You all right?"

"There's a man out there. Sick, I guess. Lying out there under the bushes across the street."

"Drunk maybe," Highhawk said. "Or stoned on crack. Usually there's three or four of them. That Department of Justice building grass is a favorite spot."

"This guy wasn't drunk."

"On crack probably," Highhawk said. "These days it's usually crack if they're dopers, or it can be anything from heroin to sniffing glue. But sometimes they're just mental cases." He considered Chee's reaction to all this. "You have them too. I saw plenty of drunks in Gallup."

"I think we have more drunks per capita than anybody," Chee said. "But on the reservation we try to pick them up. We try to put them somewhere. What's the policy here?"

But Highhawk was already limping hurriedly down the hallway, not interested in this subject, the braced leg dragging but moving fast. "Let me show you this display first," he said. "I'm trying to get it to look just like it would if it was really happening out there in your desert."

Chee followed. He still felt shaken. But now he was thinking again, and he thought that he hadn't looked for the small man around the Twelfth Street entrance to the Natural History Museum. And he thought that possibly the reason he hadn't seen the small man following him was because the small man might not have needed to follow. He might have known where Chee was going.

Henry Highhawk's exhibit was down a side hall on the main floor of the museum. It was walled off from the world of museumgoers by plywood screens and guarded by signs declaring the area TEMPORARILY CLOSED TO THE PUBLIC and naming the display THE MASKED GODS OF THE AMERICAS. Behind the screen was the smell of sawdust, glue, and astringent cleaning fluids. There was also an array of masks, ranging from grotesque and terrible to calm and sublimely beautiful. Some were displayed in groups, one group representing the varying concept of demons in Yucatán villages, and another Inca deities. Some stood alone, accompanied only by printed legends explaining them. Some were displayed on costumed models of the priests or personifiers who wore them. Some were mounted in settings illustrative of the ceremonies in which they were used. Highhawk limped past these to a diorama protected by a railing. In it stood Yeibichai himself, Talking God, the maternal grandfather of all the great and invisible *yei* who made up the gallery of the Navajo supernatural powers.

Talking God's gray-white mask, with its bristle of eagle feathers and its collar-ruff of animal fur, formed the head of a manikin. Chee had just walked past dozens of such human forms in other Smithsonian displays—of Laplanders mending reindeer harnesses, of Aztec musicians in concert, of a New Guinea hunter stalking a pig, of a Central American tribeswoman finishing a pot. But this manikin, this wearer of the Yeibichai mask, seemed alive. In fact, he seemed more than alive. Chee stood and stared at him.

"This one is mine, of course," Highhawk said. "I did some of the others, too, and helped on some. But this one is mine." He glanced at Chee, waiting a polite moment for a comment. "If you see anything wrong, you point it out," he added. He stepped across the railing to the figure and adjusted the mask, moving his fingers under the leather, tilting it slightly, then readjusting it. He stepped back and looked at it thoughtfully.

"You see anything wrong?" he asked.

Chee could see nothing wrong. At least nothing except trivial details in some of the decoration. And that was probably intended. Such a sacred scene should not be reproduced exactly except for its purpose—to cure a human being. Talking God was frozen in that shuffling dance step the *yeis* traditionally used as they approached the patient's hogan. In this display, the patient was standing on a rug spread on the earth in front of the hogan door. He was wrapped in a blanket and held his arms outstretched. Talking God's short woven kilt seemed to flow with the motion, and in each hand he carried a rattle which looked genuine. And, Chee thought, probably was. Behind Talking God in this diorama the other gods followed in identical poses, seeming to dance out of the darkness into the firelight. Chee recognized the masks of Fringed Mouth, of Monster Slayer, of Born for Water, and of Water Sprinkler with his cane and humped back. Other *yei* figures were also vaguely visible moving across the dance ground. And on both sides, the fires illuminated lines of spectators.

Chee's eyes lingered on the mask of Talking God. It seemed identical to the one he'd seen in Highhawk's office. Naturally it would. Probably it was the same one. Probably Highhawk had taken it home to prepare it for mounting. Or, if he was copying it, he would be making the replica look as much like the original as he could.

"What do you think?" Highhawk asked. His voice sounded anxious. "You see anything wrong?"

"It looks great to me. Downright beautiful," Chee said. "I'm impressed." In fact, he was tremendously impressed. Highhawk had reproduced that moment in the final night of the ceremonial called the Yei Yiaash, the Arrival of the

Spirits. He turned to look at Highhawk. "Surely you didn't get all this from that little visit out to Agnes Tsosie's Night Chant. If you did you must have a photographic memory." Or, Chee thought, a videotape recorder hidden away somewhere, like the audio recorder he had hidden in his palm.

Highhawk grinned. "I guess I read about a thousand descriptions of that ceremonial. All the anthropologists I could find. And I studied the sketches they made. And looked at all the materials we have on it here in the Smithsonian. Whatever people stole and turned over to us down through the years, I studied it. Studied the various *yei* masks and all that. And then Dr. Hartman—she's the curator who's in charge of setting up this business—she called in a consultant from the reservation. A Navajo shaman. Guy named Sandoval. You know him?"

"I've heard of him," Chee said.

"Partly we wanted to make sure we aren't violating any taboos. Or misusing any religious material. Or anything like that." Highhawk paused again. He started to say something, stopped, looked nervously at Chee. "You sure you don't see anything wrong?"

Chee shook his head. He was looking at the mask itself, wondering if there was an artificial head under it with an artificial face with an artificial Navajo expression. No reason there should be. The mask looked ancient, the gray-white paint which covered the deerskin patterned with the tiny cracks of age, the leather thongs which laced up its sides darkened with years of use. But of course those were just the details Highhawk would not have overlooked in making a copy. The mask he'd seen in the box in Highhawk's office was either this one, or an awfully close copy—that was obvious from what he had remembered. The tilt of the feathered crest, the angle of the painted eyebrows, all of those small details which went beyond legend and tradition that had lent themselves to the interpretation of the mask maker, they all seemed to be identical. Except in its ritual poetry and the sand paintings of its curing ceremonials, the Navajo culture always allowed room for poetic license. In fact it encouraged it—to bring whatever was being done into harmony with the existing circumstances. How much such license would Highhawk have if he was copying the Tano effigy? Not much, Chee guessed. The kachina religion of the Pueblo Indians, it seemed to Chee, was rooted in a dogma so ancient that the centuries had crystallized it.

"How about the basket?" Highhawk asked him. "On the ground by his feet? That's supposed to be the basket for the Yei Da'ayah. According to our artifact inventory records, anyway."

Highhawk's pronunciation of the Navajo word was so strange that what he actually said was incomprehensible. But what he probably meant was the basket which held the pollen and the feathers used for feeding the masks after the spirits within them were awakened. "Looks all right to me," Chee said.

A woman, slender, handsome, and middle-aged, had walked around the screen into the exhibit area.

"Dr. Hartman," Highhawk said. "You're working late."

"You too, Henry," she said, with a glance at Chee.

"This is Jim Chee," Highhawk said. "Dr. Carolyn Hartman is one of our curators. She's my boss. This is her show. And Mr. Chee is a Navajo shaman. I asked him to take a look at this."

"It was good of you to come," Carolyn Hartman said. "Did you find this Night Chant authentic?"

"As far as I know," Chee said. "In fact, I think it's remarkable. But the Yeibichai is not a ceremonial that I know very well. Not personally. The only one I know well enough to do myself is the Blessing Way."

"You're a singer? A medicine man?"

"Yes, ma'am. But I am new at it."

"Mr. Chee is also Officer Chee," Highhawk said. "He's a member of the Navajo Tribal Police. In fact, he's the very same officer who arrested me out there. I thought you'd approve of that." Highhawk was smiling when he said it. Dr. Hartman was smiling, too. She likes him, Chee thought. It was visible. And the feeling was mutual.

"Good show," she said to Chee. "Running down the grave robber. Sometime I must come out to your part of the country with time enough to really see it. I should learn a lot more about your culture. I'm afraid I've spent most of my time trying to understand the Incas." She laughed. "For example, if I were your guide here, I wouldn't be showing you that Night Chant display. I'd be showing you my own pets." She pointed to the diorama immediately adjoining. In it a wall of great cut stones opened onto a courtyard. Beyond, a temple rose against a mountain background. This display also offered its culturally attired manikins. Men in sleeveless tunics, cloaks of woven feathers, headbands, and leather sandals, women in long dresses with shawls fastened across their breasts with jeweled pins and their hair covered with cloths. But the centerpiece of all of this was a great metal mask. To Chee it seemed to have been molded of gold and decorated with a fortune in jewels.

"I'd been admiring that," he said. "Quite a mask. It looks expensive."

"It's formed of a gold-platinum alloy inset with emeralds and other gems," she said. "It represents the great god Viracocha, the creating god, the very top god of the Inca pantheon. The smaller mask there, that one represents the Jaguar god. Less important, I guess. But potent enough."

"It looks like it would be worth a fortune," Chee said. "How did the museum get it?" As he said it, he wished he hadn't. In his ears the question seemed to imply the acquisition might be less than honorable. But perhaps that was a product of the way he'd been thinking. No honorable

Navajo could have sold the museum that mask of Talking God he had been admiring. Not if it was genuine. Such masks were sacred, held in family custody. No one had a right to sell them.

"It was a gift," Dr. Hartman said. "It had been in the hands of a family down there. A political family, I gather. And from them it went to some very important person in the United Fruit Company, or maybe it was Anaconda Copper. Anyway, someone like that. And then it was inherited, and in the 1940s somebody needed to offset a big income tax problem." Dr. Hartman created a flourish with an imaginary wand, laughing. "Shazam! The Smithsonian, the attic of America, the attic of the world, obtains another of its artifacts. And some good citizen gets a write-off on his income tax bill."

"I guess no one can complain," Chee said. "It's a beautiful thing."

"Someone can always complain," Dr. Hartman laughed. "They're complaining right now. They want it back."

"Oh," Chee said. "Who?"

"The Chilean National Museum. Although of course the museum never actually had its hands on it." Dr. Hartman leaned against a pedestal which supported, according to its caption, the raven mask used by shamans in the Carrier tribe of the Canadian Pacific Coast. It occurred to Chee that she was enjoying herself.

"Actually," she continued, "the fuss is being raised by someone named General Huerta. General Ramon Huerta Cardona, to be formal. It was his family from which the American tycoon, whoever he was, got the thing in the first place. Or so I understand. And I imagine that if their national museum manages to talk us out of it, the good general would then file a claim to recover it for his family. And being a very, very big shot in Chilean politics, he'd win."

"Are you going to give it back?"

Highhawk laughed.

"I'm not," Dr. Hartman said. "I wouldn't give it back under the circumstances. I would be happy enough to give Henry here his bones back in the name of common sense, or maybe common decency. But I wouldn't return that mask." She smiled benignly at Henry Highhawk. "Romantic idealism I can approve. But not greed." She shrugged and made a wry face. "But then I don't make policy."

"He's coming to see it at the opening," Highhawk said. "General Huerta is. Did you notice that story about it the other day in the *Post*?"

"I read that," Dr. Hartman said. "I gather from what he told the reporter that the general is coming to Washington for some more dignified purpose, but I noticed he said he would also visit us to see"—Dr. Hartman's voice shifted into sarcasm—" 'our national treasure.' "

"That'll be a pain," Highhawk said. "Special security always screws things up."

"He's not a head of state," Dr. Hartman said. "Just the head secret policeman. We'll give him a couple of guides and a special 'meet him at the front door with a handshake.' After that, he's just another tourist."

"Except the press will flock in after him. And the TV cameras," said Highhawk, who knew a lot about such affairs.

Chee found himself liking Dr. Hartman. "He'll be seeing quite a display here," he said.

"No false modesty," Dr. Hartman said. "I think so, too. I would be good at this if I didn't have to spend so much time being a museum bureaucrat." She smiled at Highhawk. "For example, trying to figure out how to keep peace between an idealistic young conservator and the people over in the Castle who make the rules."

Chee noticed that Henry Highhawk did not return the smile.

"We have to be going," Highhawk said.

"Well," Dr. Hartman said. "I hope you're enjoying your visit, Mr. Chee. Is Mr. Highhawk showing you everything you want to see?"

This seemed to be an opportunity. "I wanted to see this," Chee said, indicating the Night Chant and the world of masks around it. "And I was hoping to see that Tano War God that I've heard about. I heard somewhere that someone at the Pueblo was hoping to get that back, too."

Dr. Hartman's expression was doubtful. "I haven't heard of that," she said, frowning. She looked at Highhawk. "A Tano fetish. Do you know anything about that? Which fetish would they mean?"

Highhawk glanced from Dr. Hartman to Chee. He hesitated. "I don't know."

"I guess you could look it up in the inventory," she said.

Highhawk was looking at Chee, examining him. "Why not?" he said. "If you want to."

They went up the staff elevator to the sixth floor, to Highhawk's airless cubicle of an office. He punched the proper information into his computer terminal and received, in return, a jumble of numbers and letters.

"This tells us the hallway, the room, the corridor in the room, the shelf in the corridor, and the number of the bin it's in," Highhawk said. He punched another set of keys and waited. "Now it tells us that it is out of inventory and being worked on. Or something."

He turned off the computer, glanced at Chee, looked thoughtful.

He knows where it is, Chee thought. He knew from the beginning. He's deciding whether to tell me.

"It should be in the conservation lab," Highhawk said. "Let's go take a look."

The telephone rang.

Highhawk looked at it, and at Chee.

It rang again. Highhawk picked it up. "Highhawk," he said.

And then: "I can't right now. I have a guest."

He listened, glanced at Chee. "No, I couldn't make the damn thing work," Highhawk said. "I'm no good with that stuff." He listened.

"I tried that. It didn't turn on." Listened again. "Look. You're coming down anyway. I'll leave it for you to fix." Listened. "No. That's a little early. Too much traffic then." And finally: "Make it nine thirty then. And remember it's the Twelfth Street entrance."

Highhawk listened, and hung up.

"Let's go," he said to Chee.

Highhawk made his limping way down a seemingly endless corridor. It was lined on both sides with higher-than-head stacks of wooden cases. The cases were numbered. Some were sealed with paper stickers. Most wore tags reading CAUTION: INVENTORIED MATERIALS or CAUTION: UNINVENTORIED MATERIALS.

"What's in all this?" Chee asked, waving.

"You name it," Highhawk said. "I think in here it's mostly early agricultural stuff. Tools, churns, hoes, you know. Up ahead we have bones."

"The skeletons you wanted returned?"

"*Want* returned," Highhawk said. "Still. We've got more than eighteen thousand skeletons boxed up in this attic. Eighteen goddamn thousand Native American skeletons in the museum's so-called research collection."

"Wow," Chee said. He would have guessed maybe four or five hundred. "How about white skeletons?"

"Maybe twenty thousand black, white, and so forth,"

Highhawk said. "But since the white-eyes outnumber the redskins in this country about two hundred to one, to reach parity I have to dig up three-point-six million white skeletons and stack them in here. That is, if the scientists are really into studying old bones—which I doubt."

Old bones was not a subject which appealed to Chee's traditional Navajo nature. Corpses were not a subject for polite discussion. The knowledge that he was sharing a corridor with thousands of the dead made Chee uneasy. He wanted to change the subject. He wanted to ask Highhawk about the telephone conversation. What was he trying to fix? What was it that wouldn't turn on? Who was he meeting at nine thirty? But it was none of his business and Highhawk would tell him so or evade the question.

"Why the seals?" he asked instead, pointing.

Highhawk laughed. "The Republicans used the main gallery for their big inaugural ball," Highhawk said. "About a thousand Secret Service and FBI types came swarming in here in advance to make sure of security." The memory had converted Highhawk's bitterness to high good humor. His laugh turned into a chortle.

"They'd unlock each case, poke around inside to make sure Lee Harvey Oswald wasn't hiding in there, and then lock it up again and stick on the seal so nobody could sneak in later."

"My God," Chee exclaimed, struck by a sudden thought. "How many keys would it take to unlock all of these?"

Highhawk laughed. "You're not dealing with the world's heaviest key ring here," he said. "Just one key, or rather copies of the same key, fits all these box locks. They're not intended to keep people from stealing stuff. Who'd want to steal a section of a Civil War rowboat, for example? It's to help with inventory control. You want in one of these cases, you go to the appropriate office and get the key off a hook by the desk and sign for it. Anyway, it all worried the Secret Service to death. About eighty million artifacts in this building, and maybe a hundred thousand of them could be used to kill somebody. So they wanted everything tied down."

"I guess it worked. Nobody got shot."

"Or harpooned, or crossbowed, or beaned with a charro lasso, or speared, or arrowed, or knitting needled, or war clubbed," Highhawk added. "They wanted all that stuff to come out too. Anything that might be a weapon, from Cheyenne metate stones to Eskimo whale-skinning knives. It was quite an argument."

Highhawk did an abrupt turn through a doorway into a long, bright, cluttered room lit by rows of fluorescent tubes.

"The conservatory lab," he said, "the repair shop for decaying cannonballs, frayed buggy whips, historic false teeth and so forth, including—if the computer was right—one Tano War God."

He stopped beside one of the long tables which occupied the center of the room, rummaged briefly, extracted a cardboard box. From it he pulled a crudely carved wooden form.

He held it up for Chee to inspect. It was shaped from a large root, which gave it a bent and twisted shape. Bedraggled feathers decorated it and its face stared back at Chee with the same look of malice that he remembered on the fetish he'd seen in Highhawk's office. Was it the same fetish? Maybe. He couldn't be sure.

"This is what the shouting's about," he said. "The symbol of one of the Tano Twin War Gods."

"Has somebody been working on it?" Chee asked. "Is that why it's here?"

Highhawk nodded. He looked up at Chee. "Where did you hear the Pueblo was asking for it back?"

"I can't remember," Chee said. "Maybe there was something in the *Albuquerque Journal* about it." He shrugged. "Or maybe I'm getting it confused with the Zuni War God. The one the Zunis finally got back from the Denver Museum."

Highhawk laid the fetish gently back in the box. "Anyway, I guess that when the museum got the word that the Pueblo was asking about it, somebody over in the Castle sent a memo over. They wanted to know if we actually had such a thing. And if we did have it, they wanted to make damn sure it was properly cared for. No termites, moss, dry rot, anything like that. That would be very bad public relations." Highhawk grinned at Chee. "Folks in the Castle can't stand a bad press."

"Castle?"

"The original ugly old building with the towers and battlements and all," Highhawk explained. "It sort of looks like a castle and that's where the top brass has offices." The thought of this wiped away Highhawk's good humor. "They get paid big money to come up with reasons why the museum needs eighteen thousand stolen skeletons. And this—" He tapped the fetish. "—this stolen sacred object."

He handed it to Chee.

It was heavier than he'd expected. Perhaps the root was from some tree harder than the cottonwood. It looked old. How old? he asked himself. Three hundred years? Three thousand? Or maybe thirty. He knew no way to judge. But certainly nothing about it looked raw or new.

Highhawk was glancing at his watch. Chee handed him the fetish. "Interesting," he said. "There's a couple of things I want to ask you about."

"Tell you what," Highhawk said. "I have a thing I have to do. We'll go back by my office and you wait there and I'll be right back. This is going to take—" He thought. "—maybe ten, fifteen minutes."

Chee glanced at his own watch when Highhawk

dropped him at the office. It was nine twenty-five. He sat beside Highhawk's desk, heels on the wastebasket, relaxing. He was tired and he hadn't realized it. A long day, full of walking, full of disappointments. What would he be able to tell Janet Pete that Janet Pete didn't already know? He could tell her of Highhawk's coyness about the fetish. Obviously it was Highhawk who had brought the War God up to the conservancy lab to work on it. Obviously he'd known exactly where to find it. Obviously he didn't want Chee to know of his interest in the thing.

Chee yawned, and stretched, and rose stiffly from his chair to prowl the office. A framed certificate on the wall declared that his host had successfully completed studies in anthropological conservation and restoration at the London Institute of Archaeology. Another certified his completion with honors of a materials conservation graduate program at George Washington University. Still another recognized his contribution to a seminar on "Conservation Implications of the Structure, Reactivity, Deterioration, and Modification of Proteinaceous Artifact Material" for the American Institute of Archaeology.

Chee was looking for something to read and thinking that Highhawk's few minutes had stretched a bit when he heard the sounds—a sharp report, a clatter of miscellaneous noises with what might have been a yell mixed in. It was an unpleasant noise and it stopped Chee cold. He caught his breath, listening. Whatever it was ended as abruptly as it had started. He walked to the door and looked up and down the hallway, listening. The immense sixth floor of the Museum of Natural History was as silent as a cave. The noise had come from his right. Chee walked down the hallway in that direction, slowly, soundlessly. He stopped at a closed door, gripped the knob, tested it. Locked. He put his ear to the panel and heard nothing but the sound his own blood made moving through his arteries. He moved down the hallway, conscious of the rows of wooden bins through which he walked, of the smells, of dust, of old things decaying. Then he stopped again and stood absolutely still, listening. He heard nothing but ringing silence and, after a moment, what might have been an elevator descending in another part of the building.

Then steps. Rapid steps. From ahead and to the left. Chee hurried to the corridor corner ahead, looked around it. It was empty. Simply another narrow pathway between deep stacks of numbered bins. He listened again. Where had the hurrier gone? What had caused those odd noises? Chee had no idea which way to look. He simply stood, leaning against a bin, and listened. Silence rang in his ears. Whoever, whatever, had made the noise had gone away.

He walked back to Highhawk's office, suppressing an urge to look back, controlling an urge to hurry. And when he reached it, he closed the door firmly behind him and moved his chair against the wall so that it faced the door. When he sat in it he suddenly felt very foolish. The noise would have some perfectly normal explanation. Something had fallen. Someone had dropped something heavy.

He resumed his explorations of the documents on Highhawk's untidy desk, looking for something interesting. They tended toward administrative documents and technical material. He selected a photocopy of a report entitled

ETHICAL AND PRACTICAL CONSIDERATIONS
IN CONSERVING ETHNOGRAPHIC MUSEUM OBJECTS

and settled down to read it.

It was surprisingly interesting—some twenty-five pages full of information and ideas mostly new to Chee. He read it carefully and slowly, stopping now and then to listen. Finally he put it back on the desk, put his heels back on the wastebasket, and thought about Mary Landon, and then about Janet Pete, and then about Highhawk. He glanced at his watch. After ten. Highhawk had been gone more than thirty minutes. He walked to the door and looked up and down the corridor. Total emptiness. Total silence. He sat again in the chair, feet on the floor, remembering exactly what Highhawk had said. He'd said wait here a few minutes. Ten or fifteen.

Chee got his hat and went out into the corridor, turning off the light and closing the door behind him. He found his way through the labyrinth of corridors to the elevator. He pushed the button and heard it laboring its way upward. Highhawk obviously had not returned by this route. On the ground floor he found his way to the Twelfth Street exit. There had been a security guard there when he came in, a woman who had spoken to Highhawk. She would know if he'd left the building. But the woman wasn't there. No one was guarding the exit door.

Chee felt a sudden irrational urge to get out of this building and under the sky. He pushed the door open and hurried down the steps. The cold, misty air felt wonderful on his face. But where was Highhawk? He remembered the last words Highhawk had said as he left him at Highhawk's office:

"I'll be right back."

15

LEAPHORN CALLED Kennedy from his hotel room and caught him at home.

"I've got him," Leaphorn said. "His name is Elogio Santillanes. But I need you to get a fingerprint check made and see if the Agency has anything on him."

"Who?" Kennedy said. He sounded sleepy. "What are you talking about?"

"The man beside the tracks. Remember? The one you got me out into the weather to take a look at."

"Oh," Kennedy said. "Yeah. Santillanes, you say. A local Hispano then, after all. How'd you get a make on him?"

Leaphorn explained it all, from St. Germain to Perez to the prescription number, including the little red-haired man who might (or might not) be watching the Santillanes apartment.

"Nice to be lucky," Kennedy said. "Where the hell you calling from? You in Washington now?"

Leaphorn gave him the name of his hotel. "I'm going to

stay here—or at least I'll be here for message purposes. Are you going to call Washington?"

"Why not?" Kennedy said.

"Would you ask 'em to let me know what they find out? And since they probably won't do it, would you call me as soon as they call you back?"

"Why not?" Kennedy said. "You going to stick around there until we know something?"

"Why not?" Leaphorn said. "It shouldn't take long with the name. Either they have prints on him or they don't."

It didn't take long. Leaphorn watched the late news. He went out for a walk in what had now transformed itself into a fine, damp, cold mist. He bought an edition of tomorrow's *Washington Post* and read it in bed. He woke late, had breakfast in the hotel coffee shop, and found his telephone ringing when he got back to the room.

It was Kennedy.

"Bingo," Kennedy said. "I am sort of a hero with the Agency this morning—which will last until about sundown. Your Elogio Santillanes was in the Agency print files. He was one of the relatively few surviving leaders of the substantially less than loyal left-wing opposition to the Pinochet regime in Chile."

"Well," Leaphorn said. "That's interesting." But what the devil did it mean? What would call a Chilean politician to Gallup, New Mexico? What would arouse in such a man an interest in a Night Chant somewhere out beyond Lower Greasewood?

"They wondered what had happened to him," Kennedy was saying. "He wasn't exactly under close surveillance, but the Agency tries to keep an eye on such folks. It tries to keep track of them. Especially this bunch because of that car bombing awhile back. You remember about that?"

"Very vaguely. Was it Chilean?"

"It was. One of this bunch that Santillanes belongs to

got blown sky-high over on Sheridan Circle, near where the very important people live. The Chilean embassy crowd didn't make enough effort to hide their tracks and the Department of State declared a bunch of them *persona non grata* and sent them home. There was a big protest to Chile, human rights complaints, the whole nine yards. Terribly bad publicity for the Pinochet gang. Anyway after that the Agency seems to have kept an eye on them. And things cooled down."

"Until now," Leaphorn said.

"It looks to me like Pinochet's thugs waited until they figured they wouldn't get caught at it," Kennedy said. "But how do I know?"

"That would explain all the effort to keep Santillanes from being identified."

"It would," Kennedy agreed. "If there's no identification, there's no static from the Department of State."

"Did you ask your people here to give me a call? Did you tell them about Santillanes' neighbor? And did you pass along what I told you about Henry Highhawk's name being in Santillanes' notebook?"

"Yes, I told them about the little man in apartment two, and yes I mentioned Henry Highhawk, and yes I asked them to give Joe Leaphorn a call. Have they called?"

"Of course not," Leaphorn said.

Kennedy laughed. "Old J. Edgar's dead, but nothing ever changes."

But they did call. Leaphorn had hardly hung up when he heard knocking at his door.

Two men waited in the hall. Even in Washington, where every male—to Leaphorn's casual eye—dressed exactly like every other male, these two were obviously Agency men.

"Come in," Leaphorn said, glancing at the identification each man was now holding out for inspection, "I've been sort of expecting you."

He introduced himself. Their names were Dillon and Akron, both being blond, Dillon being bigger and older and in charge.

"Your name is Leaphorn? That right?" Dillon said, glancing in his notebook. "You have identification?"

Leaphorn produced his folder.

Dillon compared Leaphorn's face with the picture. He examined the credentials. Nothing in his expression suggested he was impressed by either.

"A lieutenant in the Navajo Tribal Police?"

"That's right."

Dillon stared at him. "How did you get involved in this Santillanes business?"

Leaphorn explained. The body beside the tracks. Learning the train had been stopped. Learning of the abandoned luggage. Learning of the prescription number. Going to the apartment on the prescription address.

"Have you checked on the man in apartment two?" Leaphorn asked. "He fit the description of the man the attendant saw in Santillanes' roomette. And he was curious."

Akron smiled slightly and looked down at his hands. Dillon cleared his throat. Leaphorn nodded. He knew what was coming. He had worked with the Agency for thirty years.

"You have no jurisdiction in this case," Dillon said. "You never had any jurisdiction. You may have already fouled up a very sensitive case."

"Involving national security," Leaphorn added, thoughtfully and mostly to himself. He didn't intend any sarcasm. It was simply the code expression he'd been hearing the FBI use since the 1950s. It was something you always heard when the Agency was covering up incompetence. He was simply wondering if the Agency's current screwup was considered serious by Dillon's superiors. Apparently so.

Dillon stared at him, scenting sarcasm. He saw nothing on Leaphorn's square Navajo face but deep thought. Leaphorn was thinking about how he could extract information from Dillon and he had reached some sort of conclusion. He nodded.

"Did Agent Kennedy mention to you about the slip of paper found in Santillanes' shirt pocket?"

Dillon's expression shifted from stern to unpleasant. He took his lip between his teeth. Released it. Started to say something. Changed his mind. Pride struggled with curiosity. "I am not aware of that at this point in time," he said.

So there was no purpose in talking to Dillon about it. But he wanted Dillon's goodwill. "Nothing was written on it except the name Agnes Tsosie—Tsosie is a fairly common Navajo name, and Agnes is prominent in the tribe—and the name of a curing ceremonial. The Yeibichai. One of those had been scheduled to be held for Mrs. Tsosie. Scheduled about three or four weeks after the Santillanes body was found."

"What is your interest in this?" Dillon asked.

"The agent-in-charge at Gallup is an old friend," Leaphorn said. "We've worked together for years."

Dillon was not impressed with "agent-in-charge at Gallup." As a matter of fact, an agent stationed in Washington wasn't easy to impress with an agent stationed anywhere else, much less a small Western town. In earlier days agents were transferred to places like Gallup because they had somehow offended J. Edgar Hoover or one of the swarm of yeasayers with which he had manned the upper echelons of his empire. In J. Edgar's day, New Orleans had been the ultimate Siberia of the Agency. J. Edgar detested New Orleans as hot, humid, and decadent and presumed all other FBI employees felt the same way. But since his demise, his camp followers usually exiled to smaller towns agents considered unduly ambitious, unacceptably intelligent, or prone to bad publicity.

"It's still not your case," Dillon said. "You don't have any jurisdiction outside your Indian reservation. And in this case, you wouldn't have jurisdiction even there."

Leaphorn smiled. "And happy I don't," he said. "It looks too complicated for me. But I'm curious. I've got to get with Pete Domenici for lunch before I go home, and he's going to want to know what I'm doing here."

Agent Akron had sat down in a bedside chair just out of Leaphorn's vision but Leaphorn kept his eye on Dillon while he said this. Obviously, Dillon recognized the name of Pete Domenici, the senior senator from New Mexico, who happened to be ranking Republican on the committee which oversaw the Agency's budget. Leaphorn smiled at Dillon again—a conspiratorial one-cop-to-another smile. "You know how some people are about homicides. Pete is fascinated by 'em. I tell Pete about Santillanes and he's going to have a hundred questions."

"Domenici," Dillon said.

"One thing the senator is going to ask me is why Santillanes was killed way out in New Mexico," Leaphorn said. "Out in his district."

Leaphorn watched Dillon making up his mind, imagining the process. He would think that probably Leaphorn was lying about Domenici, which he was, but Dillon hadn't survived in Washington by taking chances. Dillon reached his decision.

"I can't talk about what he was doing out there," Dillon said. "Agent Akron and I are with the antiterrorist division. And I can say Santillanes was a prominent member of a terrorist organization."

"Oh," Leaphorn said.

"Opposed to the regime of President Pinochet." Dillon

looked at Leaphorn. "He's the president of Chile," Dillon added.

Leaphorn nodded. "But you can't tell me why Santillanes was out in New Mexico?" He nodded again. "I can respect that." In the code the FBI had developed down the years, it meant Dillon didn't know the answer.

"I cannot say," Dillon said. "Not at this moment in time."

"How about why he was killed?"

"Just speculation," Dillon said. "Off the record."

Leaphorn nodded, agreeing.

"The effort that was made to avoid identification suggests that it was a continuation of the Pinochet administration's war against the Communists in Chile," Dillon said. He paused, studying Leaphorn to see if this needed explanation. He decided that it did.

"Some time ago, a Chilean dissident was blown up here in Washington. A car bomb. The State Department deported several Chilean nationals and delivered a warning to the ambassador. Or so I understand." Dillon returned the same cop-to-cop smile he had received a few moments earlier from Leaphorn. "Therefore, the Chilean security people at the embassy seem to have decided they would wait until one of their targets was as far from Washington as possible before eliminating him. They would try to make sure the connection was never made."

"I see," Leaphorn said. "I have two more questions."

Dillon waited.

"What will the Agency do about the little man in apartment two?"

"I can't discuss that," Dillon said.

"That's fair enough. Does the name Henry Highhawk mean anything to you?"

Dillon considered. "Henry Highhawk. No."

"I think Kennedy mentioned him when he called the Agency," Leaphorn prompted.

"Oh, yeah," Dillon said. "The name in the notebook."

"How does this Henry Highhawk fit in? Why would Santillanes be interested in him? Why was he interested in Agnes Tsosie? Or the Yeibichai ceremonial?"

"Yeibichai ceremonial?" Dillon said, looking totally baffled. "I am not free to discuss any of that. At this point in time I cannot discuss Henry Highhawk."

But Henry Highhawk stuck in Leaphorn's mind. The name had been somehow familiar the first time he'd seen it written in the Santillanes notebook. It was an unusual name and it had rung some sort of dim bell in his memory. He remembered looking at the name in Santillanes' careful little script and trying to place it, without any luck. He remembered looking at Highhawk's photograph at Agnes Tsosie's place. He knew he had never seen the man before. When Dillon and Akron had gone away to wherever FBI agents go, he tried again. Clearly the name had meant nothing to Dillon. Clearly, Leaphorn himself must have run across it before any of this business had begun. How? What had he been doing? He had been doing nothing unusual. Just routine police administration.

He reached for the telephone and dialed the Navajo Tribal Police building in Window Rock. In about eleven minutes he had what he wanted. Or most of it.

"A fugitive warrant? What was the original offense? Really? What date? No, I meant the date of the arrest? Where? Give me his home address off the warrant." Leaphorn jotted down the Washington address. "Who handled the arrest for us? I'll wait." Leaphorn waited. "Who?"

The arresting officer was Jim Chee.

"Well, thanks," Leaphorn said. "Is Chee still stationed up at Shiprock? Okay. I'll call him there."

He dialed the number of the Shiprock subagency police

station from memory. Office Chee was on vacation. Had he left an address where he might be reached? Navajo Tribal Police rules required that he would, but Chee had a reputation for sometimes making his own rules.

"Just a second," the clerk said. "Here it is. He's in Washington, D.C. I'll give you his hotel."

Leaphorn called Chee's hotel. Yes, Chee was still registered. But he didn't answer his telephone. Leaphorn left a message and hung up. He sat on the bed, asking himself what could have possibly drawn Officer Jim Chee from Shiprock to Washington. Lieutenant Joe Leaphorn had never, never believed in coincidence.

LEROY FLECK SIMPLY couldn't get his mind relieved. He sat on the folding lawn chair in his empty apartment with the telephone on the floor beside him. In about an hour it would be time to go out to the phone booth and put in his once-a-month check-in call to Eddy Elkins. What he was going to say to Elkins was part of the problem. He was going to have to ask Elkins to wire him enough money to get Mama moved, enough to tide him over for the two or three days it would take The Client to pay up. He dreaded asking, because he was almost sure Elkins would just laugh and say no. But he had to get enough to move Mama.

Fleck had on his hat and his coat. It was cold in the apartment because he was trying to save on the utility bill. What he was doing while he was doing all this thinking normally brought him pleasure. He was hunting through the classified ad section of the *Washington Times,* looking for somebody to talk to. Normally that relieved his mind. Not tonight. Even with talking to people he couldn't get Mama out of his thoughts. The worst of it was he'd had to hurt the Fat Man. He'd had to threaten to kill the son-of-a-bitch and twisted his arm while he was doing it. There just wasn't any other way to make him keep Mama until he could find another place. But doing that had opened things up to real trouble—or the probability of it. He'd warned the man not to call the police and the bastard had looked scared enough so maybe he wouldn't. On the other hand, maybe he would. And when the police checked his address and found it was phony—well, who knows what then? They'd be interested. Fleck couldn't afford to have the police interested.

The tape recorder on the box against the wall made a whispering sound. Fleck glanced at it, his thoughts elsewhere. It whispered, and fell silent. The microphone he'd installed in the crawlspace above the ceiling of the Santillanes apartment was supposed to be voice activated. That really meant "sound activated." A lot of what Fleck was recording was Mrs. Santillanes, or whoever that old Mexican woman was, running her vacuum cleaner or clattering around with the dishes. At first, he had sometimes played the tape before sending it off to the post-office-box address Elkins had given him. He'd heard a lot of household noises, and now and then people talking. But the talking was in Spanish. Fleck had picked up a little of that in Joliet from the Hispanos. Just enough to understand that most of what he was taping was family talk. What's for dinner? Where's my glasses? That sort of stuff. Not enough for Fleck to guess why Elkins' clients wanted to keep track of this bunch. It had seemed to Fleck from very early in this assignment that these folks next door were smart enough to do their serious talking somewhere else.

He found an ad that sounded promising. It offered an Apple computer complete with twelve video games for sale by owner. Fleck knew almost nothing about computers, and cared less. But this sounded like a family where the kids had grown up and the item for sale was expensive enough so the owner wouldn't mind talking for a while. Fleck dialed the number, listened to a busy signal, and picked up the paper again. This time he selected a gasoline-powered trash shredder. A man answered on the second ring.

"I'm calling about the shredder," Fleck said. "What are you asking for it?"

"Well, we paid three hundred and eighty dollars for it, and it's just like new." The man had a soft, Virginia Tidewater voice. "But we ain't got no use for it anymore. And I think we'd come down to maybe two hundred."

"No use for it?" Fleck said. "Sounds like you're moving or something. Got anything else you're selling? Several things I need."

"Not moving," the man said. "We're just getting out of gardening. My wife's developed arthritis." He laughed. "And she's the one that did all the work."

From there, Leroy Fleck led the conversation into personal affairs—first the affairs of the owner of the item offered, and then Fleck's own. It was something he had done for years and had become very good at doing. It was his substitute for hanging out in a bar. Keeping Mama in a rest home had made bars too expensive and the people you talked to there tended not to be normal anyway. Fleck had discovered more or less by accident that it was pleasant and relaxing to talk to regular people. It happened when he decided that it would be nice for Mama to have one of those little refrigerators in her room. He'd noticed one in the want ads, and called, and got into a good-natured conversation with the lady selling it. Mama had thrown the little refrigerator on the floor and broke it, but Fleck had remembered the chat. And it had become a habit. At first he did it only when he needed to relieve his mind. But for the last few years he'd done it almost every night. Except Saturday. People didn't like to be called on Saturday night. With practice he had learned which ads to call, and how to keep the conversation going. After three or four such calls Fleck found he could usually sleep. Talking to somebody normal relieved the mind.

Usually, that is. Tonight, it didn't work. After a while the man selling the trash shredder just wanted to talk about that—what Fleck would pay for it and so forth. Fleck had then called about a pop-up-top vacation trailer which would sleep four. But this time he found himself getting impatient even before the woman who was selling it did.

After that call he just sat there on the lawn chair. To keep from worrying about Mama, he worried about those two Indians—and especially about the one who had come to his door here. Both of those men had really smelled like cops to him. Fleck didn't like having cops know where to find him. Normally in a situation like that he would have moved right out of here and got lost. But now he couldn't move. This job Eddy Elkins had got him into this time kept him tied here. He was stuck. He had to have the money. Absolutely had to have it. Absolutely had to wait two more days until the month was up. Then he'd get the ten thousand the bastards were making him wait for.

He went into the kitchen and checked the refrigerator. He had a little bit of beef liver left and two hamburger buns, but no ground beef and only two potatoes. That would handle his needs tonight. But he'd need food tomorrow. He didn't even have enough grease to fry the potatoes for breakfast. Fleck put on his hat and his coat and went out into the misty rain.

He returned with a plastic grocery sack and an early edition of the *Washington Post.* Fleck knew how to stretch his dollars. The bag contained two loaves of day-old bread, a dozen grade B eggs, a half-gallon of milk, a carton of Velveeta and a pound of margarine. He put the frying pan on the gas burner, dumped in a spoonful of margarine and the liver. Fleck's furniture consisted of stuff he could fold into the trunk of his old Chevy, which meant nothing in the kitchen except what was built in. He leaned against the wall and watched the liver fry. As it fried he unfolded the *Post* and read.

There was nothing he needed to know on the front page. On page two, the word *Chile* caught his eyes.

TOP CHILEAN POLICE BRASS VISITS;
ASKS MUSEUM TO RETURN GOLDEN MASK

He scanned the story, mildly interested in the affairs of his client. It told him that General Ramon Huerta Cardona, identified as "commander of Chilean internal security forces," was in Washington on government business and planned to deliver a personal appeal tomorrow to the Smithsonian Institution for the return of an Inca mask. According to the story, the mask was "golden and encrusted with emeralds," and the general described it as "a Chilean national treasure which should be returned to the people of Chile." Fleck didn't finish the story. He turned the page.

The picture caught his eye instantly. The old man. It was on page four, a single-column photograph halfway down the page with a story under it. Old man Santillanes.

"Oh, shit!" Fleck said it aloud, in something close to a shout.

The headline read:

KNIFE VICTIM
PROVES TO BE
CHILEAN REBEL

Fleck slammed the paper to the floor and stood against the wall. He was shaking. "Ah, shit," he repeated, in something like a whisper now. He bent, retrieved the paper, and read:

"The body of a man found beside a railroad track in New Mexico last month has been identified as Elogio Santillanes y Jimenez, an exiled leader of the opposition to the Chilean government, a spokesman for the Federal Bureau of Investigation announced today.

"The FBI spokesman said Santillanes had been killed by a single stab wound in the back of the neck and his body removed from an Amtrak train.

" 'All identification had been removed from his body—even his false teeth,' the spokesman said. He noted that this made identification difficult for the agency.

"The FBI declined comment on whether any suspects were being investigated. Two years ago, another opposition leader to the Pinochet regime was assassinated in Washington by the detonation of a bomb in his car. Following that incident, the Department of State issued a sharply worded protest to the Chilean embassy and two members of the embassy staff were deported as *personae non gratae* in the United States."

The story continued, but Fleck dropped the paper again. He felt sick but he had to think. He had guessed right about the embassy, and about why they had wanted him to kill Santillanes a long way from Washington, and why all that emphasis had been placed on preventing identification. How the hell had the FBI managed to make the connection? But what difference did that make? His problem was what to do about it.

They weren't going to send him the ten thousand now. No identification and no publicity for a month. That was the deal. A month without anything in the papers was going to be proof enough he hadn't screwed it up. And now, what was it? Twenty-nine days? For a moment he allowed himself to think that they would agree that this was close enough. But that was bullshit thinking. All they needed to screw him was the slightest excuse. They looked down on him like trash. Like dirt. Just like Mama had always told Delmar and him.

He smelled the liver burning in the frying pan, moved it off the burner, and fanned away the smoke. Elkins had told him that Mama was right. He hadn't remembered telling Elkins anything about Mama, certainly wouldn't have normally, but Elkins said he talked about it when he was coming out from under the sodium pentothal—the stuff they'd given him when they fixed him up there at the prison infirmary. Right after the rape.

Elkins had been standing beside his bed when he came to, holding a pan in case he threw up the way people sometimes do when they come up from sodium pentothal. "I want you to listen now," Elkins had told him in a whisper right by his face. "They're going to be coming in here as soon as they know you can talk and asking you questions. They're going to ask you which ones did you." And he guessed he had mumbled something about getting the score evened with the sons of bitches because Elkins had put his hand over Fleck's mouth—Fleck remembered that very clearly even now—and said: "Get even. But not now. You got to do it yourself. You tell the screws that you don't know who did you. Tell 'em you didn't get a look at anybody. They hit you from behind. If you want to stay alive in here, you don't talk to the screws. You do your own business. Like your Mama told you."

"Like your Mama told you!" So he must have been talking about Mama when he was still under the anesthesia. It was all still so very vivid.

He'd asked Elkins if they had really raped him the way he seemed to remember, and Elkins said they truly had.

"Then I got to kill 'em."

"Yes," Elkins said. "I think so. Unless you want to live like an animal."

Elkins was a disbarred lawyer with some seniority in Joliet and he understood about such things. He was doing four to eight on an Illinois State felony count. Something to do with fixing up some witnesses, or maybe it was jurors, for somebody important in the Chicago rackets. Fleck understood that Elkins had kept his mouth shut and taken the fall for it, and that seemed to be the way it worked out. Because now Eddy Elkins was important again with some Chicago law firm, even if he couldn't practice law himself.

For that matter, Elkins had been important even in the prison. He was just a trustee working as a male nurse and orderly in the prison hospital. But he had money. He had connections inside and out and everybody knew it. When Fleck came out of isolation, he found he had a job in the infirmary. Elkins had done that. And Elkins had helped him with the big problem—how to kill three hard cases. All bigger than him. All tougher. First he'd started him pumping iron. Fleck had been skinny then as well as small. But at nineteen you can develop fast if you have direction. And steroids. Elkins got him them, too. And then Elkins had showed him how a knife can make a small man equal to a big one if the small man is very, very fast and very cool and knows what to do with the blade. Fleck had always been fast—had to be fast to survive. Elkins used the life-size body chart in the infirmary office and the plastic skeleton to teach him where to put the shank.

"Always flat," Elkins would say. "Remember that. What you're after is behind the bones. Hitting the bones does you no good at all and the way past them is through the crevices." Elkins was a tall, slender man, slightly stooped. He was a Dartmouth man, with his law degree from Harvard. He looked like a teacher and he liked to teach. In the empty, quiet infirmary he would stand there in front of the skeleton with Fleck sitting on the bed, and Elkins would tutor Fleck in the trade.

"If you have to go in from the front"—Elkins recommended against going in from the front—"you have to go between the ribs or right below the Adam's apple. Quick thrust in, and then the wiggle." Elkins demonstrated the little wiggle with his wrist. "That gets the artery, or the heart muscle, or the spinal column. A puncture is usually no damn good. Any other cut is slow and noisy. If you can go in from the back, it's the same. Hold it flat. Hold it horizonal."

Elkins would demonstrate on the plastic skeleton. "The very quickest is right there"—and he would point a slender, manicured finger—"above that first vertebra. You do it right and there's not a motion. Not a sound. Very little bleeding. Instant death."

When it was time for him to go into the yard again, he went with a slender, stiff little shank fashioned of surgical steel and as sharp as the scalpel it had once been. Elkins had given him that along with his final instructions.

"Remember the number for you is three. There are three of them. If you get caught with the first one you don't do the last two. Remember that, and remember to hold it flat. What you're after is behind the bone."

He had been twenty when he did it. A long time ago. He had yearned to tell Mama about it. But it wasn't the sort of thing you could say in a letter, with the screws reading your mail. And Mama hadn't ever been able to get away to come on visiting days. He felt badly about that. It had been a hard life for her and not much he'd done had made it any easier.

The liver had that burned taste. And the hamburger buns were pretty much dried out. But he didn't like liver anyway. He only bought it because it was about half the price of hamburger. And it satisfied what little appetite he had tonight. Then he put on his hat and his still-damp coat and went out to make his call to Elkins.

"There's not a damn thing I can do for you," Elkins said.

"You know how we work. After twenty years you ought to know. We keep insulated. It's got to be that way."

"It's been more than twenty years," Fleck said. "Remember that first job?"

The first job had been while he was still in prison. Elkins was out, thanks to a lot of good time and an early parole. And the visitor had come to see him. As a matter of fact, it was the only visitor he'd ever had. A young lawyer. Elkins had sent him to give Fleck a name. It had been a short visit.

"Elkins just said to tell you to make it four instead of three. He wants you to make it Cassidy and Dalkin and Neal and David Petresky. He said you'd understand. And to tell you you'd be represented by a lawyer at the parole hearing and that he had regular work for you after that." The lawyer was a plump, blond man with greenish-blue eyes. He was not much older than Fleck and he looked nervous—glancing around all the time to see if the screw was listening. "He said for me to bring back a yes or a no."

Fleck had thought about it a minute—wondering who Petresky was and how to get to him. "Tell him yes," he said.

And now Elkins remembered it.

"That one was sort of a test," Elkins said. "They said you couldn't handle Petresky. I said I'd seen your work."

"All these years," Fleck said. "Now I need help. I think you owe me."

"I was always business," Eddy Elkins said. "You know that. It couldn't be any other way. It would just be too damned dangerous."

Dangerous for you, Fleck thought, but he didn't say it. Instead he said: "I simply got to have three thousand. I've got to have enough to get my Mama moved." Fleck paused. "Man, I'm desperate."

There was a long silence. "You say this involves your mother?"

"Yeah." In Joliet he had talked to Elkins a lot about Mama. He thought Elkins understood how he felt about her.

Another silence. "What's your number there?"

Fleck told him.

"Stay there. I'll make a contact and see what I can do."

Fleck waited almost an hour, huddled in his damp coat in the booth and, when he felt the chill stiffening him, pacing up and down the sidewalk close enough to hear the ring.

When it rang, it was The Client.

"You dirty little *hijo de puta*," he said. "You want money? You bring us nothing but trouble and you want us to pay you money for it?"

"I got to have it," Fleck said. "You owe me." He thought: *hijo de puta;* the man had called him son of a whore.

"We ought to break your dirty little neck," The Client said. "Maybe we do that. Yes. Maybe we cut your dirty little throat. We give you a simple little job. What do you do? You screw it up!"

Fleck felt the rage rising within him, felt it like bile in his throat. He heard Mama's voice: "They treat you like niggers. You let 'em, they treat you like dogs. You let 'em step on you, they'll treat you like animals."

But he choked back the rage. He couldn't afford it. He had to pick her up right away. He had to get her to a place they'd take care of her.

"I know who you are," Fleck said. "I followed you back to your embassy. I get paid or I can cause you some trouble." Then he listened.

What he heard was a stream of obscenities. He heard himself called the filthy, defecation-eating son of a whore, the son of an infected dog. And the click of the line disconnecting.

Standing in the drizzle outside the booth, Fleck spit on the sidewalk. He let the rage well up. He'd get the money another way, somehow. He'd done it in the past. Mugging. A lot of mugging to come up with three thousand dollars unless he was lucky. It was dangerous. Terribly dangerous. Only the ruling class carried big money, and some of them carried only plastic. And the police protected the ruling class. And now there was something else he had to do. It involved getting even. It involved using his shank again. It involved getting the blade in behind the bone.

"WHAT I WANT to know, for starters," Joe Leaphorn said, "is everything you know about this Henry Highhawk."

They had met in what passed for a coffee shop in Jim Chee's hotel, surrounded by blue-collar workers and tourists who, like Chee, had asked their travel agents to find them moderately priced housing in downtown Washington. Leaphorn had donned the Washington uniform. But his three-piece suit was a model sold by the Gallup Sears store in the middle seventies, and its looseness testified to the pounds Leaphorn had lost eating his own cooking since Emma's death.

With the single exception of his Blessing Way ceremonial, Jim Chee had never seen the legendary Leaphorn except in a Navajo Tribal Police uniform. He was having psychological trouble handling this inappropriate attire. Like a necktie on a herd bull, Chee thought. Like socks on a billy goat. But above the necktie knot Leaphorn's eyes were exactly as Chee remembered them—dark brown, alert, searching. As always, something in them was causing

Chee to examine his conscience. What had he neglected? What had he forgotten?

He told Leaphorn about Highhawk's job, his educational background, the charge against him for vandalizing graves, his campaign to cause the Smithsonian to release its thousands of Native American skeletons for reburial. He described how he and Cowboy Dashee had arrested Highhawk. He reported how Gomez had shown up, how Gomez had agreed to post Highhawk's bond. How yesterday Gomez had appeared at Highhawk's house. He described Highhawk's limp, his leg brace, and how Janet Pete had come to be his attorney. He touched on Janet Pete's doubts about the Tano Pueblo fetish and what he had seen in Highhawk's office-studio. But he said nothing at all about Janet Pete's doubts and problems. That was another story. That was none of Leaphorn's business.

"What do you think he was doing at the Yeibichai?" Leaphorn asked.

Chee shrugged. "He doesn't look it but he's one-fourth Navajo. One grandmother was Navajo. I guess she made a big impression on him. Janet Pete tells me he wants to be a Navajo. Thinks about himself as a Navajo." Chee considered that some more. "He wanted to be sort of initiated into the tribe. And he knew enough about the Yeibichai to show up on the last night." He glanced at Leaphorn. Did this Navajo version of pragmatist-agnostic know enough about the Yeibichai himself to know what that meant? He added: "When the *hataalii* sometimes initiates boys—lets them look through the mask. Highhawk wanted to do that."

Leaphorn merely nodded. "Did he?"

"We arrested him," Chee said.

Leaphorn thought about that answer. "Right away?"

"Well, no," Chee said. "We watched him awhile. And then when we did arrest him he asked if we could stick around a little longer. He wanted to see the part where

Talking God and Humpback and the Fringed Mouth *yei* appear. So we stuck around for that." Chee shrugged. He had been enjoying this role of knowing more than Lieutenant Leaphorn. "That's about it," he said.

Leaphorn picked up his coffee cup, examined it, looked across it at Chee, took a small sip, put it back in the saucer, and waited. "Stuck around about two hours," he said. "Right?"

"About," Chee agreed.

"You didn't just stand around. You talked. What did Highhawk talk about?"

Chee shrugged. What had they talked about?

"It was cold as hell—wind out of the north. We talked about that. He thought the people wearing the *yei* masks must get awful frostbitten with nothing on but leggings and kilts. And he asked a lot of questions. Did the paint on their bodies insulate them from the cold? Which mask represented which *yei?* Questions about the ceremonial. And he knew enough about it to ask smart questions." Chee stopped. Finished.

"About anything else?"

Chee shrugged.

Leaphorn stared at him. "That won't get it," he said. "I need to know."

Chee was not in the mood for this. He felt his face flushing. "Highhawk was taping some of it," Chee said. "He had this little tape recorder palmed. Then he'd pull it up his sleeve if anyone noticed it. You're not supposed to do that unless you square it with the *hataalii.* I let that go. Didn't say anything. And once I heard him singing the words of one of the chants. What else? He and this Gomez went into the kitchen shed once and ate some stew. And when Dashee and I arrested him, Gomez came up and wanted to know what was going on."

"If he knew as much as he seemed to know, then he

knew he shouldn't be taping without the singer's permission," Leaphorn said. "And it looked to you like he was being sneaky about it?"

"It was sneaky," Chee said. "Hiding the recorder in his palm. Up his sleeve."

"Not very polite," Leaphorn said. "Not as polite as his letter sounded." He said it mostly to himself, thinking out loud.

"Letter?" Chee said, louder than he intended. The edge in his voice was enough so that at the next table two men in Federal Express delivery uniforms looked up from their waffles and stared at him.

"He wrote a letter to Agnes Tsosie," Leaphorn said. "Very polite. Tell me about this Gomez. Describe him."

Chee was aware that his face was flushed. He could feel it, distinctly.

"I'm on vacation," Chee said. "I'm off duty. I want you to tell me about this letter. When did that happen? How did you know about it? How did you know about Highhawk? What the hell's going on?"

"Well now," Leaphorn began, his face flushing. But then he closed his mouth. He cleared his throat. "Well, now," he said again, "I guess you're right." And he told Chee about the man with pointed shoes.

Leaphorn was unusually good at telling. He organized it all neatly and chronologically. He described the body found beside the tracks east of Gallup, the cryptic note in the shirt pocket, the visit to the Agnes Tsosie place, the letter from Highhawk with Highhawk's photograph included, what the autopsy showed, all of it.

"This little man in the next apartment, he fit the description of the man in Santillanes' compartment on the train. No question he was interested in the Santillanes bunch. Any chance he and Gomez are the same?"

"Not the way you describe him," Chee said. "Gomez had

black hair. He's younger than your man sounds, and taller and slender—none of those weightlifter muscles. And I think he lost several fingers."

Leaphorn's expression shaded from alert to very alert. "Several? What do you mean?"

"He was wearing leather gloves, but on both hands some of the fingers were stiff—as if the gloves were stuffed with cotton or maybe there was a finger in it that didn't bend. I took a look every chance I got because it seemed funny. Strange I mean. Losing fingers off both hands."

Leaphorn thought. "Any other scars? Deformities?"

"None visible," Chee said. And waited. He watched Leaphorn turning these mangled fingers over in his mind. Chee reminded himself that he was on vacation and so was Leaphorn. By God, he was simply not going to let the lieutenant get away with this.

"Why?"

Leaphorn, his thoughts interrupted, looked startled. "What?"

"I can tell you're thinking those missing fingers are important. Why are they important? How does that fit with what you know?"

"Probably they're not important," Leaphorn said.

"Not good enough," Chee said. "Remember, I'm on vacation."

Leaphorn's expression shifted into something that might have been a grin. "I have some bad habits. A lot of them involve doing things to save time. A strange habit for a Navajo, I guess. But you're right. You're on vacation. So am I, for that matter." He put down his coffee cup.

"Where do I start? Santillanes didn't have any teeth. All pulled. But the pathologist who did the autopsy said there was no sign of any reason to have them pulled. No jawbone problems, no traces left by the gum diseases that cause you to lose your teeth. I wondered how Santillanes lost his teeth.

You wondered how Gomez lost his fingers." Leaphorn took the final sip of his coffee, signaled the waiter. "You see a connection?"

Chee hesitated. "You mean like they both might have been tortured?"

"It occurs to me. I guess they're Chilean leftists. The right wing's in power. There's been a lot of reporting of the secret police, or maybe the army, knocking people off. People disappearing. Political prisoners. Murder. Torture. Some really hideous stuff causing investigations by Amnesty International."

Chee nodded.

"I think we should go talk to Highhawk," Leaphorn said. "Okay?"

"If we can find him," Chee said. "I called this morning. Called his house. Called his office. No answer. So I called Dr. Hartman. She's the curator he's working for at the museum. She hadn't seen him either. She was looking for him."

"Let's go try to find him anyway," Leaphorn said. He picked up the check.

"I didn't tell you about last night," Chee said. He described how Highhawk had taken the telephone call, then left saying he'd be right back, and never returned.

"I think we should go on out there. See if we can find the man. Try his house and if he's not there, we'll try the Smithsonian."

Chee put on his hat and followed.

"Why not?" he said, but even as he said it he had a feeling they weren't going to find Henry Highhawk.

They took a cab to Eastern Market.

"Stick around a minute until we see if our party is home," Leaphorn said.

The cabby was a plump young man with a mass of curly brown hair and fat, red lips. He pulled a paperback copy of

Passage to Quivera off the dashboard and opened it. "It's your money," he said. "Spend it any way you like."

Leaphorn punched the doorbell. They listened to it buzz inside. He punched it again. Chee walked back down the porch steps and rescued the morning paper from where it had been thrown beside the front walk. He showed it to Leaphorn. He nodded. Punched the doorbell again. Chee walked to the window, shaded the glass with his hands. The blinds were up, the curtains open. The room was empty and dark on this dreary, overcast morning.

"What do you think?" Chee said.

Leaphorn shook his head, rang the bell again. He tried the doorknob. Locked.

"Curtains open, blinds up," Chee said. "If he came home last night, maybe he didn't turn on the lights."

"Maybe not." Leaphorn tried the door again. Still locked. "I know a cop here," he said. "I think we'll give him a call and see what he thinks."

"FBI?" Chee asked.

"A real cop," Leaphorn said. "A captain on the Washington police force."

They took the cab to the public phone booths at the Eastern Market Metro station. Leaphorn made his call. Chee waited, watching the cabby read and trying to decide what the hell Highhawk was doing. Where had he gone? Why had he gone? How was Bad Hands involved in this? He thought of Bad Hands in the role of revolutionary. He thought of how it would feel to have your fingers removed by a torturer trying to make you talk. Leaphorn climbed back into the cab.

"He said he would meet us at a little coffee place in the old Post Office building."

The cabby was awaiting instructions. "You know how to find it?" Leaphorn asked.

"Is the Pope a Catholic?" the cabby said.

They found Captain Rodney awaiting them just inside the coffee shop door, a tall, bulky black man wearing bifocals, a gray felt hat, and a raincoat to match. The sight of Leaphorn provoked a huge, delighted, white-toothed grin.

"This is Jim Chee," Leaphorn said. "One of our officers."

They shook hands. Rodney's craggy, coffee-colored face usually registered expression only when Rodney allowed it to do so. Now, just for a moment, it registered startled surprise. He removed the fedora, revealing kinky gray hair cropped close to the skull.

"Jim Chee," he said, memorizing Chee's face. "Well, now."

"Rodney and I go way back," Leaphorn said. "We survived the FBI Academy together."

"Two misfits," Rodney said. "Back in the days when *all* FBI agents had blue eyes instead of just most of them." Rodney chuckled, but his eyes never left Chee. "That's when I first learned that our friend here—" he indicated Leaphorn with a thumb—"has this practice of just telling you what he thinks you have to know."

They were at a table now and Leaphorn was ordering coffee. Now he looked surprised. "Like what?" he said. "What do you mean by that?"

Rodney was still looking at Chee. "You work for this guy, right? Or with him, anyway."

"More or less," Chee said, wondering where this was leading. "Now I'm on vacation."

Rodney laughed. "Vacation. Is that a fact. You just happen to be three thousand miles east of home at the same time as your boss. I think maybe I was blaming Joe for something that's a universal Navajo trait."

"What are we talking about here?" Leaphorn asked.

"About the Navajo Tribal Police sending two men"—he pointed a finger at Leaphorn and then at Chee—"two men, count 'em, to Washington, Dee, Cee, which is several miles out of their jurisdiction, to look for a fellow which us local cops didn't even yet know there was a reason to be looking for."

"Nobody sent us here," Leaphorn said.

Rodney ignored the remark. He was staring at Chee. "What time did you leave the Smithsonian last night?"

Chee told him. He was baffled. How did this Washington policeman know he had been at the museum last night? Why would he care? Something must have happened to Highhawk.

"Which exit?"

"Twelfth Street."

"Nobody checked you out?"

"Nobody was there."

Surprise again registered on Rodney's face.

"Ah," he said. "No guard? No security person? How did you get out?"

"I just walked out."

"The door wasn't locked."

Chee shook his head. "Closed, but unlocked."

"You see anything? Anybody?"

"I was surprised no one was there. I looked around. Empty."

"You didn't see a young woman in a museum guard's uniform? A black woman? The guard who was supposed to be keeping an eye on that Twelfth Street entrance?"

Chee shook his head again. "Nobody was around," he said. "Nobody. What's the deal?" But even as he asked the question, he knew the deal. Highhawk was dead. Chee was just about the last person who'd seen him alive.

"The deal is"—Rodney was looking at Leaphorn now—"that I get a call from my old friend Joe here to check on whether there's any kind of report on a man named Henry Highhawk and I find out this Highhawk is on a list of people

Homicide would like to talk to." Rodney shifted his gaze back to Chee. "So I come down here to talk to my old friend Joe, and he introduces me to you and, what do ya know, you happen to be another guy on Homicide's wish list. That's what the deal is."

"Your homicide people want to talk to Highhawk," Chee said. "That means he's alive?"

"You have some reason to think otherwise?" Rodney asked.

"When you said you had a homicide I figured he was the one," Chee said. He explained to Rodney what had happened last night at the Smithsonian. "Back in just a minute, he said. But he never came back. I went out and wandered around the halls looking for him. Then finally I went home. I called him at home this morning. No soap. I called his office. The woman he works for was looking for him too. She was worried about him."

Rodney had been intent on every word.

"Went home when?"

"I told you," Chee said. "I must have left the Twelfth Street entrance a little before ten thirty. Very close to that. I walked right back to my hotel."

"And when did Highhawk receive this telephone call? The call just before he left?"

Chee told him.

"Who was the caller?"

"No idea. It was a short call."

"What about? Did you hear it?"

"I heard Highhawk's end. Apparently he had been trying to tell Highhawk how to fix something. Highhawk had tried and it hadn't worked. I remember he said it 'didn't turn on,' and Highhawk said since he was coming down anyway the caller could fix it. And then they set the nine-thirty time and Highhawk told him to remember it was the Twelfth Street entrance."

"Him?" Rodney said. "Was the caller a man?"

"I should have said him or her. I couldn't hear the other voice."

"I'm going to make a call of my own," Rodney said. He rose, gracefully for a man of his bulk. "Pass all this along to the detective handling this one. I'll be right back." He grinned at Chee. "Quicker than Highhawk, anyway."

"Who's the victim?" Leaphorn asked.

Rodney paused, looking down on them. "It was the night shift guard at the Twelfth Street entrance."

"Stabbed?" Leaphorn asked.

"Why you say stabbed?"

Now Leaphorn's voice had an impatient edge in it. "I told you about what brought me here," he said. "Remember? Santillanes was stabbed. Very professionally, in the back of the neck."

"Oh, yeah," Rodney said. "No. Not stabbed this time. It was skull fracture." He made another move toward the telephone.

"Where did they find the body?" Chee asked. "And when?"

"A couple of hours ago. Whoever hit her on the head found the perfect place to hide her." Rodney looked down at them, the tale teller pausing to underline his point. "They laid her out on the grass there between the shrubbery and the sidewalk, and got some old newspapers out of the trash bin there and threw them over her."

Chee understood perfectly the sardonic tone in Rodney's voice, but Leaphorn said: "Right by the sidewalk and nobody checked all morning?"

"This is Friday," Rodney said. "In Washington, the Good Samaritan comes by only on the seventh Tuesday of the month." And he walked away to make his telephone call.

The only remaining sign that a corpse had been on

display under the shrubbery adjoining the Twelfth Street entrance to the Smithsonian Museum of Natural History was a uniformed policeman who stood beside a taped-off area. He was whistling idly, and he glanced at Rodney without a sign of recognition. Probably too young.

Inside, Rodney's badge got them through the STAFF ONLY doorway. They took the elevator to the sixth floor and found that Dr. Hartman was not in. A young woman who seemed to be her assistant said she was probably down on the main floor at her mask exhibition. And no, the young woman said, Henry Highhawk had not showed up for work.

"Did you hear what happened?" she asked. "I mean about the guard being killed?"

"We heard," Rodney said. "Do you know where we can get the key to Highhawk's office?"

"Dr. Hartman would probably have one," she said. "But wasn't that dreadful? You don't expect something like that to happen to someone you know."

"Did you know her?" Rodney said.

The young woman looked slightly flustered. "Well I saw her a lot," she said. "You know. When I worked late she would be standing there."

"Her name was Alice Yoakum," Rodney said, mildly. "Mrs. Alice Yoakum. Is there a way we can page Dr. Hartman? Or call down there for her somehow?"

There was, but Dr. Hartman proved to be either unreachable or too busy to come to the telephone.

"It might not be locked," Chee said. "It wasn't when I left. If he didn't come back who would lock it?"

"Maybe some sort of internal security," Rodney said.

But nobody had locked it. The door opened under Rodney's hand. The room was silent, lit by an overhead fluorescent tube, the blinds down as Chee remembered them. Highhawk's gesture at keeping his light from leaking out into the night was now holding out the daylight.

"You leave the light on last night?" Rodney asked.

Chee nodded. "He said he was coming back. I thought he might. I just pulled the door closed."

They stood inside the doorway, inspecting the room.

"Everything look like you left it?" Rodney asked.

"Looks like it," Chee said.

Rodney picked up the telephone, dialed, listened. "This is Rodney," he said. "Get hold of Sergeant Willis and tell him I'm calling from Henry Highhawk's office on the sixth floor of the Smithsonian Museum of Natural History. He's not here. Nobody's seen him. Tell him I have Jim Chee with me. We're going to look around up here and if I don't hear from him before then, I'll call back in—" he glanced at his watch "—about forty-five minutes." He cradled the telephone, sat in Highhawk's chair, looked at Leaphorn who was leaning against the wall, then at Chee by the window.

"Either one of you have any creative thoughts?" he asked. "This isn't my baby—nor yours either for that matter—but here we are knee deep in it."

"I'm asking myself some questions," Leaphorn said. "We have this Highhawk vaguely connected to the knifing of a terrorist, or whatever you want to call him, out in New Mexico. Just the name in the victim's notebook. Now we have him disappearing, I guess, the same night this guard is killed here. But do we know when the guard was killed?"

"Coroner said the first glance looked like it was before midnight," Rodney said. "He may get closer when they have the autopsy finished."

Leaphorn looked thoughtful. "So it might have been either shortly before, or shortly after, Highhawk walked out of here. Either way?"

"Sounds like it," Rodney said. He glanced at Chee. "How about you?"

"I'm thinking that this is the world's best place to hide a body," Chee said, slowly. "Tens of thousands of cases and containers lining the halls. Most of them big enough for a body."

"But locked," Rodney said. "And some of them, I noticed, were sealed, too."

"They all use the same simple little master key," Chee said. "At least most of them must use the same key, or you'd need a truck to haul your keys around. I think you just pick up a key, sign for it, and keep it until you're finished with it. Something like that."

"You know if Highhawk had a key?"

"I'd guess so," Chee said. "He was a conservator. He would have been working with this stuff all the time."

Leaphorn put his forefinger on a hook which had been screwed into the doorjamb. "I'd been wondering what this was for," he said. "I'd guess it was where Highhawk hung his key."

No key hung there now, but the white paint below the hook was discolored with years of finger marks.

"Let's go look around," Rodney said. He got up.

"He took it when he left," Chee said. "And before we go looking, why not make a telephone call first? Call maintenance, or whoever might know, and ask them if they found anything unusual this morning."

Rodney paused at the doorway, looking interested. "Like what?"

Chee noticed that Leaphorn was looking at him, smiling slightly.

"Chee's a pessimist," Leaphorn said. "He thinks somebody killed Highhawk. If somebody did, it would be tough to drag him out of the building—even with the guard dead. Not many people around at night in here, I'd guess, but it would only take one to see you."

Rodney still looked puzzled. "So?"

"So this place is jammed with bins and boxes and cases and containers where you could hide a body. But they're probably all full of things already. So the killer empties one out, puts in the body, and then he relocks it. But now he's stuck with whatever came out of the bin. So he looks for a place and dumps it somewhere."

Rodney picked up the telephone again. He dialed, identified himself, and said: "Give me the museum security office, please." Judging from the Rodney end of the conversation, Museum Security had no useful information. The call was transferred to maintenance. Chee found himself watching Leaphorn, thinking how quickly his mind had worked. Leaphorn was still standing beside the open door and as Chee watched, he shifted his weight from one foot to the other, grimacing slightly. He was wearing black wing-tip shoes burnished to a high gloss. Leaphorn's feet, as was true of Chee's, would be accustomed to boots and more breathing space. Chee guessed Leaphorn's hurt and that made him conscious of the comfort of his own feet, at home in the familiar boots. He felt slightly superior. It served Leaphorn right for trying to look like an Easterner.

"A what?" Rodney was saying. "Where did they find it?" He listened. "How large is it?" Listened again. "Where did it come from?" Listened. "Okay. We'll check. Thanks." He hung up, looked at Chee.

"They found a fish trap," he said. "Thing's made out of split bamboo by somebody-or-other. They said it had just sort of been pushed up into a passage between two stacks of containers."

"How big?" Leaphorn asked.

Rodney was dialing the telephone again. He glanced up at Leaphorn and said: "Big as a body."

FIRST, LEROY FLECK called his brother. It was something he rarely did. Delmar Fleck had made it very clear that he couldn't afford to have contacts with a convict—particularly one known to be his relative. Delmar's wife answered the telephone. She didn't recognize his voice and Leroy didn't identify himself to her because if he did, he was pretty sure she would hang up on him.

"Yeah," Delmar said and Leroy got right to the point.

"It's me. Leroy. And I got to have some help with Mama. They're kicking her out of the home here in the District and the one I found to move her into wants more advance money down than I can handle."

"I told you not to call me," Delmar said.

"I just got to have some help," Leroy said. "I was supposed to get a payment today, but something held it up. Ten thousand dollars. When I get it next week, I'll pay you right back."

"We been over this before," Delmar said. "I don't make

hardly anything at the car lot, and Faye Lynn just gets tips at the beauty shop."

"If you could just send me two thousand dollars I could come up with the rest. Then next week I'll send it back to you. Western Union." Next week would take care of itself. He would think of something by then. Elkins would have another job for him. Elkins always had jobs for him. And until Elkins came through with something bigger, he'd just have to go on the prowl for a few days.

"No blood in this turnip," Delmar said. "It's already squeezed. I couldn't raise two thousand dollars if my life depended on it. We got two car payments, and rent, and the credit card, and medical insurance and—"

"Delmar. Delmar. I just got to have some help. Can you borrow something? Just for a week or so?"

"We been all over this. The government takes care of people like Mama. Let the government do it."

"I used to think that, too," Leroy said. "But they don't actually do it. There's no program for people like Mama." Silence on the other end. "And, Delmar, you need to find a way to come and visit with her. It's been years and she's asking about you all the time. She told me she thought the Arabs had you a hostage somewhere. She thinks that to keep her feelings from being hurt. Her mind's not what it used to be. Sometimes she don't even recognize me."

There was still only silence. Then he heard Delmar's voice, sounding a long ways off, talking to someone. Then he heard a laugh.

"Delmar!" he shouted. "Delmar!"

"Sorry," Delmar said. "We got company. But that's my advice. Just call social services. I'd help you if I could, but I'm pressed myself. Got to cut it off now."

And he cut it off, leaving Fleck standing at the telephone booth. He looked at the telephone, fighting down first the despair and then the anger, trying to think of who else he could call. But there wasn't anyone.

Fleck kept his reserve money in a child's plastic purse tucked under the spare tire in the trunk of his old Chevy—a secure enough place in a society where thieves were not attracted to dented 1976 sedans. He fished it out now, and headed across town toward the nursing home, counting it while he waited for red lights to turn green.

He counted three hundreds, twenty-two fifties, eleven twenties, and forty-one tens. With what he had in his bill-fold it added up to $2,033. He'd see what he could do with that with the Fat Man at the rest home. He didn't like going back there like this. It sure as hell wasn't the way he had it planned, or would plan anything for that matter. He normally would have been smart enough not to make an enemy of a man when you were going to have to ask him a favor. But maybe a combination of paying him and scaring him would work for a little while. Until he could pull something off. He could make a hit out at National Airport. In the men's room. The blade and then off with the billfold. People going on planes always carried money. It would be risky. But he could see no choice. He'd try that, and then work on the tourists around the Capitol Building. That was risky, too. In fact, both places scared him. But he had made up his mind. He would fix something up with the Fat Man to buy a little time and then start collecting enough to get Mama someplace safe and decent.

The Fat Man wasn't in.

"He went out to get something. Down to the Seven-Eleven, I think he said," the receptionist told him. "Why don't you just come on back later in the day? Or maybe you better call first." She was looking at the little sack Fleck was carrying, looking suspicious, as if it was some sort of dope. Actually it was red licorice. Mama liked the stuff and Fleck always brought her a supply. The receptionist was some kind of Hispanic—probably Puerto Rican, Fleck guessed. And she looked nervous as well as suspicious while she talked to him. That made Fleck nervous. Maybe she would call the police. Maybe she had heard something the last time he was here when he told the Fat Man he would kill him if he didn't hold onto Mama until he could find her another place. But he hadn't seen her that day, and he'd kept his voice low when he explained things to the fat bastard. Maybe she was around somewhere listening. Maybe she wasn't. There was nothing he could do about it. He didn't have any options left.

"I'll just go on back there to the parlor and visit with Mama until he gets back," Fleck said.

"Oh, she's not there any more," the receptionist said. "She fights with the other ladies all the time. And she hurt poor old Mrs. Endicott again. Twisted her arm."

Fleck didn't want to hear any more of that kind of talk. He hurried down the hallway to Mama's room.

Mama was sitting in her wheelchair looking at the little TV Fleck had bought for her, watching some soap opera which Fleck thought might be "The Young and the Restless." They had her tied in the chair, as they did all the old people, and it touched Fleck to see her that way. She was so helpless now. Mama had never been helpless until she'd had those strokes. Mama had always been in charge before then. It made Fleck unhappy when he came to see her. It filled him with a kind of dreary sorrow and made him wish he could get far enough ahead so that he could afford a place somewhere and take care of her himself. And he always started trying to think again how he could do it. But there was simply no way. The way Mama was, he would have to be with her all the time. He couldn't just go off and leave her tied in that chair. And that wouldn't leave him with any way to make a living for them.

Mama glanced at him when he came through the door.

Then she looked back at her television program. She didn't say anything.

"Hello," Fleck said. "How are you feeling today?"

Mama didn't look up.

"I brought you some licorice, Mama," Fleck said. He held out the sack.

"Put it down on the bed there," Mama said. Sometimes Mama spoke normally, but sometimes it took her a while to form the words—a matter of pitting indomitable will against a recalcitrant, stroke-damaged nervous system. Fleck waited, remembering. He remembered the way Mama used to talk. He remembered the way Mama used to be. Then she would have made short work of the Fat Man.

"You doing all right today, Mama?" he asked. "Anything I can do for you?"

Mama still didn't look at him. She stared at the set, where a woman was shouting at a well-dressed man in poorly feigned anger. "I was," Mama said, finally. "People keep coming in and bothering me."

"I guess I could put a stop to that," Fleck said.

Mama turned then and looked at him, her eyes absolutely without expression. It occurred to him that maybe it was him she meant. He studied her, wondering if she recognized him. If she did, there was no sign of it. She rarely did in recent years. Well, he would stay and visit anyway. Just keep her company. All her life, as far back as Fleck could remember into his childhood, Mama had had pitifully little of that.

"That girl there's got on a pretty dress," Fleck said. "I mean the one on TV."

Mama ignored him. Poor woman, Fleck thought. Poor, pathetic old woman. He stood beside the open door, examining her profile. She had been a good-sized woman once—maybe 140 pounds or so. Strong and quick and smart as they come. Now she was skinny as a rail and stuck in that wheelchair. She couldn't hardly talk and her mind was not working well.

"How about me giving you a push?" Fleck asked. "Would you like to go for a ride? It's raining outside but I could push you around inside the building. Give you a little change."

Mama still stared at the TV. The angry woman on "The Young and the Restless" had left, slamming the door behind her. Now the man was talking on the telephone. Mama hitched herself forward in the chair. "I had a boy once who had a four-door Buick," she said in a clear voice that sounded surprisingly young. "Dark blue and that velvety upholstery on the seats. He took me to Memphis in that."

"That would have been Delmar's car," Fleck said. "It was a nice one." Mama had talked of it before but Fleck had never seen it. Delmar must have bought it while Fleck was doing his time in Joliet.

"Delmar is his name, all right," Mama said. "The A-rabs got him hostage in Jerusalem or someplace. Otherwise he'd come to see me, Delmar would. He'd take care of me right. He was all man, that one was."

"I know he would," Fleck said. "Delmar is a good man."

"Delmar was all man," Mama said, still staring at the TV set. "He wouldn't let nobody treat him like a nigger. Do Delmar and he'd get you right back. He'd make you respect him. You can count on that. That's one thing you always got to do, is get even. If you don't do that they treat you like a goddamn animal. Step right on your neck. Delmar wouldn't let anybody not treat him right."

"No Mama, he wouldn't," Fleck said. Actually, as he remembered it, Delmar wasn't much for fighting. He was for keeping out of the way of trouble.

Mama looked at him, eyes hostile. "You talk like you know Delmar."

"Yes Mama. I do. I'm Leroy. I'm Delmar's brother."

Mama snorted. "No you ain't. Delmar only had one brother. He ended up a damn jailbird."

The room smelled stale to Leroy. He smelled something that might have been spoiled food, and dust and the acidic odor of dried urine. Poor old lady, he thought. He blinked, rubbed the back of his hand across his eyes.

"I think it would be nice for you to get out in the halls at least. Get out of this room a little bit. See something different just for a change."

"I wouldn't be in here at all if the A-rabs hadn't got to Delmar. He'd have me someplace nice."

"I know he would," Fleck said. "I know he'd come to visit you if he could."

"I had two boys, actually," Mama said. "But the other one he turned out jailbird. Never amounted to shit."

It was just then that Leroy Fleck heard the cop. He couldn't make out the words but he recognized the tone. He strained to listen.

But Mama was still talking. "They said that one turned fairy up there in the prison. He let them use him like a girl."

Leroy Fleck leaned out into the hallway, partly to see if the voice which sounded like a cop really was a cop. It was. He was standing beside the receptionist and she was pointing down the hall. She was pointing right at Leroy Fleck.

Elkins had always told him he was naturally fast. He could think fast and he could move like lightning. "It's partly in your mind, and it's partly in your reflexes," Elkins had told him. "We can get your muscles built up, build up your strength, by pumping iron. But anybody can do that. That quickness, that's something you gotta be born with. That's where you got the edge if you know how to use it."

He used it now. He knew instantly that he could not let himself be arrested. Absolutely not. Maybe he'd come clear on the Santillanes affair. Probably not. Why else were those two Indian-looking cops dogging him? But even if they didn't make him on that one, as soon as they matched his prints, they'd make him on something else. He'd worked for Elkins on too many jobs, and been on the prowl in too many airports and nightclubs, to ever let himself be arrested. He'd survived only by being careful not to be. But now the Fat Man, that fat bastard, had put an end to that. He'd have to get even with the Fat Man. But there was no time to think of that now. Within what was left of the same second, Fleck had decided how he would talk his way out of this. It would help that the Fat Man wasn't here to press his case. The receptionist apparently had orders to call the law anytime he showed up, but she was minimum-wage help. She wouldn't care what happened next.

Fleck moved back into the room and sat on the bed. "Mama," he said softly, "you're going to have some more company in just a minute. It's a policeman. I want to ask you to just keep calm and be polite."

"Policeman," Mama said. She spit on the floor by the television set.

"It's important to me, Mama," Fleck said. "It's awful important."

And then the policeman was at the door, looking in.

"You Dick Pfaff?"

It took Fleck the blink of an eye to remember that was the name he'd used when he'd checked Mama in here.

Fleck stood. "Yes sir," he said. "And this here is my Mama."

The policeman was young. He had smooth, pale skin and a close-cropped blond mustache. He nodded to Mama. She stared at him. Where was his partner? Fleck wondered. He would be the old hand on this team. If Fleck was lucky, the partner would be resting out in the patrol car, letting the rookie handle this pissant, nothing little complaint. If they thought there was any risk at all of it being serious they would both be in here. In fact, Fleck suspected the police rules probably required it. Somebody was goofing off.

"We have a complaint that you caused a disturbance here," the policeman said. "We have a statement that you threatened to kill the manager."

Fleck produced a self-deprecatory laugh. "I'm ashamed of that. That's the main reason I came today—to apologize for the way I behaved." As he said it, Fleck became aware that Mama was no longer watching the television set. Mama was watching him.

"That's a pretty serious offense," the officer said. "Telling a man you're going to kill him."

"I doubt if I really quite said that," Fleck said. "But you notice how it smells in here? My Mama here, she hadn't been properly cleaned up. She had bedsores and all that and I just lost my temper. I had told him about it before."

Clearly the policeman was aware of the smell. Fleck could tell from his face that he'd switched from cautiously hostile to slightly sympathetic.

"If he's got back yet, I'll go out there and apologize to him. I'm sorry for whatever I said. Just got sore about the way they was treating Mama here."

The policeman nodded. "I don't think he's here anyway," he said. "That woman said he was off somewhere. I'll just check you for weapons." He grinned at Fleck. "If you didn't come in here armed, I'd say it's a pretty good argument on your side since he's about four times your size."

"Yes sir," Fleck said. He resisted the prison-learned instinct to spread his legs and raise his arms. The cop would never find his shank, which was in the slot he'd made for it inside his boot, but getting into the shakedown stance would tip off even this rookie that he was dealing with an ex-con.

"What do you want me to do?" Fleck asked.

"Just turn around. And then lock your hands over the back of your neck," the policeman said.

"Get down—" Mama began. Then it broke off into a sort of incoherent stammer. But she kept trying to talk and Fleck looked away from the policeman and looked at her instead. Her face was filled with an expression of such fierce contempt that it took Leroy Fleck back to his childhood.

"—and lick his goddamn shoes," Mama said.

He had made his decision even before she forced it out. "Now, Mama," he said, and bending down, he slid the blade out of his boot into his palm. He gripped it flat-side horizontal and as he stepped toward the policeman he was saying: "Mama had a stroke—" and with the word "stroke" the blade was driving through the uniform shirt.

It sank between the policeman's ribs with the full force of Fleck's weightlifter muscles behind it. And there, in that terribly vulnerable territory Elkins had called "behind the bone," Fleck's weightlifter's wrist flicked it, and flicked it and flicked it. Cutting artery. Cutting heart. The officer's mouth opened, showing white, even teeth below the yellow mustache. He made a kind of a sound, but not very loud because the shock was already killing him. It was hardly audible above the shouting that was going on in "The Young and the Restless."

Fleck released the knife handle, grabbed the policeman's shoulders, and lowered him to his knees. He removed the knife and wiped it on the uniform shirt. (If you do it all properly, Elkins would say, the bleeding is mostly inside. No blood all over you.) Then Fleck let the body slide to the floor. Face down. He put the knife back in his boot and turned toward Mama. He intended to say something but he didn't know what. His mind wasn't working right.

Mama was looking at the policeman, then she looked up at him. Her mouth was partly open, working as if she was trying to say something. Nothing came out but a sort of an odd sound. A squeaking sound. It occurred to him that Mama was afraid. Afraid of him.

"Mama," Leroy Fleck said. "I got even. Did you see that? I didn't let him step on me. I didn't kiss any boot."

He waited. Not long but more time than he could afford under the circumstances, waiting for Mama to win her struggle to form words. But no words came and Fleck could read absolutely nothing in her eyes except fear. He walked out the door without a glance toward the reception desk, and down the narrow hallway toward the rear exit, and out into the cold, gray rain.

MUSEUM SECURITY had located Dr. Hartman, and Dr. Hartman had located possible sources of the fish trap. It was a matter of deciding in what part of the world the trap had originated (obviously in a place which produced both bamboo and good-sized fish) and then knowing how to retrieve data from the museum's computerized inventory system. The computer gave them thirty-seven possible bamboo fish traps of appropriate antiquity. Dr. Hartman knew almost nothing about fish and almost everything about primitive construction methods and quite a bit about botany. Thus she was able to organize the hunt.

She pushed her chair back from the computer terminal, and her hair back from her forehead.

"I'm going to say this Palawan Island tribe is the best bet, and then we should check, I'd say, this coastal Borneo collection, and then probably Java. If none of those collections is missing a fish trap, then it's back to the drawing board. That must be a Smithsonian fish trap and if it is then we can find out where it was stored."

She led them down the hallway, a party of five now with the addition of a tired-looking museum security man. With Hartman and Rodney leading the way, they hurried past what seemed to Leaphorn a wilderness of branch corridors all lined with an infinity of locked containers stacked high above head level. They turned right and left and left again and stopped, while Hartman unlocked a door. Above his head, Leaphorn noticed what looked like, but surely wasn't, one of those carved stone caskets in which ancient Egyptians interred their very important corpses. It was covered with a sheet of heavy plastic, once transparent but now rendered translucent with years of dust.

"I have a thing with locks," Dr. Hartman was saying. "They never want to open for me."

Leaphorn considered whether it would be bad manners to lift the plastic for a peek. He noticed Chee was looking too.

"Looks like one of those Egyptian mummy cases," Leaphorn said. "What do you call 'em? But they wouldn't have a mummy here."

"I think it is," Chee said, and lifted the sheet. "Yeah, a mummy coffin." His expression registered distaste. "I can't think of the name either."

Dr. Hartman had solved the lock. "In here," she said, and ushered them into a huge, gloomy room occupied by row after row of floor-to-ceiling metal shelving racks. As far as Leaphorn could see in every direction every foot of shelf space seemed occupied by something—mostly by what appeared to be locked canisters.

Dr. Hartman examined her list of possible fish trap locations, then walked briskly down the central corridor, checking row numbers.

"Row eleven," she said, and did an abrupt left turn. She stopped a third of the way down and checked bin numbers.

"Okay, here we are," she said, and inserted her key in the lock.

"I think I had better handle that," Rodney said, holding his hand out for the key. "And this is the time to remind everyone that we may be interested in fingerprints in here. So don't be touching things."

Rodney unlocked the container. He pulled open the door. It was jammed with odds and ends, the biggest of which was a bamboo device even larger than the fish trap found by the janitor. It occupied most of the bin, with the remaining space filled with what seemed to be a seining nets and other such paraphernalia.

"No luck here," Rodney said. He closed and locked the door. "On to, where was it? Borneo?"

"I'm having trouble with making this seem real," Dr. Hartman said. "Do you really think someone killed Henry and left his body in here?"

"No," Rodney said. "Not really. But he's missing. And a guard's been killed. And a fish trap was located out of place. So it's prudent to look. Especially since we don't know where else to look."

The Borneo fisherman's bin, Dr. Hartman's second choice, happened to be only two aisles away.

Rodney unlocked it, pulled open the door.

They looked at the top of a human head.

Leaphorn heard Dr. Hartman gasp and Jim Chee suck in his breath. Rodney leaned forward, felt the man's neck, stepped aside to give Chee a better view. "Is this High-hawk?"

Chee leaned forward. "That's him."

Some of the homicide forensic crew was still out at the Twelfth Street entrance and got there fast. So did the homicide sergeant who'd been working the Alice Yoakum affair. Rodney gave him the victim's identification. He explained about the fish trap and how they had found the body. Dr.

Hartman left, looking pale and shaken. Chee and Leaphorn remained. They stood back, away from the activity, trying to keep out of the way. Photographs were taken. Measurements were made. The rigid body of Henry Highhawk was lifted out of the bin and onto a stretcher.

Leaphorn noticed the long hair tied into a Navajo-style bun, he noticed the narrow face, sensitive even in the distortion of death. He noticed the dark mark above the eye which must be a bullet hole and the smear of blood which had emerged from it. He noticed the metal brace supporting the leg, and the shoe lift lengthening it. Here was the man whose name was scrawled on a note in a terrorist's pocket. The man who had drawn a second terrorist all the way to Arizona, if Leaphorn was guessing correctly, to a curing ceremonial at the Agnes Tsosie place. Here was a white man who wanted to be an Indian—specifically to be a Navajo. A man who dug up the bones of whites to protest whites digging up Indian bones. A man important enough to be killed at what certainly must have been a terrible risk to the man who killed him. Leaphorn looked into Highhawk's upturned face as it went past him on the police stretcher. What made you so important? Leaphorn wondered. What made Mr. Santillanes polish his pointed shoes and pack his bags and come west to New Mexico looking for you? What were you planning that drew someone with a pistol into this dusty place to execute you? And if you could hear my questions, if you could speak, would you even know the answer yourself? The body was past now, disappearing down the corridor. Leaphorn glanced at Chee. Chee looked stricken.

Chee had found himself simultaneously watching what had been Henry Highhawk emerge from the container and watching his own reaction to what he was seeing. He had been a policeman long enough to have conditioned himself to death. He had handled an old woman frozen in her hogan, a teenaged boy who had hanged himself in the restroom at his boarding school, a child backed over by a pickup truck driven by her mother. He had been investigating officer of so many victims of alcohol that he no longer tried to keep them sorted out in his memory. But he had never been involved with the death of someone he'd known personally, someone who interested him, someone he'd been talking to only a matter of minutes before he died. He had rationalized his Navajo conditioning to avoid the dead, but he hadn't eliminated the ingrained knowledge that while the body died, the *chindi* lingered to cause ghost sickness and evil dreams. Highhawk's *chindi* would now haunt this museum's corridors. It would haunt Jim Chee as well.

Rodney had been inspecting the items removed from the container where Highhawk's body had rested. He held up a flat, black box with something round connected to it by wires. "This looks a little modern for a Borneo fishing village," he said, showing the box to all of them. The box was a miniature Panasonic cassette tape recorder.

"I think it's Highhawk's tape recorder," Chee said. "He had one just like that when he was at Agnes Tsosie's place. And I saw it again in the office at his place." Chee could see now that tape recorder was wired to one of those small, battery-operated watches. It was much like the nine-dollar-and-ninety-nine-cent model he was wearing except it used hands instead of digital numbers.

"I think it's wired to turn on the recorder," Leaphorn said. "Possibly that's what Highhawk was talking about on that telephone call. Getting that thing fixed."

Rodney inspected it carefully. He laughed. "If it was, it wasn't fixed very well," he said. "If Highhawk did this he doesn't know any more about electricity than my wife. And she thinks it leaks out of the telephone." He unwound the wires and removed the watch. Holding it carefully by the edges he opened the recorder and popped out the miniature tape. He weighed it in his hand, examined it, and put it back in the machine. "Let's see what we have on this," he said. "But first, let's see what else we have in this container."

Rodney sorted gingerly among the fish nets, bamboo fish spears, canoe paddles, clothing, and assorted items that Chee couldn't identify. Pressed against the side of the bin, partly obscured by folded twine of fish netting, was something white. It looked like leather. In fact, to Chee it looked like it might be a *yei* mask.

"I guess that's it," Rodney said. "Except your team will come along and do a proper search and find the murder weapon in there, and the killer's photograph, fingerprints, and maybe his business card."

"We'll catch that later," the sergeant said. "We'll get somebody from the museum who knows what's supposed to be in there and what isn't."

Chee leaned past Rodney and turned the white leather between his fingers. The mask of Talking God stared up at him.

"This is the mask Highhawk had been working on," Chee said. "Or one of them."

The sergeant retrieved it, turned it over in his hands, examined it. "What'd you say it was?" he asked Chee, and handed it to him.

"It's the Yeibichai mask. A Navajo religious mask. Highhawk was working on this one, or one just like it, for that mask display downstairs."

"Oh," the sergeant said, his curiosity satisfied and his interest exhausted. "Let's get this over with."

They followed Highhawk's body into the bright fluorescent lighting of the conservancy laboratory. When the sergeant finished whatever he wanted to do with him, Henry Highhawk would go from there to the morgue. Now the cause of death seemed apparent. The blackened round mark of what must be a bullet hole was apparent above the left eye. From it a streak of dried blood discolored the side of Highhawk's face.

The sergeant went through Highhawk's pockets, spreading the contents on a laboratory table. Wallet, pocketknife, a half-used roll of Tums, three quarters, two dimes, a penny, a key ring bearing six keys, a crumpled handkerchief, a business card from a plumbing company, a small frog fetish carved out of a basaltic rock.

"What the hell is this?" the sergeant said, pushing the frog with his finger.

"It's a frog fetish," Leaphorn said.

The sergeant had not been happy to have two strangers and Rodney standing around while he worked. The sergeant had the responsibility, but obviously Rodney had the rank.

"What the hell is a frog fetish?" the sergeant asked.

"It's connected with the Navajo religion," Leaphorn said. "Highhawk was part Navajo. He had a Navajo grandmother. He was interested in the culture."

The sergeant nodded. He looked slightly less hostile.

"No bin key?" Chee asked.

The sergeant looked at him. "Bin key?"

"When he left his office last night, he took the key that unlocks all these bins off a hook beside his door and put it in his pocket," Chee said. "It was on a little plain steel ring." The killer probably had taken Highhawk's key to open the bin and to relock it. Unless of course the killer was another museum employee with his (or her) own key.

"You saw him put the key in his pocket?"

Chee nodded. "He took it off the hook. He put it in his right front pants pocket."

"No such key in his pocket," the sergeant said. "What you see here is everything he had on him. From the car keys he was carrying, it looks like he was driving a Ford. You know about that? You know the license number?"

"There was a Ford Mustang parked in the driveway by his house. I'd say about five or six years old. I didn't notice the license. And I don't know if it was his," Chee said.

"We'll get it from Motor Vehicle Division. It's probably parked somewhere close to here."

Rodney put the tape recorder beside Highhawk's possessions on the laboratory table. "I unwired the recorder from the watch. Just in case," he said. "You want to hear it?"

He removed a pencil from his inside coat pocket, held it over the PLAY key, and glanced up at the sergeant, awaiting a response.

The sergeant nodded. "Sure."

The first sounds Chee heard sent him back into boyhood, into the winter hogan of Frank Sam Nakai on the west slope of the Chuska Mountains. Bitter cold outside, the cast-iron wood stove under the smoke hole glowing with heat. Frank Sam Nakai, brother of his mother, teaching the children how the Holy People saved the Holy Boy and his sister from the lightning sickness. His uncle sitting on the sheepskin, legs crossed, head back against the blanket hung against the log wall, eyes closed, singing. At first, the voice so low that Cousin Emmett and little Shirley and Chee would have to lean forward to hear them:

"Huu tu tu. Huu tu tu," Frank Sam Nakai would sing, the sound of night birds, the sound of Talking God summoning the *yei* to attend to the affair at hand. And the voice rising: *"Ohohoho, hehehe heya haya—"* The sound of his fellow spirits answering. And by now the children would know that these were not words in any human language. They were the words of the gods.

From the tiny speaker of the tiny recorder Chee was hearing the same chant. Talking God summoning the *yei* to the Naakhai ceremony on the final night of the Yeibichai, calling them for the ritual which would heal Mrs. Agnes Tsosie and restore her to harmony. Not cure her, because Agnes Tsosie was dying of liver cancer. But heal her, return her to *hozro,* to harmony with her fate. As he listened, Chee became aware that Henry Highhawk had been recording a long time before Chee had caught him at it. Chee remembered the moment. Highhawk had been standing beside one of the rows of bonfires which lined the dance ground. Through the chant Chee heard the crackle of burning sage and piñon, and the startled exclamation of a woman who had suddenly found her blanket smoldering from a spark. And then came the voices of Water Sprinkler, and the male *yeis,* forming sounds which—being the sounds gods make—would not produce any meaning mere humans could understand.

Chee noticed that both Rodney and the sergeant were looking at him, awaiting an explanation.

"It's chanting from the Yeibichai," Chee said. "The Night Chant." That, obviously, explained nothing. "Highhawk was at this ceremonial the night I arrested him," Chee said. "He was recording it."

As he said it, the sound of the chanting was replaced by the voice of Henry Highhawk.

"The song you have been hearing is the beginning of one of hundreds of songs which make up the poetry of a Navajo curing ceremony," the voice of Highhawk said. "White people call it the Night Chant. Navajos call it the Yeibichai—or Talking God. Talking God is one of the powerful supernatural spirits of that great tribe, one of the connections between the Navajo and the great all-powerful Creating God. We could compare him with the figure of the Archangel Raphael in Jewish/Christian creation mythology."

There was silence. Chee glanced up. Rodney said: "Well, now—" and then Highhawk's voice resumed:

"I, I being Talking God, ask you who have come to look at this display of masks to look around you in this exhibition, and throughout this museum. Do you see a display of the masks of the gods of the Christian, or of the Jew, or of Islam, or of any other culture strong enough to defend its faith and to punish such a desecration? Where is the representation of the Great God Jehovah who led the Jews out of their bondage in Egypt, or the Mask of Michael the Archangel, or the Mother of the Christian God we call Jesus Christ, or a personification of Jesus himself? You do not see them here. You have here in a storage room of this museum the Tano Pueblo's representation of one of its holy Twin War Gods. But where is a consecrated Sacred Host from the Roman Catholic cathedral? You will not find it here. Here you see the gods of conquered people displayed like exotic animals in the public zoo. Only the overthrown and captured gods are here. Here you see the sacred things torn from the temples of Inca worshippers, stolen from the holy kivas of the Pueblo people, sacred icons looted from burned tepee villages on the buffalo plains."

Highhawk's voice had become higher, almost shrill. It was interrupted by the sound of a great intake of breath. Then a moment of silence. The ambulance crew picked up Highhawk's stretcher and moved out—leaving only his voice behind. The forensic crew sorted his possessions into evidence bags.

"Do you doubt what I say?" Highhawk's voice resumed. "Do you doubt that your privileged race, which claims such gentility, such humanity, would do this? Above your head, lining the halls and corridors of this very building, are thousands of cases and bins and boxes. In them you find the bones of more than eighteen thousand of your fellow humans. You will find the skeletons of children, of mothers, of grandfathers. They have been dug out of the burials where their mourning relatives placed them, reuniting them with their Great Mother Earth. They remain in great piles and stacks, respected no more than the bones of apes and . . ."

Rodney hit the OFF button and looked around him in the resulting silence.

"What do you think? He was going to broadcast this somehow with that mask display he was working on? Was that the plan?"

"Probably," Chee said. "He seems to be speaking to the audience at the exhibition. Let's hear the rest of it."

"Why not?" Rodney said. "But let's get out of here. Down to Highhawk's office where I can use the telephone."

The items from Highhawk's pockets were in evidence bags now, except for the recorder.

"I've got to get moving," the sergeant said. "I still have some work to do on the Alice Yoakum thing."

"I'll bring in the recorder," Rodney said. "I'll clean up here."

"I'll need to talk to—" The sergeant hesitated, searching for the name. "To Mr. Chee here, and Mr. Leaphorn. I'll need to get their statements on the record."

"Whenever you say," Leaphorn said.

"I'll bring them in," Rodney said.

In Highhawk's office, Rodney put the recorder on the desk top and pushed the PLAY button. Rodney, too, was anxious to hear the rest of it.

"—antelopes. Their children have asked that these bones be returned so that they can again be reunited with their Mother Earth with respect and dignity. What does the museum tell us? It tells us that its anthropologists need our ancestral bones for scientific studies. Why doesn't it need the ancestral bones of white Americans for these studies? Why doesn't it dig up your graves? Think of it! Eighteen thousand human skeletons! Eighteen thousand! Ladies and gentlemen, what would you say if the museum looted your cemeteries, if it dug up the consecrated ground of your graveyards in Indianapolis and Topeka and White Plains and hauled the skeletons of your loved ones here to molder in boxes and bins in the hallways? Think about this! Think about the graves of your grandmothers. Help us recover the bones of our own ancestors so that they may again be reunited with their Mother Earth."

Silence. The tape ran its brief miniature-recorder course and clicked off. Rodney pushed the REWIND button. He looked at Chee. "Quite an argument."

Chee nodded. "Of course there's another side to it. An earlier generation of anthropologists dug up most of those bones. And the museum has given a few of them back. I think it sent sixteen skeletons to the Blackfoot Tribe awhile ago, and it says it will return bones if they were stolen from regular cemeteries or if you can prove a family connection."

Rodney laughed. "Get those skeletons in the lineup," he said. "Get the kinfolks in and see if they can pick their grannie out from somebody's auntie." About a millisecond before he ended that jest, Rodney's expression shifted from amused to abashed. In the present company, maybe this was no laughing matter. "Sorry," Rodney said. "I wasn't thinking."

Now Chee looked amused. "We Navajos aren't into this corpse fetish business," he said. "Our metaphysics turns on life, the living. The dead we put behind us. We avoid old bones. You won't find Navajos asking for the return of their stolen skeletons."

It was now Leaphorn's turn to look amused. "As a matter of fact, we are. The Navajo Tribe is asking the museum to send us our skeletons, if the museum has any of them. I think somebody in the tribal bureaucracy decided it was a chance to make a political point. A little one-upmanship on Washington."

"Any reason to hear this again?" Rodney asked. He

slipped the recorder into an evidence bag, sealed it, leaned heavily against the edge of the table, and sighed. He looked tired, Chee thought, and unhappy.

"I don't enjoy being involved in things I don't understand," Rodney said. "I don't have the slightest goddamn idea why somebody killed this Highhawk bird, or whether it ties in with that guard being killed, or whether this tape has a damned thing to do with anything. That tape sounds like the Smithsonian Museum might have a motive to knock him off." Rodney rubbed the back of a hand across his forehead and made a wry face. "But I gather that museums tend to wait until you're dead and then go after your skeleton. So I'd guess that tape doesn't have much to do with this. And—"

"I'd guess it does," Chee said.

Leaphorn studied him. He nodded, agreeing. "How?"

"I haven't thought it through," Chee said. "But think about it a minute. Highhawk goes to a lot of trouble to get to that Yeibichai to make this tape." He glanced at Leaphorn. "He wrote to Old Lady Tsosie, didn't he? He'd have to find a way to run down her address."

"She was in that big Navajo Reservation article *National Geographic* ran," Leaphorn said. "That's where he got her name."

"Then he goes all the way out there from Washington, and finds out how to find Lower Greasewood, and the Tsosie place, dreams up that bullshit story about wanting to be a Navajo, and—"

"Maybe not bullshit," Leaphorn said. "From what you told me about him."

"No," Chee said, thoughtfully, "I think maybe not. I think now that might have been part of the genuine Highhawk package. But anyway, it involved a lot of trouble. He must have written that oration he gave we just heard, and then got it dubbed in on the tape. Now why? What's he going to do with it? I think it's obvious he was planting it in that mask exhibit, in his Talking God exhibit. The tape practically says that. And Highhawk has a track record of knowing how to get publicity. The kind to put the heat on the Smithsonian. That tape was sure well designed to do that. Zany enough to make the front page."

"Yeah," Rodney said. "The Talking God actually talking."

"Did he have it with him when he left you in his office?" Leaphorn asked.

"He had a cardboard box. About three times the size of a shoebox. Anyway, it was big enough for the mask and all. He picked it up just as he was leaving."

"And that tells us what?" Rodney asked. He shook his head, thinking about it.

Silence in the room. Rodney now slouched in Highhawk's swivel chair; Chee leaning against the wall in the practiced slouch of a man who had done a lot of leaning against things, a lot of waiting for his age; Joe Leaphorn sitting on the edge of the desk, looking uncomfortable in his three-piece suit, his gray, burr-cut head bowed slightly forward, his expression that of a man who is listening to sounds inside his own head. The quiet air around them smelled of dust and, faintly, of decay.

"Officer Chee here, he and I, we have a problem," Leaphorn said—half to Rodney and half to the desk. "We are like two dogs who followed two different sets of tracks to the same brush pile. One dog thinks there's a rabbit under the brush, the other thinks it's a bobcat. Same brush pile, different information." He glanced at Chee. "Right?"

Chee nodded.

"As for my end of it, I see the body of a worn-out, toothless man who keeps his old shoes polished. His body is under a chamisa bush in New Mexico. And in the shirt pocket is a note mentioning Agnes Tsosie's Yeibichai ceremony. When I get out to Agnes Tsosie's place, I run into the name of Henry Highhawk. He's coming out. I follow those pointed shoes back to Washington and I find a little den of Chilean terrorists—or, maybe more accurately, the victims of Chilean terror. And right in the next apartment to this den is a little man with red hair and freckles and the torso of a weightlifter who just happens to fit the description of the guy who probably killed Pointed Shoes with his knife. But I've come to a dead end. Good idea who killed my man, now. I think that surely the man's widow, his family, they'll tell me why. No such luck. Instead of that, they act like they never heard of him."

Leaphorn sighed, tapped his fingers on the desk top, and continued without a glance at either of his listeners. "I get a make on Mr. Pointed Shoes' identity from the FBI. It turns out he's one of the big ones in one of the factions that's sort of at war with the right-wing government in Chile. Turns out the ins have already killed one of his bunch earlier. So now the mystery is solved. I know who Pointed Shoes is. His name is Santillanes. I know who killed him—or I think I do—and I think I know why. But now I've got a new problem. Why were Santillanes' kinfolks acting that way? It looked like they didn't want anyone to know the man had been killed."

Leaphorn's droning voice stopped for several seconds. "Now why in the world would that be?" he said. He was frowning. He shook his head, looked at Rodney and Chee. "Either one of you want to break in here?"

Neither one did.

"So," Leaphorn said. "So, I'm almost to the brush pile. Now my question is what the hell is going on here? And for some reason I can't get Highhawk out of my head. He doesn't seem to fit anywhere. I think I know how Santillanes found out he should go to the Navajo Reservation to find Highhawk. But I don't understand why."

Leaphorn paused again, looked at Chee. "Do you know about this? Right after Highhawk pulled that business of digging up the graves and mailing the bones to the museum, he got the big splash of publicity he wanted. But before anybody could serve a warrant on him, he had dropped out of sight. All his friends and his neighbors could tell anybody looking for him that he was going to Arizona to attend a Yeibichai ceremonial for some relative named Agnes Tsosie. I think Santillanes probably read about his exploits in the paper and went looking for him about the same time the police did. Santillanes got the word that Henry was heading west for the Yeibichai. But he didn't know it was a month in the future."

Leaphorn stopped again, inhaled hugely, exhaled, drummed his fingers against the desk top, thinking. Rodney made a sentence-opening sound but cut it off without actually saying anything. But he looked at his watch.

"Why would Chilean politicians want to meet with Henry Highhawk?" Leaphorn asked himself the question. "They had to want to contact him badly enough to send someone three thousand miles, and get him killed, and then send somebody else to complete the mission. And post his bail." He glanced up at Chee. "That's right, isn't it? And Highhawk called that guy with the missing fingers his friend, didn't he? Any idea how long they'd known each other?"

"They didn't," Chee said. "Highhawk was lying. They hadn't met until the Yeibichai."

"You sure?" Leaphorn asked.

"I watched them meet," Chee said. "I'm sure."

Rodney held up a hand. "Friends, I've got to go and do some things. Two or three in fact. I was going to be back at the office about an hour ago. Stick around. I'll be back." He slipped off the desk and disappeared into the hallway.

"Every effect has its cause," Leaphorn said to Chee.

"Once in a while, maybe, a star just falls at random. But I don't believe in random. The Santillanes bunch had a hell of a good reason to chase after Highhawk. What was it?"

"I don't know," Chee said. "All I know about the Santillanes bunch is from seeing Bad Hands a couple of times. I got here by a totally different route. And I've got a different question under your brush pile." He sat on the desk about where Rodney had been leaning, thinking, deciding how to explain this premonition, this hunch that had been making him uneasy.

"I keep remembering Highhawk at the Yeibichai," Chee said. "I was curious about him so I was watching him, standing just a little off to the side where I could see his face. He was cold—" He laughed, glanced at Leaphorn. "Of course he was cold. Everybody's cold at a Night Chant, but he was colder than most of us because, you know, if you come from the East you think desert country is supposed to be hot, so he wasn't dressed like us. Just had on a leather jacket. Anyway, he was shivering." Chee stopped. Why was he telling Leaphorn all this? Highhawk standing, shaking with cold, hugging himself, the wind blowing dust across the dance ground around his ankles, the wavering light from the bonfires turning his face red. His expression had been rapt, and Chee had noticed his lips were moving. Highhawk was singing to himself. Agnes Tsosie had been standing on a blanket spread on the packed earth in front of the medicine hogan attended by the *hataalii.* Talking God, Humpback God, and Water Sprinkler had been making their slow, stately approach. Chee had edged closer, close enough to hear what Highhawk was chanting. "He stirs. He stirs. He stirs. He stirs," Highhawk had been singing. "Now in old age wandering, he stirs." It had been words from the "Song of Waking" which the *hataalii* would have sung on the first midnight of the ceremonial, summoning the spirit in the mask from its cosmic sleep to take its part in the ritual. He remembered noticing as Highhawk sang that while some of the words were wrong, the man's expression was deeply reverent.

Now he noticed that Leaphorn's expression was puzzled. "He was cold," Leaphorn said. "Yes, but you haven't made your point."

"He was a believer," Chee said. "You know what I mean. Some people come to a ceremonial out of family duty, and some come out of curiosity, or to meet friends. But to some it is a spiritual experience. You can tell by their faces."

Leaphorn's expression was still puzzled. "And he was one of those? He believed?"

Yes, Chee thought, Highhawk was one of those. You're not one, lieutenant. You don't believe. You see the Navajo Way as a harmless cultural custom. You would be one of those who go only as a family duty. But this crazy white man believed. Truly believed.

"He did," Chee said. "He was moved. He even knew words to the song that awakens the spirit of Talking God in the mask. He was singing it at the wrong time, but he knew the words. And the point I'm trying to make with all this—the point is I'm puzzled about this mask we found."

Leaphorn waited for that to be explained.

"Maybe I'm wrong but I don't think so. I don't think Highhawk would use the *yei* mask like that. I don't think he would put it on the head of a manikin in a public display. I don't think the museum would approve of that either. Despite what Highhawk said. For example, they brought in a *hataalii,* a man named Sandoval, brought him in to check out the exhibit and make sure Henry wasn't doing anything sacrilegious. So—" Chee paused, thinking about it.

"Go on," Leaphorn said.

"So Highhawk was making a duplicate mask. A replica of the genuine Yeibichai mask in the museum's collection.

A copy. He must have had both of them here last night." Chee picked up the *yei* mask by its fur collar ruff and held it up, facing Leaphorn.

"This mask we have here, it's not the genuine Yeibichai mask," Chee said. "It's just about an exact replica. Highhawk made it because he wouldn't use the real one in a public display, and he certainly wouldn't have rigged up his tape player inside of it."

"It looks old as the mountains to me," Leaphorn said. "Cracked and worn."

"He's good at that," Chee said. "But take a look at it. Up close. Look for pollen stains, along the cheeks where the medicine man puts it when he feeds the mask, and on the end of the mouthpiece. And down into the leather tube that forms the mouth. It's not there. No stains. He dried the buckskin somehow, or got an old piece, and dried out the paint, but why bother with the pollen stains? Nobody would notice it."

"No," Leaphorn said slowly. "Nobody would. So the mask on exhibit downstairs is the genuine Yeibichai mask."

"What else could it be? And there has to be a mask on the Talking God manikin. Dr. Hartman was down there this morning checking everything. She couldn't find Highhawk so she must have checked his display carefully. You naturally would. If Talking God didn't have his mask on, she sure as hell would have noticed that. But she wouldn't be able to tell the genuine mask from Highhawk's counterfeit."

"So who put it there?" Leaphorn mused. "Whoever killed Highhawk must have put it there, wouldn't you say? But—" Leaphorn stopped, midsentence. "Where is that Yeibichai display?"

"It's sort of off to one side, to the left of the center of the mask exhibition. Right across from it is an exhibition of Andean stuff, Incan and so forth. The high point is a gold and emerald mask which some Chilean general is trying—" Now it was Chee's turn to halt, midthought. "My God!" he said. "Dr. Hartman said this Chilean general—I think he's the head of their political police—was supposed to come in to today to look at the thing."

"Is this Chilean exhibit right across from Talking God?" Leaphorn asked. "Is that it?"

He moved toward the door while he was still asking the question, amazingly fast for a man of his age in a three-piece suit. And Jim Chee was right behind him.

20

LEROY FLECK WALKED the block and a half to where he'd parked the old Chevy sedan. He walked briskly, but without breaking into a trot, without any sign of urgency that anyone who saw him might remember. The important point was to keep any connection from being made between the crime and the car. If that happened he was a goner. If it didn't, then he had time to do the things he had to do.

He drove just at the speed limit, careful at the lights, careful changing lanes, and as he drove he listened to the police scanner on the seat beside him. Nothing much exciting except for a multivehicle, multi-injury accident on the Interstate 66 exit ramp at the Theodore Roosevelt Bridge. He was almost downtown before the call came. A slight strain showed in the laconic voice of the dispatcher and Fleck recognized the address of the nursing home and the code. It meant officer down. It meant nothing else would matter much for a while in D.C. law enforcement. A policeman had been killed. Within fifteen minutes, probably less, Fleck's description would be broadcast to every police car in the district. The noon newscasts would carry it big. But nobody had his picture and he still had time.

His first stop was at Western Union. The message he sent to Delmar was short: TAKE CARE OF MAMA. TELL HER I LOVE HER. AM SENDING MONEY ORDER.

He gave the girl at the desk the message and then opened the plastic purse and counted out $2,033. He thought for a moment. He had almost half a tank of gasoline but he might need to make a telephone call, or pay an admission fee somewhere. He saved the three ones, stuffed them in his shirt pocket. He asked the girl to subtract the transmission fees and make out a money order for the rest. Then he drove to the Chilean embassy.

He parked down the street at a place where he could watch the entrance gate. Then he walked through the drizzle to the pay booth, dialed the embassy, and gave the woman who answered the word that The Client had given him for emergencies.

"I need Stone," he said. He always wondered why the man used that for a code name. Why not something in Spanish?

"Ah," the woman said. "One little moment, please."

Then he waited. He waited a long time. The rain was mixed with snow now, big wet flakes which stuck to the glass of the booth for a second and then slid down the pane. Fleck went over his plan, but there was nothing much to go over. He would try to lure The Client out where he could reach him. If The Client wouldn't come out, he would wait. He would get him eventually. He would get as many as he could. He would get ones as important as possible. It was all he could do. He knew The Client wasn't his own man. He was taking his orders from somebody up the ladder. But it didn't matter to Fleck. Like Mama said, they were all the same.

"Yes," the voice said. It was not The Client's voice.

"I got to talk to Stone," Fleck said.

"He is not available. Not now."

"When then?" Fleck asked.

"Later today."

Perhaps, Fleck thought, he could get someone else. Someone more important. That would be as good. Even better.

"Let me talk to his superior then."

"Just a moment." Fleck could hear a distant-sounding voice, asking questions.

"They are getting ready to go," the man said. "They have no time now."

"I have to talk to somebody. It's an emergency."

"No time now. You call back. This evening."

The line went dead.

Fleck looked at it. Hung it up gently. Walked back to his car. It made no difference at all really. He could wait.

He had waited less than five minutes when the iron driveway gate creaked open and the limousine emerged. After it came another, equally black. They turned downtown, toward Capitol Hill.

Leroy Fleck trailed them in his rusty Chevy.

The limos did left turns on Constitution Avenue, rolled past the National Gallery of Art, and pulled to a stop at the Tenth Street entrance to the Museum of Natural History. Fleck pulled his Chevy into a No Parking zone, turned off the ignition, and watched.

Seven men emerged from the two limos. Fleck recognized The Client. Of the others, one carried cameras and a camera bag, and two more were burdened by a movie camera, tripods, and what Fleck guessed must be sound recording equipment. The remaining three were a short, plump man in a fur-collared coat; a tall, elegantly dressed man with a mustache; and a burly, hard-looking weightlifter type with a crooked nose. The driver from the front limo held a black umbrella over Mustache, protecting him from the wet snowflakes until the entourage reached the shelter of the museum entrance. Fleck sat a moment, sorting them out in his mind. The plump man would probably be the ambassador himself, or at least someone high on the power ladder. The elegant man would be a visiting Very Important Person, the one he'd read about in the *Post*. Judging from who got the umbrella, the visitor outranked the ambassador and rated the personal attention of The Client. The weightlifter type would be the VIP's personal muscle. As for The Client, Fleck had pegged him long ago as the man in charge of security at the embassy. In all they made a formidable bunch.

Fleck climbed out of the Chevy without bothering to take the key out of the ignition or to lock the door. He was finished with the Chevy now. No more need for it. He trotted up the museum steps and into the entrance foyer. The last two cameramen from the limo delegation were disappearing through a doorway into the central hall. They hurried into a side hallway to his right, under a banner which read THE MASKED GODS OF THE AMERICAS. Fleck followed.

There were perhaps fifty or sixty people in the exhibit of masks. Two-thirds of them looked to Fleck like a mixture of standard tourists. The rest were reporters and television cameramen and museum functionaries who must have been here waiting for Big Shot and his followers to appear. Now they were clustered around the elegant man. The Client stood a little aside from the central knot. He was doing his job. He was watching, his eyes checking everyone. They rested a moment on Fleck, then dismissed him and moved on.

The Client would have to be first, Fleck decided. He was the professional. Then he would go for the VIP. Fleck was conscious that he held two advantages. None of them had ever seen him and they wouldn't be expecting an attack. He would have total surprise on the first one he hit, and maybe a little surprise left on number two if there was enough confusion. He would need more luck than he could expect to take out the third one, but it was worth a try.

A cameraman's strobe flash lit the scene. Then another one. They were setting up some sort of filming apparently, with the VIP over by the display of South American stuff. Beside Fleck was an exhibit of masked dancers, big as life. Apparently some sort of American Indians. Fleck stooped, slipped the shank out of his boot, and held it in his palm, the honed blade hidden by his sleeve. Then he waited. He wanted the crowd to be exactly big enough. He wanted the time to be exactly right.

"THIS MIGUEL SANTERO, was that his name? This guy with the mutilated hands, did you see any sign of him around here last night?"

Leaphorn was standing exactly in front of the vertical line formed by the junction of the elevator doors, staring at the crack as he asked the question. It seemed to Chee that the elevator was barely moving. Why hadn't they looked for the stairs? Six flights. They could have run down six flights while this incredibly slow elevator was dropping one.

"I didn't see him," Chee said. "I just had a feeling that it was Santero on the telephone."

"I wish we knew for sure how he connects," Leaphorn said, without relaxing his stare at the elevator door. "Three slim threads is all we have—or maybe four—tying him to the Santillanes bunch. The FBI connects him, but the FBI has a bad habit of buying bad information. Second, after Santillanes was killed going to find Highhawk, Santero went out and found him. Maybe that was just a coincidence.

Third, the little red-headed man who killed Santillanes seems to have been following Santero too."

The elevator's floor indicator passed three and sank toward two. Leaphorn watched it. He got Chee to explain how the displays were arranged. He told Chee what he'd seen in the *Post* about General Huerta Cardona demanding return of the Incan mask. If he felt any of the anxiety which was causing Chee to chew relentlessly on his lower lip, he didn't allow it to show.

"What's the fourth?" Chee said.

Leaphorn's mind had left this part of the puzzle to explore something else. "Fourth?"

"You said maybe four thin threads."

"Oh. The fourth. Santero's mangled hands and Santillanes' teeth. They were broken out, I think. The pathologist said there was nothing wrong with the man's gums." He looked at Chee. "I think that's what decides me. Santero is one of the Santillanes people. The FBI had this one right. Describe him to me again."

Chee described Bad Hands in detail.

"What do you think we're dealing with here?"

"I'd guess a bomb," Chee said.

Leaphorn nodded. "Probably," he said. "Plastic explosive in the mask, and someone there to detonate it when the general is in exactly the right place."

The elevator creaked to a halt at the ground floor.

"I'll get the mask," Chee said. "You look for Santero."

Finding Santero proved to be no problem.

They rushed out of the elevator, through the door into the museum's main-floor public display halls and down the corridor toward the MASKED GODS OF THE AMERICAS banner—Chee leading, Leaphorn puffing along behind. Chee stopped.

"There he is," he said.

Santero had his back to them. He was standing beside an exhibit of Toltec masks, watching the crowd, which was watching television crews at another exhibit. Bright lights flashed on—a television crew preparing for action.

Chee turned his hurried walk into a run, dodging through the spectators, staggering a teenaged girl who backed into his path, being staggered in turn by a hefty woman whose shoulder grazed him as he passed. The Yeibichai itself had drawn only a few lookers. Curiosity about the television crews and the celebrity at the Incan display was the magnet but Chee had to push his way through the overflow to reach the exhibit. He was forcing himself not to think two terrible, unthinkable thoughts. He would reach the mask and there would be a bomb under it and Bad Hands would detonate it in his face. He would reach the mask and tear it off and there would be nothing under it. Only the molded plastic head of the manikin. In the first thought he would be instantly dead. In the second he would be hideously, unspeakably, terminally humiliated—living out his life as a public joke.

Chee pushed aside a boy and vaulted over the guardrail into the Yeibichai display. Up close, the manikin representing Talking God seemed even larger than he'd remembered. He gripped the fur ruff at the throat of the mask. Behind him he heard a voice shouting: "Hey! You! Get out of there." He pulled up on the leather. (It will explode, he thought. I will be dead.) Through his fingers, the mask and head seemed to be one—a single entity. The stiff leather wouldn't pull loose.

"Hey!" he heard behind him. "Get away from that. What the hell are you doing!" A security guard was climbing over the railing.

Chee jerked at the mask, tilting the manikin against him. He jerked again. The mask, the head, all of it came off in his arms. The headless manikin toppled with a crash. "Hey!" the guard shouted.

Leroy Fleck had several terrible weaknesses and several terrible strengths. One of his strengths was in stalking his prey, attaining the exact place, the exact time, the exact position, for using his shank exactly as Eddy Elkins—and his own subsequent experience—had taught him to use it. The secret of Leroy Fleck's survival had been finding a way to make his kill instant and silent. And Fleck had managed to survive seventeen years since his release from prison.

He was stalking now. While he watched the crowd and waited for the moment, he slipped the shank out of his sleeve and an envelope out of his pocket. He put the shank in the envelope, and carried it in his right hand, deep in his right coat pocket where it would be ready. The envelope had been Elkins' idea. "If witnesses see an envelope, they react like they're seeing somebody handing somebody a letter. Same with the victim. But if people see a knife coming, it's a totally different reaction." That had been proved true. And the paper didn't get in the way at all, or slow things down. With the handle of the shank ready between his thumb and forefinger, he watched The Client carefully, and the VIP, and the VIP's muscleman, and the ambassador, and the rest of them. He concluded from the way the man moved, and the way he watched, that the still photographer was also the ambassador's bodyguard. Partially on the basis of that he had changed his strategy. The VIP would go first. The Client second. The VIP was the one that mattered, the one who would best demonstrate that Leroy Fleck was a man, and not a dog that could be spit on without retribution.

He could do it right now, he thought, but the situation was improving. It became clear to Fleck what was happening. The VIP had called some sort of press conference here at the Incan display. That brought in the television cameras, and TV crews attracted the curious. The bigger the crowd got, the better the odds for Fleck. It would multiply the confusion, improve his chances of getting two, and maybe even three.

Then he saw Santero—the man who always wore gloves. It was clear to Fleck almost immediately that Santero was also stalking. Fleck watched. Santero seemed to have two objectives. He was keeping out of the line of vision of The Client, and he was keeping the VIP in sight. Fleck considered this. It didn't seem to matter. Santero was no longer the enemy. The man had probably come here to try something. But if he did, it could only be helpful to Fleck. He could see no problem in that.

Just as he had decided that, he saw the two Indian cops. They hurried into the exhibit hall together. Then the tall one broke into a run toward him, and the older one headed for Santero. Here Fleck could definitely see a problem. Both of these men had seen him, the older one clearly and in good light. No more time to wait for a bigger crowd. Fleck pushed his way past a man in a raincoat, past a television light technician, toward the VIP. The VIP was standing with a well-dressed fat man wearing bifocal glasses. They were studying a sheet of paper, discussing it. Probably, Fleck thought, they were looking at notes for the statement he intended to make. If he could handle it, Fleck decided he would take the VIP from the back. He slipped his right hand from his pocket, crumpling one end of the envelope as he gripped the shank handle. Then he moved, Fleck fashion, like lightning.

Leaphorn always thought things through, always planned, always minimized the opportunity for error. It was a lifelong habit, it was the source of his reputation as the man to handle impossible cases. Now he had only a few seconds to think and no time at all to plan. He would have to presume that there was a bomb, that Santero held the detonator, that Santero was working alone because only one person would be needed. Santero's presence, lurking where he could watch the general, seemed to reinforce some of that thinking. The man was waiting until the general moved up to the position closest to the bomb. And the detonator? Probably something like the gadget that turned his television on and changed the channels. Grabbing him wouldn't work. He'd be too strong and agile for Leaphorn to handle, even with surprise. He'd simply point the thing and push the button. Leaphorn would try confusion.

Santero heard him rushing up and whirled to face him. His right hand was in his coat pocket, the arm rigid.

"Señor Santero," Leaphorn said, in a loud, hoarse, breathless whisper. *"Venga conmigo! Venga! Pronto! Pronto! Venga!"*

Santero's face was shocked, bloodless. The face of a man interrupted at the moment of mass murder.

"Come with you?" he stammered. "Who are you?"

"Los Santillanes sent me," Leaphorn said. "Come. Hurry."

"But what—" Santero became aware that Leaphorn had gripped his right arm. He jerked it away, pulled out his right hand. He wore a black glove on it, and in the glove he held a small, flat plastic box. "Get away from me," Santero said, voice fierce.

There was a clamor of voices from the crowd. Someone was shouting: "Hey! You! Get out of there." Santero turned from Leaphorn, backing away, starting at the sound of a second shout: "Hey! Get away from that."

Santero took another step backward. He raised the box.

"Santero," Leaphorn shouted. *"El hombre ahí no esta el general. No esta El General Huerta Cardona. Es un—"*

Leaphorn's Arizona–New Mexico Spanish included no Castilian noun for "stand-in" or even "substitute." *"Es un* impostor," he concluded.

"Impostor?" Santero said. He lowered the box a little. "Speak English. I can't understand your Spanish."

"I was sent to tell you they were using a stand-in," Leaphorn said. "They heard about the plot. They sent someone made up to look like the general."

Santero's expression shifted from doubtful to grim. "I think you're lying," he said. "Stop trying to get between me and—"

From the crowd at the display came the sound of a woman screaming.

"What the devil—?" Santero began. And then there were shouts, another scream, and a man's voice shouting: "He's fainted! Get a doctor!"

Leaphorn's move was pure reflex, without time to think. His only advantages were that Santero was a little confused, a little uncertain. And the hand in which Santero held the control box had only two fingers left inside that glove. Leaphorn struck at the hand.

Leroy Fleck said, "Excuse me. Excuse me, please," and pushed past the woman he had been using as a screen and went for the general's back. But he did it just as the general was turning. Fleck saw the general staring at him, and the general's bodyguard making a quick-reflex move to block him. His instincts told him this was not going well.

"A letter—" he said, striking at the general's chest. He felt the paper of the envelope crumple against his fist as the steel razor of the shank slit through the general's vest, and shirt, and the thin muscle of the chest, and sank between the ribs.

"—from an admirer," Fleck said, as he slashed back and

forth, back and forth, and heard the general gasp, and felt the general sag against him. "He's fainted!" Fleck shouted. "Get a doctor!"

The Muscle had grabbed him by the shoulder just as he shouted it, and struck him a terrible blow over the kidneys. But Fleck hugged the general's sagging body, and shouted again, "Help me!"

It caused confusion, exactly as Fleck had hoped. The Muscle released Fleck's arm and tried to catch the general. The Client was there now beside them, bending over the slumping body. "What?" he shouted. "What happened? General!"

Fleck withdrew the shank, letting the crumpled envelope fall. He stabbed The Client in the side. Stabbed him again. And again.

The bodyguard was no longer confused. He shot Fleck twice. The exhibit echoed with the boom of the pistol, and the screams of panicking spectators.

Chee was only dimly aware of the shouts, the screams, the general pandemonium around him. He was numb. He turned the mask in his hands and looked into it, with no idea what to expect. He saw two dangling wires, one red, one white, a confusing array of copper-colored connections, a small square gray box, and a heavy compact mass of blue-gray dough.

The security officer clutched his arm. "Come on!" he shouted. "Get out of here!" The security officer was a plump young black man with heavy jowls. The screams were distracting him. "Look," Chee said, turning the open end of the mask toward him. "It's a bomb." While he was saying it, Chee was tearing at the wires. He dropped them to the floor, and sat on the back of the fallen manikin, and began carefully peeling the Yeibichai mask from the mass of blue-gray plastic which had been pressed into it.

"A bomb," the guard said. He looked at Chee, at the mask, and at the struggle at the adjoining Incan exhibit. "A bomb?" he said again, and climbed the railing and charged into the Incan melee. "Break it up," he shouted. "We have a bomb in here."

And just then General Huerta Cardona's bodyguard shot Leroy Fleck.

Chee looked up to see what was happening. And then he finished brushing the fragments of plastic out of the mask of Talking God, and straightening the bristling row of eagle feathers and the fox-fur ruff. He picked it up in one hand, and the ball of plastic explosive in the other, and climbed over the railing and out of the exhibit. He wanted to show Leaphorn they'd guessed right.

Joe Leaphorn's hand knocked the control box out of Santero's grip. It clattered to the marble floor between them. Santero reached for it. Leaphorn kicked it. It went skittering down the corridor, spinning past the feet of running people. Santero pursued it, running into the crowd stampeding out of the exhibition hall. Leaphorn followed.

A man with a camera collided with him. "He killed the general," the photographer shouted to someone ahead of him. "He killed the general." On the floor near the wall Leaphorn saw fragments of black plastic and an AA-size battery. Someone had trampled the detonator. He stopped, backed out of the stampede. Santero had disappeared. Leaphorn leaned against the wall, gasping. His chest hurt. His hip hurt where the heavy camera had slammed into it. He would go and see about Jim Chee. But first he would collect himself. He was getting too damned old for this business.

22

JIM CHEE SAT on his bed, leaned back on his suitcase, and tried to cope with his headache by not thinking about it. He was wearing the best shirt and the well-pressed trousers he had hung carefully in the closet when he unpacked to save in the event he needed to look good. No need now to save them. He would wear them on the plane. It was a bitch of a headache. He had slept poorly—partly because of the strange and lumpy hotel mattress (Chee being accustomed to the hard, thin padding on the built-in bed of his trailer home), and partly because he had been too tense to sleep. His mind had been too full of horrors and terrors. He would doze, then jerk awake to sit on the edge of the mattress, shaking with the aftereffects of shallow, grotesque dreams in which Talking God danced before him.

Finally, about a half-hour before the alarm was scheduled to rescue him from the night, he had given up. He had taken a shower, packed his stuff, and checked again with the front desk to see if he had any messages. There was one from Leaphorn, which simply informed him that Leaphorn had returned to Window Rock. That surprised Chee. It was a sort of courtly thing for the tough old bastard to have done. There was a message from Janet Pete, asking for a call back. He tried and got no answer. By then the headache was flowering and he had time to kill. Downstairs he drank two cups of coffee—which usually helped but didn't this morning. He left the toast he'd ordered on the plate and went for a walk.

The mild early-winter storm which had been bringing Washington rain mixed with snow yesterday had drifted out over the Atlantic and left behind a grim gray overcast with a forecast for high broken clouds and clearing by late afternoon. Now it was cold and still. Chee found that even in this strange place, even under these circumstances, he could catch himself up in the rhythm of the fast, hard motion, of heart and lungs hard at work. The nightmares faded a little, coming to seem like abstract memories of something he might have merely dreamed. Highhawk had never really existed. There were not really eighteen thousand ancestors in boxes lining hallways in an old museum. No one had actually tried to commit mass murder with the mask of Talking God. He walked briskly down Pennsylvania Avenue, and veered northward on Twelfth Street, and strode briskly westward again on H Street, and collapsed finally on a bench in what he thought, judging from a sign he'd noticed without really attending, might be Lafayette Square. Through the trees he could see the White House and, on the other side, an impressive hotel. Chee caught his breath, considered the note from Leaphorn, and decided it was a sort of subtle gesture. (You and I, kid. Two Dineh among the Strangers.) But maybe not. And it wasn't the sort of thing he would ever ask the lieutenant about.

A dove-gray limousine pulled up under the hotel's entryway roof, and after it a red sports car which Chee couldn't identify. Maybe a Ferrari, he thought. Next was a long black Mercedes which looked like it might have been custom built. Chee was no longer breathing hard. The damp low-country cold seeped up his sleeves and around his socks and under his collar. He got up, inspired half by cold and half by curiosity, and headed for the hotel.

It was warm inside, and luxurious. Chee sank into a sofa, removed his hat, warmed his ears with his hands, and observed what his sociology teacher had called "the privileged class." The professor admitted a prejudice against this class but Chee found them interesting to observe. He spent almost forty-five minutes watching women in fur coats and men in suits which, while they tended to look almost identical to Chee's untrained eye, were obviously custom made. He saw someone who looked exactly like Senator Teddy Kennedy, and someone who looked like Sam Donaldson, and a man who was probably Ralph Nader, and three others who must have been celebrities of some sort, but whose names eluded him.

He left the hotel warm but still with the headache. The material splendors, the fur and polished leather of the hotel's guests, had replaced his nightmares with a depression. He hurried through the damp cold back to his own hotel room.

The telephone was ringing. It was Janet Pete.

"I tried to call you last night," she said. "How are you? Are you all right?"

"Fine," Chee said. "We had trouble down at the museum. The FBI got involved and—"

"I know. I know," Janet said. "I saw it on television. The paper is full of it. There's a picture of you, with the statue."

"Oh," Chee said. The final humiliation. He could see it in the Farmington *Times:* Officer Jim Chee of Shiprock, New Mexico, seen above wrestling with a representation of Talking God, from which he has removed the head, in the Smithsonian Museum in Washington, D.C.

"On television, too. On the ABC morning news. They had some footage of you with the mask. But I'm not sure people who didn't know how you were dressed would know it was you."

Chee could think of nothing to say. His head still ached. He wished with a fervent longing to be back in New Mexico. In his trailer under the cottonwood on the bank above the San Juan River. He would take two aspirin and sprawl out on his comfortable, narrow bed and finish reading *A Yellow Raft on Blue Water.* He'd left it opened to page 158. A hard place to stop.

"They said Henry Highhawk was dead," Janet Pete said in a small voice.

"Yes. The police think Santero killed him," Chee said. "It seems fairly obvious that it must have been Santero."

"Henry was a sweet man," Janet said. "He was a kind man." She paused. "He was, wasn't he, Jim? But if he was, how did they talk him into being a part of this—of this horrible bomb thing?"

"I don't think they did," Chee said. "We'll never know for sure, I guess. But I think they conned him, and used him. Probably they saw the story in the *Post* about Highhawk digging up the skeletons. They needed a way to kill the general and they had a way of knowing their target would be visiting the Smithsonian, so they went out and made friends with Henry."

"But that doesn't explain why he would help them."

"I think Highhawk thought Santero was sympathetic to what Henry was trying to do. In fact, I'd be willing to bet that planting the tape recorded message in the mask was dreamed up by the Santillanes bunch. Maybe they knew he'd need technical help with the timer on the tape recorder and all that."

"I'd like to think you're right," Janet said. "I'd like to think I wasn't a complete fool. Wanting to help him when he was helping murder a lot of innocent people." But her tone was full of doubt.

"If I wasn't right— If you weren't they wouldn't have had to kill him," Chee said. "But they did kill him. Maybe he noticed something and caught on. Maybe they just couldn't leave him around to tell all to the police."

"Sure," Janet said. "I didn't think of that. I feel better. I guess I needed to keep believing Henry just wanted to do good."

"I think that's right," Chee said. "It took me a while, but I've decided that, too."

"What are you going to do now?"

"I have a flight this afternoon back to Albuquerque. Then I catch the Mesa Airlines flight to Farmington, and pick up my car and drive back to Shiprock," Chee said.

Janet Pete correctly read the tone of that.

"I'm sorry," she said. "I had no idea what I was getting you into. I never would have—"

Chee, a believer in the Navajo custom of never interrupting anyone, interrupted her.

"I wanted to come," he said. "I wanted to see you."

"Do you still want to see me? I'll come over and take you to the airport." A long pause. "If you really do have to go. You're on vacation, aren't you?"

"I'd like that," Chee said. "A ride to the airport."

So now he waited again. He was able now to think about what had happened yesterday. The D.C. police would probably catch Santero sooner or later. He found he had no interest in that. But he wondered what Leaphorn had done to keep Santero from pushing the button. Chee retraced it all in his memory. Handing the museum guard the ball of plastic explosive. ("Here. Be careful with this. It was a bomb. Give it to the cops.") He'd walked back to the STAFF ONLY elevator carrying Talking God's mask. He had pushed his way through the uproar of scurrying and shouting. He'd gotten off at the sixth floor and walked back to Highhawk's office. He'd emptied an assortment of leather, feathers, and bones out of a box beside Highhawk's chair. He placed the mask gently in the box and closed it. Then he searched the office, quickly and thoroughly, without finding what he wanted. That left two places to look.

He picked up the replica mask Highhawk had made, laid it atop the box, and carried it down the elevator to the exhibit hall.

By then the spectators were gone and two D.C. policemen were guarding the corridor. He saw Rodney, and Rodney let him through. Rodney was holding the plastic explosive.

"What the hell happened?" Rodney had asked. "Joe tells me this bomb was under the mask and you pulled it off. That right?"

"Yes," Chee said. He handed the replica to Rodney. "Here," he said. "Whoever did it sort of molded the plastic into the mask. Jammed it in."

Leaphorn was standing there, his face gray. "You all right?" he asked.

"I'm fine," Chee said. "But you don't look so hot."

On the floor between the Yeibichai exhibit and the Incan display three men were sprawled in that totally careless attitude that only the dead can manage. One of them matched Leaphorn's description of the little redhead with the shape of a weightlifter. Sooner or later he would wonder about what the redhead was doing here, and what had happened. When he did, he'd ask Leaphorn. Now it didn't seem to matter. And then the morgue crew began arriving. And more plainclothes cops, and men who had to be, by their costume, the feds.

Chee had not been in the mood for the Federal Bureau of Investigation. He walked out of the Tenth Street entrance and around the building. He checked parked cars. A wrecker was hauling an old Chevy sedan away from the towaway fire zone, but Chee was looking for Highhawk's Ford Mustang. He finally found it in a staff parking lot.

It was locked. What he was looking for wasn't visible inside, and it was too large to fit under the seat and out of sight. If it wasn't in the car, he'd have to take a cab out to Highhawk's place and look for it there. But first he'd check the trunk. Locked, of course. Chee found a slab of broken concrete near the sidewalk. He slammed it down on the trunk lid, springing it open. There was a box inside, wrapped in an old pair of coveralls. Chee took off the lid and looked in. The fetish representing the Tano War Twin smiled its sinister, malicious smile up at him. He took Talking God's mask out of the box from Highhawk's office, packed it carefully in with the fetish, put the empty box in the trunk, and closed it.

Two young men, each holding a briefcase, were standing beside a nearby car watching him break into the Mustang. Chee nodded to them. "Had to get this fetish out," he said, and walked back to the Natural History Museum. He had left the box in the checkroom and went back to the exhibit.

There the FBI had taken over. Chee had unchecked his box and walked to his hotel.

Now, in his room, he was coming to terms with yesterday when the telephone rang again.

"Jim?"

It was Mary Landon's voice.

"Yes," he said. "It's me, Mary."

"You weren't hurt? On the news they said you weren't hurt."

"No. Not at all."

"I'm coming to Washington. To see you," she said. "I called you yesterday. At the police station in Shiprock. They said you were in Washington and told me your hotel. I was going to call you and come. And then last night— That was terrible."

Jim Chee was having trouble analyzing his emotions. They were turbulent, and mixed.

"Mary. Why do you want to see me?" He paused, wondering how to phrase it. "I got your letter," he said.

"That was why," she said. "I shouldn't have said that in a letter. It's the sort of thing that you say in person. That was wrong. It was stupid, too. I know how you feel. And how I feel."

"How do you feel about living on the reservation? About the reservation being home?"

"Oh, Jim," she said. "Let's not—" She left it unfinished.

"Not get into that? But that's always been our problem. I want you to come and live with me. You know how I am. My people are part of me. And you want me to come out to the world and live with you. And that's only fair. But I can't handle it."

A moment passed before she spoke again, and her voice was a little different. "I wish I hadn't told you in a letter. That's all. That was cruel. I just didn't think. Or, I did think. I thought it would hurt too much to see you like that, and I would be all confused about it again. But I should have told you in person."

There was not much to say after that, and they said good-bye. Chee washed his face, and looked out his window into the window of the office across the narrow street. The man into whose office Chee's window looked was looking down at the passing cars, still with his vest and tie neatly in place. The man and Chee were looking at each other when Janet Pete tapped at his half-opened door and came in.

He offered her the chair, and she took it.

"You don't look like you feel like doing a lot of talking,"

she said. "Would you like to just check out now, and drive on out to the airport?"

"No hurry," he said. She was not exactly a beautiful woman, he thought. She did not have the softness, the silkiness, the dark blue, pale yellow feminine beauty of Mary Landon. Instead she had a kind of strong, clean-cut dignity. A classy gal. She was proud, and he identified with that. She had become his friend. He liked her. Or he thought he did. Certainly, he pitied her. And he was going to do something for her. What was happening to her here in Washington was nothing but miserable. He hated that.

"And before we go," Chee added, "there's something I want to give to you."

Chee got off the bed and unsnapped the suitcase. He took out the hotel laundry sack in which he'd wrapped it and extracted the fetish.

He handed it to her. "The Tano War God," he said. "One of the twins."

Janet Pete stared at it, and then at Chee. She made no move to accept it.

"I didn't think he should be so far away from home," Chee said. "He has a twin somewhere, and people who miss him. It seemed to me that the Smithsonian has plenty of other gods, stolen from other people, and they could keep the replica Highhawk made and get along without this one. I thought this one should go back to its kiva, or wherever the Tanos keep him."

"You want to give it to me?" Janet asked, still studying his face.

"That way he will get home," Chee said. "You can turn him over to John McDermott, and John gives him to what's-his-name—Eldon Tamana, wasn't it? That lawyer from Tano. And Tamana, he takes it home."

Janet Pete said nothing. She looked down at her hands, and then up at him again.

"Or," Chee added softly, "whatever you like."

Janet held out her hands. Chee laid the Twin War God in them.

"I guess we should go now," Chee said, and he relocked the suitcase. "I think I've been in this town long enough for a country boy Navajo."

Janet Pete was rewrapping the Twin War God in the laundry sack. "Me too," she said. "I have been here for months and months and months. So long it seems like a lifetime." She put her hand on Chee's sleeve.

"I will take this little fellow home myself," she said.

BOOKS BY TONY HILLERMAN

THE BLESSING WAY
Available in Paperback, Mass Market, and eBook

DANCE HALL OF THE DEAD
Available in Paperback, Mass Market, and eBook

LISTENING WOMAN
Available in Paperback, Mass Market, and eBook

PEOPLE OF DARKNESS
Available in Paperback, Mass Market, and eBook

THE GHOSTWAY
Available in Mass Market and eBook

SKINWALKERS
Available in Mass Market and eBook

A THIEF OF TIME
Available in Mass Market, and eBook

TALKING GOD
Available in Paperback, Mass Market, eBook, and Digital Audio

COYOTE WAITS
Available in Paperback, Mass Market, and eBook

SACRED CLOWNS
Available in Paperback, Mass Market, eBook, and Digital Audio

THE FALLEN MAN
Available in Mass Market, eBook, and Digital Audio

THE FIRST EAGLE
Available in Mass Market and eBook

HUNTING BADGER
Available in Mass Market, eBook, and Audiobook CD

THE WAILING WIND
Available in Mass Market, eBook, and Audiobook CD

THE SINISTER PIG
Available in Mass Market

SKELETON MAN
Available in Mass Market and eBook

THE SHAPE SHIFTER
Available in Mass Market, eBook, Audiobook CD, and Large Print

THE BEST OF THE WEST
Available in Paperback

SELDOM DISAPPOINTED
Available in Paperback and eBook

BOOKS BY ANNE HILLERMAN

SPIDER WOMAN'S DAUGHTER

A Leaphorn, Chee & Manuelito Novel

Available in Paperback, eBook, Mass Market, Large Print, and Digital Audio

"Chip off the literary block—there are a lot of things Tony taught his daughter, Anne, and one of them was how to tell a good story. *Spider Woman's Daughter* is a proud addition to the legacy, capturing the beauty and breath of the Southwest as only a Hillerman can."
—Craig Johnson, author of the Walt Longmire Mysteries

ROCK WITH WINGS

A Leaphorn, Chee & Manuelito Novel

Available in Paperback, eBook, Mass Market, Large Print, and Digital Audio

"Hillerman uses the southwestern setting as effectively as her late father did while skillfully combining Native American lore with present-day social issues." —*Publishers Weekly*

SONG OF THE LION

A Leaphorn, Chee & Manuelito Novel

Available in Paperback, eBook, Mass Market, Large Print, and Digital Audio

"Hillerman seamlessly blends tribal lore and custom into a well-directed plot, continuing in the spirit of her late father, Tony, by keeping his characters (like Chee) in the mix, but still establishing Manuelito as the main player in what has become a fine legacy series." —*Booklist*

CAVE OF BONES

A Leaphorn, Chee & Manuelito Novel

Available in Hardcover, Mass Market, eBook, Large Print, and Digital Audio

"This fictional universe now belongs firmly in the hands of Anne Hillerman." —*New York Journal of Books*

TONY HILLERMAN'S LANDSCAPE

On the Road with Chee and Leaphorn

Available in Hardcover and eBook

Narrated by his daughter, Anne Hillerman, with original photos from Don Strel, *Tony Hillerman's Landscape* is a timely showcase of a hauntingly beautiful region that captured one man's imagination for a lifetime, and is a daughter's loving tribute to her father.